A MAP OF THE SKY

Claire Wong

LION FICTION

A MAP OF THE SKY

"A brilliant and sensitively written portrayal of the adult world through the eyes of a curious, loveable eleven-year-old boy. This book tackles adult issues but without the overanalysis that comes with adulthood. Very enjoyable."

Polly Courtney, novelist and screenwriter

"A lovely story about the confusion of trying to understand the big wide world through a child's eyes. A Map of the Sky *is so well written it made me feel young again! It captures the beauty and drama of the North Yorkshire coast as though you are there, allowing readers to escape the hurry of modern life. Highly recommended."*

CL Smith, author of the *Kadogos* trilogy

Published by
Lion Hudson Limited
Wilkinson House, Jordan Hill Business Park,
Banbury Road, Oxford OX2 8DR, England
www.lionhudson.com

ISBN 978 1 78264 269 5

e-ISBN 978 1 78264 270 1

First edition 2019

A catalogue record for this book is available from the British Library

Printed and bound in the UK, June 2019, LH26

to Benjamin…
with a lifetime of adventures ahead

ACKNOWLEDGMENTS

Thank you to Jessica Gladwell, whose advice and discernment helped this story grow into what it is, to Rachel Ashley-Pain for her astute editing, to Joy Tibbs for guiding me through the manuscript's transformation into a book, and to everyone at Lion Hudson who worked on this project.

Writing is often a solitary pursuit, but it cannot be done alone. I am grateful to so many people, especially to Emma and Emily, for helping me better understand life with chronic illness. Thank you also to Hannah, whose knowledge helped me find Kit's voice, to Jenny for lending her thoughtful perspective, and to my Mum who is always willing to be one of my first readers.

Thanks also to Susanna for the French translations, to Joss for the lesson in Yorkshire history, and to my wordsmith colleagues, Marianne, Hayley, Gemma, Crispin, and Michelle, who humoured my last-minute vocabulary queries.

CHAPTER ONE

ASKFELD

THE INTREPID NORTHERN ADVENTURES OF CHRISTOPHER SHACKLETON FISHER, AGED ELEVEN.

A record of the places I will discover and the mysteries I am going to solve this summer. Not to be read by rival explorers or older sisters (that means you, Juliet).

The North Sea heaved and rolled against the rocks far below. Without a moment's delay, Kit ran to the window of his new room and flung it wide open. You had to lean out into the cold air and crane your head round at an awkward, neck-aching angle, but it was just possible to see the waves from up here. He grinned at the feeling of mist-like rain on his face.

"Stop that and get back inside." His mother did not look up from examining a scratch on one of the suitcases in the doorway, while her overloaded handbag balanced on top of another. "You could fall out."

The land dropped sharply away from Askfeld Farm Guest House's crag-top perch to where the great grey water stretched out under a stony sky. Between sea and air was a space that was alive with darting shapes of the auks and gannets that skimmed the waves.

"When Dad arrives, we can go to the beach," said Kit. He closed the window; the white curtains stopped billowing and settled back into place. The smell of the sea air lingered. Then, though he knew it would provoke a reaction, or perhaps precisely because of that, he added, "When *does* Dad get here?"

"Not now!" his mother snapped with a fierceness he had rarely heard her use. It was not the first time he had asked since they set out that morning, but he was pretty certain the question had not yet been answered properly. Each time the response had been sharper and shorter, which made no sense at all.

"Your second room is just next door, Mrs Fisher." Sean Garsdale, who owned the guest house at Askfeld Farm, appeared behind them, saving Kit from any further reprimand. That was one of the Fisher family rules: no arguing or shouting in front of strangers. While his mother and sister followed Sean out, Kit stayed behind and assessed what he had seen of their host so far. He was quite a young sort of adult, if you looked past the smart shirt and polite conversation: the kind that might still be fun enough to want to play football or talk about games.

Kit opened his suitcase and pulled out a stack of comics. Sandwiched between the brightly coloured exploits of superpowered heroes was a red notebook, whose use he had been planning ever since he stumbled, bleary-eyed, into the car six hours ago. He yawned, sat down cross-legged on the bed, and wrote in black ink on the cover: *The Intrepid Northern Adventures of Christopher Shackleton Fisher, aged eleven* (it had been his birthday two weeks ago and he had finally caught up with the rest of his year group at school). Then he opened it to the first blank page.

Through the adjoining wall of their two rooms, the voices were half muffled, but Kit prided himself on his sharp ears, and he could make out most of what they were saying. Sean was apologizing for the weather.

"You picked a grey day to arrive and I hope it doesn't put you off. We had bright July sunshine last week. There's beautiful walks to be had on the moors or the coastal path when it's warm."

"Oh, that's not a problem; we can cope with a little rain," Kit's mother replied with the indomitable determination of someone who has resolved to be cheerful. "Besides, we need to get used to all kinds of weather here. I mentioned to your wife on the phone when I booked that we're actually moving to the area. The house isn't quite ready for us yet, but we were so keen to come and explore our new home, weren't we?"

"Yes, of course; we've heard so many lovely things about this place," Juliet agreed, in a tone that made Kit involuntarily roll his eyes. People always mistook his sister for much older than she was, because she knew how to talk like a grown-up.

At the top of the page, he wrote *Day One: Mysteries* and then paused, the pen still pressed down so that the ink at the foot of the "s" began to spread and bleed through the paper. Would a single sheet be enough to list all the questions racing around in his head? When he thought back over the past couple of weeks, it was one long saga of being on the wrong side of a closed door, sent outside or to a friend's house while urgent conversations were conducted. Even worse were the false smiles when he was allowed back into the room: the bright tone with which he was told "Time to start packing!" without explanation. Overnight, asking questions had become re-categorized as bad behaviour. It earned you only a frown and an evasive comment. But Kit would get to the bottom of it all. He knew he was clever: not as clever as Juliet, of course, but he was sure he could find out the truth.

The floorboards on the landing creaked a warning. Kit squirrelled the book away under his pillow as the others returned to the room. He smiled blankly at the three of them and hoped they could not guess what he had been thinking. As it happened, no one looked directly at him as Juliet and their mother collected luggage from where it lay on the threshold.

"Just come and find me if there's anything else you need," Sean was saying to Kit's mother. "This here's a key for the front door, in case you want to go out before seven or come in after ten. And here's a card with some useful phone numbers. Top one's for the house. See where it says Sean and Beth Garsdale? That's me and my wife. Breakfast is seven until nine-thirty. And although it says on the website we're a bed and breakfast, we do now serve hot meals throughout the day. You'll find the day's specials written up on the chalkboard in the dining room."

"How long have you and your wife owned this place?" his mother asked, taking the card but not looking at it. Kit noticed she was talking down to him. When he had addressed her as Mrs Fisher earlier, she had not told him to call her Catherine, as she usually did when meeting new people.

"Been about four years now. We bought it just after we got married. Needed a lot of work done, but my wife Beth has a good eye for decorating. All this," he motioned around the white-painted room with its sturdy oak furnishings and a framed watercolour of seashells on the adjacent wall, "is her design. We had to rename the place too. The last owner, he had a bit of a strange sense of humour, you see, and he thought, because of us being so near all the seaside resorts here, it'd be funny to call this place The Last Resort! Doubt it did his bookings much good. So we took that sign down as soon as we moved in, and went back to the old name of Askfeld. That's what this house was called back when it was a working farm."

"Very nice." Kit's mum nodded approvingly. "Local history is so important."

"I'll leave you to settle in, unless there's anything else you need now."

"The wifi password?" Juliet asked. Their mother sniffed sharply, but to Kit's surprise gave no voice to her disapproval. Normally she was quick to tell her children they should spend less time staring at screens. In her day, she liked to remind them, people read books or talked to one another. Kit always wanted to argue that people still did those things, just combined with better technology, but he knew better than to answer back. Sean pointed her to a little printed card on the bedside table, and Juliet swept it up, hurrying to key the code into her phone. She was now lost to them, in another world populated by friends her own age and conversations that interested her.

"Are there whales and sharks in the sea here?" Kit blurted out as Sean turned to leave.

He chuckled. "Oh, they're out there all right, but you won't often see them from the shore. You'd have to go out in a boat, or have a really good telescope, I reckon."

Kit pictured himself aboard a pirate ship, a brass spyglass to his eye, shouting "Sharks ahoy!" while his family hoisted sails and swabbed decks. Except that Juliet would probably get seasick and his mother would insist everyone went to bed on time despite the adventure at hand.

Sean left the room, and Catherine clapped her hands together in a way that always meant instructions would soon follow.

"Juliet, why don't you go and have a rest in our room? I'll be along in just a minute to unpack our things and test the kettle. I've brought our own teabags, because you never know whether places like this will have anything good."

Kit was not sure what she meant by "places like this". As far as he knew, they had never stayed in a guest house before. Without a word, Juliet left the room. Once they were alone, and the door into the next room had clicked shut, Catherine leaned forward to his eye level and dropped her voice low. "Now, Kit, I hope you're going to be very grown up and helpful while we're here. Can you do that for me?"

Her seriousness came as a surprise; he wondered what he might have done wrong to make his mother worry he would be anything else. He nodded wordlessly. She smiled and drew herself back up.

"I knew you'd understand."

But Kit was not at all sure he did.

Catherine frowned and attempted to neaten her son's dark hair, which was getting too long now. He ducked out of the way as he always did when this happened, while his mother muttered something about wishing she had booked him a haircut before they moved. She left the room, and through the shared wall Kit could soon hear the soft roar of a portable kettle boiling. He took out his exercise book and pen again.

Day one: Mysteries. One: why have we moved early? We weren't supposed to come here until after school finished for the summer, and the house isn't even ready. Two: why isn't Dad with us?

Kit pictured his father trapped somewhere in a seventh-floor office, looking for a way to escape and be reunited with his family. For some reason the whole subject made his mother cross. When he had asked her about it earlier, from the back seat of the car on the motorway, he had not been able to see her expression, but he had noticed the muscles in her neck and jaw grow tense. He paused to decide what to list next. The topic of Juliet's exams was also off limits, but that was less mysterious: she tended to turn slightly pale and walk out of the room if you mentioned them. Fortunately, Kit thought exams were a very boring subject anyway. Then there was this place: Askfeld Farm Guest House, the only establishment near their new house in Utterscar with rooms available at such short notice. On the way upstairs they had passed a ground floor room that seemed to be full of books and paintings, but when Kit asked about it Sean had quickly closed the door and told him that room was private and for the use of staff only. But it did not look like any staffroom Kit had ever seen, and he suspected Sean Garsdale was not telling them everything.

Three: what is hidden in the secret room downstairs? There at least was a secret he stood a chance of figuring out without getting into trouble for asking more forbidden questions. He looked at the pile of comic books strewn across the duvet. Not one of the cape-clad characters looking out from the covers would shirk the chance to solve these mysteries. What's more, they would certainly find a way to fix the problem of his family's sudden strange behaviour. If Kit was going to be helpful, it wasn't because his mother had told him to; it was because it was just what a hero would do in this situation.

"Mum! Can I go and explore?" Kit put his head round the door of his mother and sister's room. "I've unpacked! Well, mostly." Technically, he had put his comic book collection on top of the bedside table, but that had to count for something. His clothes could stay in the case until he actually needed to wear them.

Catherine held up a hand to tell him to wait. She was pressing the phone to her ear with one hand, while hanging up a silk blouse with the other. Juliet was arranging her school files on the windowsill, their bright colours obscuring the view outside. She did not turn around or seem to have noticed Kit come into the room.

"Laura? Can you hear me all right? I'm sorry, the reception is terrible here. Listen, you'll need my report for tomorrow's meeting with the directors. I left a copy on Colin's desk, but he won't think to bring it – in fact, it's probably already buried in his bombsite of an in-tray – so I'm going to email it to you as well. No, it's no trouble at all. It should all be self-explanatory, but if you need me to go through it before the meeting, have Debbie set up a conference call. Yes, we've arrived safely, thank you. The place where we're staying is ever so quaint! Real rustic charm, and fabulous views of the sea. But the owner – he's just so *young*. Well, he's probably close to thirty and I'm showing my age, but when we first arrived, I thought we were being met by the work experience student! OK, I'll let you get back to work now. But if you need anything else for the directors, just let me know."

She finished off her call and asked Kit to repeat his question.

"Is it OK if I go looking around?"

"Only indoors, and don't go disturbing the other guests." She smoothed invisible creases out of her navy blue dress: the one she wore to important meetings. She liked to tell Kit and Juliet that people took her seriously in that outfit, though Kit could not imagine anyone daring not to take his mother seriously, whatever she wore. She wasn't the sort of person you ignored.

"Thanks, Mum!"

The house was old, which Kit liked. Their mother had told them on the journey up that it had once been a farmhouse, built hundreds of years ago, and only recently converted into a bed and breakfast. Kit ran his hand along the white-painted wall of the stairwell, wondering what history the stones remembered. What wars, storms, and famines had they weathered? They were cold to the touch, with an uneven finish that meant the wooden stairs had been cut into odd shapes with awkward angles so they would fit in the available space.

His mother had said to stay indoors, and not to bother the other guests. She had said nothing about the staff or secret rooms. It was time to investigate what mysteries Askfeld hid.

CHAPTER TWO

ADVENTURES IN STILLNESS

DAY ONE, MYSTERY NOTES:

For a secret room, it doesn't look very well guarded. No sign of motion sensors, infra-red cameras or guard dogs so far. Can guard dogs be trained not to bark so you don't know they're there? I don't mind friendly dogs, but the big police dogs they brought into school last year looked like they could bite your arm off.

The hallway was empty. Through the glass pane next to the front door, he could see Sean striding away across the grass towards a dilapidated building that might once have been stables. A draught slipped in through a window frame's ageing timbers and rattled the frayed twine garland of seashells that hung along the opposite wall. He was willing to bet that the out-of-bounds room was not even locked. There was only one way to test his theory. He reached for the handle and the door opened easily, just as he had predicted.

The room was lit only by daylight pouring in through a wide window. The bookcases Kit had glimpsed through the doorway earlier lined the wall nearest him. By the opposite wall was a table set up with watercolours and a sketchbook. Paintings lay propped up in corners or against furniture; an empty canvas leaned against the table and in one corner an easel had been set up with a half-finished picture of a ship at sea. Beside the window sat a woman in a wicker chair, with a gingham blanket over her legs. She was young and pretty, with a bob of brown hair framing the sort of face that probably looked friendly even when it wasn't thinking about anything in particular.

"Hello."

She looked round at the sound of Kit's voice and smiled. "Hello. What's your name?"

"I'm Kit."

"Nice to meet you, Kit. My name's Beth. You look like you're exploring."

What was she doing? Her hands rested on the arms of the chair. There was no book open in her lap, no screen or headphones in sight to entertain her. It seemed to be just Beth and the window.

"Yeah, I'm only allowed to look around indoors today though. Mum says."

"Oh well, rules are rules," she sighed sympathetically.

"Are you on holiday here?" Kit wondered if this conversation would count as bothering the other guests.

"No, I live here. Did you meet Sean when you arrived?"

Kit nodded.

"Well, he and I are married, and we own Askfeld Farm."

That was good news. He had not been forbidden from talking to the owners. It occurred to him that Beth had the same accent as Sean. He liked the sound of it: it was less brisk and clipped than the way his parents and teachers spoke.

"Are you looking for something out there?" Kit pointed at the window Beth's chair was facing. It looked out on a stretch of overgrown grass leading to the edge of the cliff and then the great grey sea rising and falling in flecks of white foam. It was not bright and beautiful, the way a picture-perfect summer holiday snap might be, but it was striking in its vastness all the same. *Like discovering a giant*, Kit thought: at once both frightening and incredible, so that it was impossible to look away.

"Nothing in particular. But it's a good view, isn't it?"

"Why are you sitting there then?"

She gave a conspiratorial smile. "I'm learning about stillness today."

"What do you mean?"

She leaned forward in her chair as though about to tell him a deep secret, and Kit instinctively stepped towards her to hear it. "Have you ever noticed how people rush around in such a hurry all the time? Everything has to happen right now. No one knows how to listen to the stillness any more."

Now that she mentioned it, this place held a deeper silence than Kit had encountered before. When he stopped to notice, he found there was no background rush of traffic sweeping past Askfeld on distant roads, no siren screeches or shouts from outside. He had not noticed their absence until now. It was disconcerting.

"When I have to sit still and be quiet in school, I get bored. Don't you get bored?"

Beth laughed, making the string of blue and yellow beads around her neck shake with a clackety sound. "Sometimes, yes! But when you're stuck in a chair for days or weeks at a time, you learn ways to deal with boredom. I've read a lot of books. On good days, I paint too, and bring the outside world in to me."

There was a pile of books on the table in the corner: a strange mix of ancient leather-bound tomes and thin paperbacks. Beside them was a small sketchbook and a handful of pencils. Kit stared at this woman, trying to decide what it was that meant she could not get up and go outside. He could see no crutches in the room, no plaster cast on her legs to indicate an injury. Then he spotted the bump under her dress.

"Are you going to have a baby? Is that why you can't go out?"

"Yes and no. I am going to have a baby. But I can't go outside because I'm not well. And I was ill before I knew this little one was on the way."

"What kind of not well?" Without thinking, he took half a step backwards. Kit's mother was always telling him to be careful about germs. She carried a bottle of antibacterial handwash in her bag and would produce it after any interaction with potential hazards, such as dirt or the outside world. Beth did not answer straight away, but looked off into the distance, as if searching for the right words. She twisted the string of beads around her hand and tilted her head to one side.

"The kind with a very long name that's hard to pronounce, where your arms and legs don't want to work properly most days. And all of you is tired."

"Maybe you should have a nap," he suggested, seeing that she already had a good selection of pillows propping her up.

She laughed again, but it was a different sound this time, somehow heavier and more introspective. "If only," she murmured. Then she shifted in her chair, raising herself up and wincing slightly at the movement of her shoulder muscles. "Well, tell me something about yourself, Kit."

"Like what?"

"Hmm, good question. Let's not bother with what school year you're in or what you want to be when you're older. I bet grown-ups ask you that all the time. I used to want to be a dancer. Do you like reading? I liked reading when I was about your age."

"Yes. I prefer playing in the park, but if I can't go because it's raining, then books are more fun than homework."

"What's your favourite kind of book then?"

This was easy to answer. "I like the ones with superheroes and adventures. Especially comic books, though Mum says she wishes I'd read more of the classics instead. She says they make you a more rounded person. I like the King Arthur stories too. I think they're cool."

Beth smiled, as if this information somehow told her more about Kit than just his reading habits. But it was not as if he had admitted to her that, aged seven, he had been known to run around the house in a cape fashioned from a duvet cover. He was too old for that now, of course, and beginning to be embarrassed by the memory.

"Well, you are welcome to borrow any of those, if you want them." She pointed to the bookcases. "I'm sure there are some classics on there that would keep your mum happy."

"Thanks!" Kit bounded to the shelves and searched through volumes whose titles promised excitement and journeys. There was even one about the knights of the Round Table. Not many of them had pictures, but Kit knew (thanks to his mum's frequent reminders during their Saturday morning library trips) he was getting to an age where he was not supposed to be interested in books with illustrations. They were childish, apparently. He pulled the book about King Arthur out first, and then selected *Odysseus' Adventures: An Epic Retelling for Young Readers*, which had beautiful gold letters on the cover. The pages were yellowing at the edges, but when he opened it, the letters on the page were reassuringly large and rounded.

"Can I come back again?" he asked. "When I've finished these, to return them to you, I mean?"

"Of course you can."

If he had Beth's permission to come back, it surely would not matter that Sean had said the room was out of bounds, or that his mother did not like him bothering people. Askfeld's secret was not so terrible after all, but it brought him a gleeful kind of excitement to know it when his mother and sister did not. He would not tell them about meeting Beth just yet. After all, they were clearly keeping secrets from him, about this move and why his dad had stayed behind, so why should he tell them everything?

As he left the room, he looked over his shoulder at Beth, who was sitting perfectly motionless, a silhouette against the window. She had gone back to whatever had occupied her thoughts before he interrupted them.

Kit was so distracted tearing down the corridor with his new books under his arm that he almost collided with a man leaving the guests' sitting room.

"Steady there, lad!" the stranger cried with a laugh. He wore a brown tweed jacket, and trousers whose cuffs were flecked with dried mud. His grey hair was dishevelled and his blue eyes sparkled with amusement.

"Sorry. I didn't see you."

"Clearly. To have the single-minded energy of youth again! On holiday with your family here, are you?" He peered down at Kit, the way one might study a particularly curious museum artefact. Kit rearranged the books in his arms so he would not drop them.

"Not exactly. We're supposed to be moving up here. But the house wasn't ready. Or we moved too soon. I'm not sure. But anyway, it was something like that, and Mum says we need to stay here for a while."

"I see," said the stranger. Kit resisted an urge to reply "said the blind man", which was what his dad always liked to say after this phrase. "Well, let me think; it's July, so you must be enjoying the start of your school holidays. Am I right?" He smoothed out the now-crumpled newspaper he had been carrying under his arm.

"Almost. Holidays don't properly start until next week for my school." The school play was on Thursday and someone else would have to take over his part now that he was going to miss it. It was hard not to be cross, after he had spent weeks learning the lines.

"So you're getting an extra week's grace, lucky lad. I thought it was near impossible to take holiday in term time these days. However did you parents manage that?"

It had taken many phone calls and a visit to the school office to secure it. His friends, though sad to see him go, had been clearly envious that Kit got to go away before the end of term – something that was forbidden in almost all circumstances. But when they asked him what was so important that he couldn't stay till the end of term, especially since it was their last term together before everyone moved up to secondary school, Kit had been forced to shrug and plead ignorance, which nobody in his class believed. His best friend Toby had seemed quite hurt by it, suspecting that Kit was betraying their seven-year friendship by keeping this secret from him. Nothing Kit could say would convince him that they were both equally in the dark.

The stranger glanced at the borrowed books. "That's an impressive reading list for someone so young. Nice to meet a fellow intellectual. If you're looking for a good spot to enjoy your books, I can highly recommend the blue armchair in the corner by the fireplace."

He pointed through the doorway to the guests' sitting room. It was cosy and inviting, with woollen blankets draped over chairs facing an oak mantelpiece.

"The name's Bert, by the way. Or Professor Albert Sindlesham, if you're talking to any of my colleagues. But you look a bit short to be an academic just yet. Mind you, I swear the post-doctoral assistants are getting younger with every passing year." He shook his head as if the inevitability of this saddened him.

"I'm Kit. What's a post-doctor… what did you call it?"

"Kit? Bit of an unusual name. What's that short for?" Bert asked, missing the question that came first.

"Christopher, but I only get called that when I'm in trouble. It's after this man who wrote plays a long time ago. Mum and Dad like the stuff he wrote, I think. They used to go to the theatre a lot, before they had children. My middle name's Shackleton, after the explorer. Dad thought it should be Ernest instead, because that's a real name at least, but Mum said she didn't want people thinking I was named for an Oscar Wilde character."

His mother had told him it was a cultured name that would never go out of fashion, because they had wanted to give him the best chance of succeeding in life. Apparently there were too many bad role models in the world these days, which was why he was named after famous men who had done remarkable things with their time on earth.

"Hmm. Strange thing to lump your child with, if you ask me, but each to their own!"

Kit was about to say that he had never minded his name, and if you were going to feel sorry for anyone, it should be Juliet, whose namesake was only famous for dying tragically, but they were interrupted by the sound of raised voices from the reception desk around the corner.

"I don't see why it's any of your concern!" a woman could be heard declaring. Bert raised his greying brows at the aggressive tone, but there was a definite sparkle of curiosity and amusement in his eyes as the two of them listened in.

"Ms Morley, I was only –" Kit recognized that voice: it was Sean Garsdale, and his efforts to reason with this angry woman did not appear to be working.

"If I want to extend my stay here, and frankly it's clear that you need the bookings, then what more is there to talk about? Really, if you learned to respect your guests' privacy perhaps you'd run a more successful business!"

"I'm sorry to have offended you." Sean's voice turned quiet and controlled. "Let me assure you I meant to be polite, not to pry."

"Well!" the woman began, but having no more to add, she ended the conversation there and came storming round the corner to find Kit and Bert, who could not feign nonchalance quickly enough to convince her they had not overheard everything. Flustered, Kit met her eyes with what he feared was quite a guilty expression.

"See, this is exactly what I'm talking about!" she fumed. "Even the other guests are eavesdropping now. Nobody knows how to mind their own business these days."

Kit's face flushed red with embarrassment. Bert coughed and looked away until she had marched past them and stamped up the stairs to her room. Somewhere above them, a door slammed. Kit jumped at the noise, but Bert merely chuckled.

"That's Maddie Morley. Don't mind her; she's barely smiled once at anyone here. It's curious, though. She was already a guest at Askfeld when I arrived last week, and that's the second time she's extended her stay."

"Doesn't she want to go home?" Surely you would only draw out a holiday if you were enjoying it, which Maddie clearly was not.

Bert glanced up, as if assessing the soundproof qualities of the ceiling, before confiding in a low voice, "From what I hear, she hasn't got much of a home to go to any more. Not sure of the details, but the current guest house rumours are that there was some kind of incident at work, and she's not welcome back there. Though best to pretend you don't know anything about that, of course." Bert gave a knowing look to underline the secrecy of this information.

"Of course," Kit nodded. He saw no reason why he would want to make Maddie shout at him any more than she already had.

"Well, I'd best be off before anyone else accuses me of loitering and spying. Got a professional reputation to salvage somehow, after all. I'm sure I'll see you again, Kit. Cheerio."

And with that, Bert strolled away. Kit went through into the sitting room and sat in the recommended armchair. Its high back forced him to sit up straight and formally, as though he were overseeing an important gathering. He liked the feeling.

The cover of *Odysseus' Adventures* showed a bearded man alone at sea. The waves looked almost like tentacles grasping at the ship. He thought of Maddie, with no home to return to, and wondered if that took the fun out of travelling. Then he opened the book and forgot about her and everyone else at Askfeld. For the next hour, the room around him vanished and Kit was transported to the island of Ithaca, to white sandy bays and olive groves, where young Prince Telemachus waited on the seashore for his father to return home, while Queen Penelope wove tricks together to placate the people around her. And then Odysseus himself burst into the story in the middle of a storm, struggling to find his way to land while the boat rose and fell with each surging wave of the raging Mediterranean Sea. When Kit pictured Odysseus in his mind's eye, it was with his own father's face.

CHAPTER THREE

THE UNFINISHED MAP

DAY TWO

What would be the coolest superpower to have if you could pick one?

I think I'd go for either flight, because then you could get anywhere really fast, or else mind-reading, so you'd always know what secrets other people were trying to keep.

Over the next twenty-four hours, the rest of the Fisher family seemed to completely forget they were in an exciting new place. Far from being eager to go out and explore the coastline or meet their new neighbours (if indeed there were any people to meet; Askfeld was so isolated on its cliff perch, you could imagine that there was no one else for miles), Juliet blocked out the world with her headphones and a history textbook, while Catherine sent emails and muttered under her breath about her former colleagues' incompetence.

"I thought you said you were leaving your job when we moved," said Kit, when he came next door to borrow the toothpaste after breakfast. His mother looked up sharply as if about to tell him off for the remark, then relented.

"I know I did, but it's not a case of simply walking out of the office and leaving it all behind. That's not how things work. When you give your resignation, you have to hand over everything to your colleagues so that they can manage without you. I didn't quite get round to finishing that off, so I want to make sure they have what they need from me. It's just a few loose ends. I was very senior in the company, after all. Not that any of that has stopped Colin from swooping in like a vulture to try to snatch up everything I worked so hard to build. As if he's even capable of taking over my job. We Fishers work hard for our rewards."

That was one of Catherine's favourite sayings. The Fisher family were not lazy or entitled: they all worked hard. Catherine believed in high expectations, the virtue of keeping busy, and in speaking to her children as if they were adults. As a result, Kit knew a lot of long words, and enjoyed surprising people with them. All the same, there was a lot that his mum said that still made no sense to him. If moving early was so troublesome to her job, then why had she been the one to insist on it? It didn't seem to benefit anyone. Then again, there was a lot about grown-up jobs that Kit could not get his head around, like how you no longer got the summer off after you left school, but nobody seemed to mind.

"Can I help you?" It was meant to be a kind of holiday, and he did not like to see his mother surrounded by so much work.

"That's sweet of you, but it's all very complicated, I'm afraid. I'll just have to keep working through my list until it's all sorted out. When it's done, I promise we can go out and do something fun." She drew in a deep breath, readied her manicured nails over the keyboard, and began to type.

"OK," said Kit. "Jules, want me to help you revise?" He tilted his head round to try to make out the title of her book. Sometimes she would let him read out quick-fire questions to test her. It wasn't the most exciting game, but over the last few months he had learned a lot about cloud formations and the Cold War this way.

Today, however, Juliet shook her head and continued sticking fluorescent-orange notes to the chapter she was reading.

He sighed in frustration. Everyone was being so boring.

"I bet Dad wouldn't carry on working all day if he was here."

"All right, that's enough! If you're going to be this difficult, then go back to your room and find a book or a game to keep you busy." Catherine's eyes had hardened, the familiar set of her jaw telling Kit that there was no negotiation to be had on this. Was it the accusation that she worked too much, or the mention of his father that had annoyed her?

He shrugged and left the room. It had been explained to him on more than one occasion that his parents had very important jobs. His mother was head of a department in a recruitment company, and his father was a management consultant. When Kit had asked what that meant, his dad said he solved other people's problems for them. It also meant that his parents were busy and could not always attend school plays or sports days, but Kit was proud of them all the same. "Fishers work hard." He must have heard those words a hundred times. "If we didn't work so hard, we couldn't go on fun holidays or have such a big house in this part of London."

But they weren't in London any more. They were in a centuries-old farmhouse with only a short stretch of grass between them and the cliff edge. They had no friends' houses to visit or cinemas to go to: just acres of sea and sky stretching out beyond them. It was wonderful, and yet, on days like today, he wondered if it had the potential to be a little dull too. Certainly his family's response to it was uninspiring. After all the talk of this move being an exciting adventure, a fresh start for them all, they might just as easily have been shut away in a hotel room down the road from their old house.

Back in his own room, he sat down heavily on the bed and picked up the book about Odysseus' voyage. When his back grew stiff and his legs ached from staying still too long, he stood up and stretched. He needed to walk around, or he might go mad with cabin fever, so he went downstairs.

All Askfeld's rooms were airy and cool, largely because the front door was often propped open during daylight hours to let in the breeze. The smell of salt water and sea kelp clung to its walls. There was no one in the guests' sitting room this morning. Kit had hoped to see Bert again, though he was relieved there was no sign of Maddie Morley. Still, there was one other person he would like to speak to, so he left the sitting room.

"Where do you think you're going?" Sean stopped sweeping sand and dust from the floor tiles and straightened up to block Kit's way down the corridor.

"To see Beth." He decided to stay resolute in face of this question. Beth had, after all, said he was allowed to come back. If Sean was surprised that Kit knew his wife's name or that she was in the out of bounds room, he did not show it.

"Not so fast. I told you that room was private for a reason. Beth's not well. She needs lots of rest. That's why she has her own sitting room away from everyone else. I don't want you going and making her exhausted with all your noise and running around."

It was the first time Kit had seen Sean look stern, and he wondered for a moment if he dared answer back. It seemed wiser not to, so he ran up the stairs and sat on the landing with his face pressed between the bars of the bannister railing, listening to what went on below him. He heard Sean go into the kitchen, and come back out again a few minutes later, rolling up his sleeves and laughing at something the chef had said. He reached the reception desk at the precise moment Maddie stepped through the front door.

"Good morning."

"Does this place have DIY tools available for guests to use?" Maddie scraped her boots clean on the doormat and did not return the greeting. There was a pause, probably as Sean processed this strange question. Kit tried to imagine what this angry woman could be building while on holiday.

"I'm afraid not."

"As I expected. Well, do you know where I might hire or buy some?"

"What are you looking for exactly?"

Maddie raised her voice. "Look, if you don't know or won't help me, just say so! There's no need for this interrogation and deflection."

Kit actually felt slightly sorry for Sean, who was once again the target of Maddie's anger. However, it had all played out in his favour, since he was also now confident that Askfeld's owner was too busy to notice someone sneaking back downstairs. Kit seized his opportunity and tiptoed all the way to the door of Beth's room. He was almost surprised to find that Sean had not locked it to keep out unwanted visitors after their last conversation, but once again the handle turned easily and he tapped against the frame as he stepped inside.

Beth seemed more lively today, though she was still in her wicker chair supported by lots of cushions. An easel was set up in front of her. The broad piece of paper it displayed was painted as brown as coffee or parchment and there was an ornate compass in the top right corner, but the centre remained largely blank, like a wilderness of uncharted territory. Beth was not looking at this map: she was hunched over a sketchbook on her lap, scribbling notes round the edge of something she had drawn.

"What are you doing?" Kit asked from the doorway.

"Come in, Kit. I'm just trying to remember something."

"What have you forgotten?"

"A lot of things, thanks to a brain that gets easily confused these days. But specifically, right now, I'm trying to remember the shape of the lake where I used to skim stones with my dad when I was your age."

Kit stood beside Beth's chair to watch what she was working on. The sketch she was adding to was a rough outline of a map much like the one on her easel, but with more detail. He took a closer look and saw that the north-east part of the page was all sea. Along the wavy black line of the coast were small pictures and notes. One read *Find fossils here*, while another said *Secret short cut to the lookout point*, but had a couple of arrows and question marks pointing to different locations on the paper. It was when he spotted a small sketch of a house with the word *Askfeld* next to it that he realized what he was seeing.

"It's a map of here!"

There was the guest house, perched high on the cliffs, and the wavering line where the land met the sea. Spreading out from here were notes about the best beaches, and arrows towards places of interest. But from the look of Beth's scribblings, she was having trouble getting the map right. There were question marks and crossings-out where she had changed her mind about where something should be. Some of her notes had been transferred to the map on the easel, which sported a beautifully intricate border and calligraphic annotations, but the much busier sketched version remained a mess of uncertainty.

"I'm trying to plot out all the places I used to play when I was younger. I've had so many adventures, down by the sea or running across the moors, and I want to record them all."

"Because you can't go out and see those places any more?"

"Exactly. And most of all, I want to pass on those memories to this one," she patted her bump, "so my child can enjoy all these places too. Sean can take him or her out for walks, and then when they come home I'll get to hear the stories of what they've done and seen."

It had not occurred to Kit before, but it suddenly struck him as very sad that she might not be able to run around outside with her child when he or she was old enough, or play hide and seek. Beth squinted at the easel and pressed her lips together, and then began to paint a ship onto the sea. Before Kit's eyes, it grew into a longboat with a striped sail and a dragon-like figurehead at the prow.

"But you can't remember where all the different places are, or what they look like?"

"No," she sighed, dipping her brush into a pot of gold ink and then dotting it along the side of the ship. "It's frustrating for my memory to let me down now. I remember all the games and the exploring, even the parkin wrapped up in tin foil my dad would bring for us to eat on the walk home, but not the useful details. Like this lookout point, for example. I know there's a hidden path from the road, with trees either side. It's not an official path, so it's not on the Ordnance Survey I've looked at. You have to be small or else crouch low to fit through it in places, but you come out on the top of the cliffs and it's the most incredible view out to sea, with the headland in the distance to the south. I suppose I'll make my best guess as to where it is and one day my son or daughter will come and tell me whether I was right."

"So when will you get better?"

She balanced the brush over a water-filled jam jar. It dripped paint onto the sketchbook. "Well… It's not like when you have a cold or chicken pox; this is different."

"Different how? Are you going to die?" He was suddenly gripped with anxiety that his new friend would meet a tragic end before the summer was out.

Beth laughed. "No, it's not like that. There are some illnesses that don't act like the ones you're thinking of. They aren't the sort that kill you, but at the same time there isn't a medicine you can take to make it all go away. And I might get better one day, but I might not."

This made Kit uneasy. He had never heard of such a thing before. Illnesses were either slight enough to mean that you got a day off school, or serious enough to involve trips to hospital and solemn voices. In books they were normally the latter, whereas in real life he had only experienced the first kind. But here was something unsettling and new. What was he to do with an illness that just lingered, making no promises about its endpoint or trajectory? And what should he think of Beth now, whose story might be neither a happy ending of recovery nor a terrible tragedy, but something slower and more confined?

Still, if there was one thing that reading myths and adventure stories had taught him, it was that a hero should never give up hope, even when the situation looked impossible or unchanging. Odysseus kept persevering to get home, even though it took him ten years of storms and monsters. In that moment, Kit made a decision: he would not let this mysterious illness win. He was going to help Beth finish her map. If she could not go out to find the places she half remembered, then he would discover them for her. It would be a surprise, so he said nothing, but studied the picture very hard to memorize as much as he could.

Day two of my adventures, he later wrote in his book. *I have identified my quest.*

CHAPTER FOUR

VIEWS AND VILLAINS

TOP FOUR THINGS A HERO NEEDS FOR HIS QUEST:

1. Something to find (like Excalibur or a place on a map).

2. Someone to rescue from trouble (Beth).

3. A friendly and helpful sidekick (in the past I'd have said this was Juliet, but she's not as friendly or helpful these days. I wish Mum had let us get a dog).

4. A villain or monster to defeat.

"Isn't this nice?" Catherine said for the sixth or seventh time. "What a lot of fresh air and beautiful scenery!"

It might have been Kit's imagination, but he thought she watched Juliet's expression each time she said it, as if looking for a particular response. Juliet said nothing. Their mother glanced to her left and right as if searching for something else lovely to remark upon and continue the conversation. Absent-mindedly, her hand went to one of her gold earrings and turned it around, as she often did when she was thinking; as if she were turning the cogs of her brain.

"It is pretty cool," said Kit, supplying an answer to fill the silence. And it was. Sean had lent them a guidebook to the Cleveland Way, the far-reaching coastal path that passed through Askfeld's grounds, and they had decided to walk a short stretch of it leading south from the guest house. To their right lay green fields edged with lichen-flecked stone walls. In some the grass was grazed short by flocks of sheep with black faces and horns that curled like seashells, while others grew tall and unkempt with purple thistle heads and delicate stars of shepherd's needle. To the left, a narrow line of gorse and low, wind-beaten trees was all that separated them from the cliff edge plunging down into the North Sea. On a cold day it might have been bleak and shelter-less, the perfect spot for a brooding walk while you agonized over your misfortunes with an upturned collar against the pelting rain, but today was clear and fine. Insects hummed among the grasses and birdsong warbled down from the trees.

In spite of her unwillingness to sing the Cleveland Way's praises, Juliet was relaxed enough to list for their mother the things she wanted to bake as soon as they were moved into their own house with a proper kitchen. Kit was not especially interested in macaroons or choux pastry, so he ran on ahead.

The best thing about being at the front of the group was that you could imagine you were exploring uncharted territory. The path became a track through the overgrown wilderness, and Kit was discovering it all for the first time. There might be any number of wild beasts lurking nearby, ready to burst out of the gorse in a flurry of claws and teeth, or the ground might suddenly give way and hurl him down onto the rocks below. *Kit Fisher: intrepid explorer* sounded rather good. His grandmother had always said he had the sort of name that he could go far with, and now they certainly were far from home.

There was an added delicious secret to today's exploring: Kit was on a mission. Every stride he took was full of purpose. As he delved around in this new terrain, he paid particular attention to the vegetation on his left. Beth had spoken of a narrow pathway leading to a viewpoint on the cliff edge, somewhere south of Askfeld. It had to be near here. Maybe he could find it. He ran his hand over the uneven surface of the low wall and was surprised to find its stones were warm under his fingers where they had soaked up sunlight.

"Shall we turn back now?" his mother called ahead. It was a rhetorical question, and Kit knew he was supposed to agree without further discussion, but he still had not found the path, so he decided to feign misunderstanding.

"Just a bit further!" he called back. There was something up ahead that might be a gap. He ran up to it, ignoring the shouts that followed him. He crouched down. There was definitely a space between the slender trunks of two buckthorn trees. Kit squeezed between them, realizing that there must have been a good many years for the tunnel to become choked with spiny branches and thick greenery since Beth could have crawled through it as a child, if it even was the same one she had described.

As Kit clambered on, the tunnel grew wider and the thicket began to draw back, until abruptly it opened out and at once he knew he had found the right place.

He was at the top of the cliffs. The sea before him was a deep dark blue, flat and serene under the clear sky. The wind was blowing in off the waters, and the smell of salt and seaweed hit him more squarely here where it was unfiltered by the gorse. Gold grasses bobbed their feathered heads about his knees, and the gulls wheeled and swooped down to the waves with shrill yikkering cries to one another.

The strange mix of being alone before a breathtaking view and knowing that he had succeeded in his mission to find the secret path made him giddy with triumph. He would bring news of this place back to Beth and it would make her illness easier to bear, knowing she could pass on the knowledge to her child. He laughed aloud into the wind and the cackling calls of gulls. But the noise was overheard, and his family's voices came drifting through the gorse, sounding concerned and impatient.

"Kit, where are you? Come back!"

He could not stay here, in this window onto a world where anything was possible. If he did not return to the path, the others would worry. He turned his back on the sea, pivoting on the ball of one foot in a perfect spin. But the ground between the grasses was softer than it looked, and betrayed him.

Kit skidded back through the mud and fell sprawling forward. In a panic, he flung out his arms to grab at anything nearby, but only felt thin stems brush between his fingers. How close had he been to the edge? How far was he falling? He wanted to cry out, but something stopped the sound in his throat. With a thump, he hit the ground face first, his fingers tightly wound round clumps of yellow grass. *It's OK, I'm on solid ground. I can't have been that close to the edge after all. Just breathe slowly and don't make any noise to scare the others.* Still clinging to the vegetation, he turned his head to look backwards, and felt his stomach lurch: he might have landed safely, but his feet were dangling in mid-air over the side of the cliff!

He dragged himself forward, dislodging loose stones that bounced off the cliff and made no audible sound as they collided with the ground far below. Pulling his legs in, he sat on the grass and took a deep, steadying breath. Now that he knew he was safe, a curious, or maybe morbid, impulse compelled him to take one last glance over the edge: to know exactly how far he would have fallen. His stomach churned. It must be over a hundred metres down to sea level and the dark rocky platform that would have marked the end of his descent. What would it have been like? He had never been afraid of heights, but suddenly an instinct for survival kicked in and he found himself scrambling back from the edge as fast as he could.

"Kit! I won't ask you again. Come back here now!"

His mother's exasperated tone cut through that wave of fear, bringing him back to an ordinary world. Nothing had changed. He stood up and tried to brush down his trousers, but there was no cleaning the mud that had embedded itself into their turn-ups and the soles of his shoes.

When he returned through the tunnel to the main path, Catherine and Juliet were a short distance away, calling his name while scanning the fields and gorse.

"It's OK, I'm here!" Stepping back onto the sunny Cleveland Way, he waved to his family, and noticed an angry red line carved across the back of his hand. It stung sharply, but did not bleed. He must have caught it on the gorse thorns when he reached out to stop his fall. It would be best if his mother did not see, so he lowered his hand and hid the mark.

"Kit! What were you thinking, running off like that? And leaving the path. It's not safe on the edge of the cliffs; you have to stay on the level ground. The rocks give way all the time – Sean warned us about it this morning. What if you'd fallen?"

It would have been a sudden end to his quest, but Kit supposed it might have briefly felt like flying. He did not think his mother would appreciate this response.

"Sorry, Mum. I must have taken a wrong turning."

"Oh well, at least you're safe. But look at the state of you!" She took in the mud caked around his feet. "What were you doing? Jumping in a peat bog? You'll have to take those shoes off before we get indoors, or you'll be explaining to Sean why there are muddy footprints all over his nice clear floor." She sighed and ran her hand through her hair. Kit did his best to look contrite, which was not easy when he was still shaking off the horror of his fall. It must have been enough though, because Catherine brightened up. "Let's go back now, and no more running out of sight this time! When we've had a rest from our walk, we can talk about what colour you both want your rooms painted when we get our new house."

Kit knew his mother would keep an eye on him the whole way back, so he walked ahead to make it easier for her. While Catherine and Juliet discussed cupcake recipes, Kit began to count his steps, measuring the distance back in strides.

"One, two, three," he muttered under his breath so the others would not overhear.

"So what was all that about today then?" Juliet asked. She had relocated to Kit's room for the afternoon and sat on the wooden floor beneath the window with her knees pulled up to her chin. Most of the time she was distracted by her phone, but periodically she would say something without looking up that showed she had not forgotten her brother was there too.

"What was what?" Kit examined his hand where he had grazed it against the gorse. The scratch had raised itself up into a thin red ridge across his skin that only stung when he remembered it was there. At least it was clean and wouldn't become infected: that was one small advantage to having a mother who made you wash your hands every time you came back in from outdoors.

Juliet's line of inquiry was not derailed by his nonchalance. "I saw what you were up to. When you disappeared for a bit, you didn't get lost like you claimed – that was deliberate, wasn't it?"

She raised her dark eyes from the phone screen and fixed him with a stare he could not avoid. For all that she might try to behave like their mother, Kit always found that Juliet was much better at knowing what was going on. She had a way of spotting his excuses or knowing when he was hiding something, which his parents did not. He knew she would not give up asking questions until he told her the truth, so he explained about Beth who lived in the secret room downstairs and how he had decided to collect what she needed to finish her map.

"It's such a cool place, Jules. You can forget everything up there, and just imagine what it's like being a bird flying over the sea. I found it for Beth, so she can remember where it is."

He decided not to tell her the rest: how the magical lookout point could be treacherous if you let down your guard or overlooked your footing. Juliet needed more reasons to like their new home, not fewer; only this morning, on learning that Askfeld did not generally stock oat milk for its coffee selection, she had described the guest house as "prison conditions, but with fewer social opportunities". Sean had even offered to source some dairy alternatives specially, but Juliet had insisted she couldn't let him go to such trouble for her sake, and then contacted her school friends to shock them with tales of her ordeals in the North.

"That was… nice of you, I suppose. Why did you do it?"

"To help her," Kit replied, which was a true answer, if not a complete one. He hoped it would be enough to deflect suspicion.

Juliet made a scornful noise: the short "huh" that she used when she lacked the motivation to properly laugh at something. "I overheard Mum say you had to be helpful while we're here. I'm not sure this is what she meant."

"No, it's not that," Kit protested, resenting the insinuation that he only did anything right when instructed to by adults. Being kind to others was just something he did, the way being brilliantly hard-working was what came naturally to Juliet. Not that he was stupid. His mum always made a fuss of his school marks and house points. It was just that he could never match his sister's achievements, and had realized after one too many parents' evenings in Juliet's shadow that maybe he could instead carve out a space for himself by protecting classmates from bullies and collecting exercise books for Mrs MacAllister. "It's like… it's like this." He grabbed his copy of *Legends of King Arthur* and held it up for Juliet to see. "They get quests in this book. Tasks they have to complete. Because they're knights, and they have a code of honour, and they've sworn to serve the king but also to help others in need."

"Right. So this Beth is what – a princess in need of rescuing? By you, the noble Sir Christopher, I suppose." Her lips twisted into a thin, wry smirk. "What about monsters? Every knight has to face a villain or a monster on their quest. Have you decided who that is yet?"

Kit thought about this. Though he knew her question was meant to mock him, Juliet was right: heroes always had an enemy to defeat before they could reach their goal. He had not met anyone at Askfeld who acted like a villain, but then some monsters could disguise themselves. Was there anyone who might harbour ulterior motives? Maddie was fearsome but avoidable; Bert seemed friendly and harmless. That left one person.

"I think it's Sean," he said, remembering how he had blocked the way to his wife's room. "He doesn't want me to help Beth, or even to see her. Don't know why though."

"That's stupid. Why would he not want someone to help her? He's her husband. It's not as if he's locked her away like Mrs Rochester. You're making too much drama out of it. You always overthink things."

"I don't know." Kit did not know who Mrs Rochester was either, but did not want to admit this and earn his sister's scorn. He stared into the distance as he tried to imagine why Sean would oppose any efforts to be kind to Beth. "But I guess if I keep on finding the places for Beth's map, I'll find out sooner or later."

Juliet rolled her eyes and checked her phone again. A moment later she threw it down in frustration. Kit considered telling Juliet about the other reason, but decided she would object to it. He had not shaken the thought that there must be a way to bring their dad to join them here sooner. There was no escaping the sense that something was not right in the Fisher family, and that was surely because they were separated by hundreds of miles. That was not how it should be, and Kit felt the ache of that wrongness growing each day. He saw it in the rest of his family too, in his mother's shortness of temper and his sister's strange behaviour. But he meant to fix it.

His father just needed convincing that he wanted to live here instead of in the city. It must be hard, as an adult, to leave an important job and move to somewhere comparatively quiet and remote. Kit would find a way to persuade his dad that Askfeld was not so bad, not as grey and bleak as his mum would joke from time to time, and that they could be happy in their new home. Beth's unfinished map was like a promise of shared adventures to come, not just for the Garsdales' child but also for Kit and his family. He would be the one to reunite the Fishers and set everything back to the way it should be.

First, he needed to find a way to sneak past Sean to see Beth and set his plan into motion.

CHAPTER FIVE

NORTH AND SOUTH

DAY THREE

Top three things about our new home that Dad will love when he gets here:

1. All the open space for playing football – you don't have to share the beaches and moors with a million dog walkers and joggers like in Richmond Park.

2. Being right next to the sea. That's where people usually go in the summer for a weekend, but now we're going to live by it all the time, Dad will get to feel like he's always on holiday.

3. If everyone's as friendly as Beth and Bert, then it will be easy for him to make new friends. Dad likes having lots of people to talk to and tell jokes with, so Askfeld will be great for that. Note – Mum always says Dad is good for her because he reminds her to go out and have fun from time to time. So we need Dad here or she'll never stop phoning her old office.

This time, Kit waited until he had seen Sean abandon the reception desk for the kitchen. He might have been reading too much into the situation, but it was interesting timing, the way Sean left just as Maddie returned to Askfeld from her shopping trip. Maddie let herself in, muttering phrases Kit sometimes heard at school but wasn't allowed to repeat at home as she stomped on the doormat to dislodge mud from her walking boots. As Kit leaned forward in his chair by the fireplace, he could see what had annoyed her. The shopping bag she was using had split, jettisoning its contents. She now carried the bundle of her new purchases in her arms, still wrapped in the bag's shredded remains. There looked to be a few tins with metal lids and a plane like the one Kit's dad kept in the garage for sanding down wood. A hammer rested in the crook of her arm, the way a wealthy landowner might carry a shotgun around his estate, and the weight of it had pulled her raincoat off that shoulder so that she looked dishevelled and flustered.

What was she up to? A summer holiday was hardly the time to start building furniture, but Kit could not see what else this new selection of tools could be intended for: he had seen his father use similar ones when he made a coffee table for Kit's mother as an anniversary gift. That table was now in storage, waiting to be unloaded into their new house one day. Maybe Maddie wanted a coffee table to make her room at Askfeld feel more homely, since she had nowhere else to go, according to Bert. And yet there were enough more pressing mysteries at hand, without investigating someone so easily enraged. Kit was not sure it would be worth it, to risk being shouted at again. He decided to let this particular puzzle remain.

She glanced around, checking that no one had seen her come in, and as she looked through the doorway into the sitting room, Kit jolted back against his chair so hard he made it rock on its hind legs. He opened a book and pretended to be engrossed in it.

The bravest of all Arthur's men was raised by Nimue, the Lady of the Lake. She trained the orphan

Lancelot in all he would need to know to become a knight at Camelot.

Nimue probably taught more useful skills than he had learned at school. Lancelot would not have needed to worry about subordinate clauses or modifying adverbs, as long as he had courage and good manners. Knowing how to wield a sword probably got you further in life than memorizing times tables.

Satisfied that no one was spying on her for once, Maddie marched up the stairs, and through the ceiling overhead Kit could hear the creak of floorboards as she crossed the landing to her room. The coast was clear at last.

Kit snapped the book shut and headed off to see Beth. As he reached the door, it opened from the other side and he jumped back to avoid a collision with the person exiting.

"Who's this then?" A woman in her fifties looked down at Kit without smiling. The lines on her face drew out an expression so stern that his first thought was that she might easily be Sean's mother.

"I'm Kit. I've come to see Beth. Can I go in please?"

She did not move.

"Is that Kit?" Beth's voice called from within the room.

"That's what he's saying." The older woman did not look round to answer, but fixed Kit with a piercing stare.

"Well, don't go scaring him away, Mum!" Beth laughed, and Kit stared, trying to see any family resemblance in this unfriendly expression. They had the same round face shape, now that he looked again, and perhaps the same nose.

"In you go then; don't just stand there gawpin'," she said impatiently, as if Kit had been dawdling out here keeping everyone waiting, rather than recoiling from the stony greeting he'd received. He squeezed past her into the room.

"I'll see you next Thursday," Beth's mother said. "Don't forget to tell Sean I said not to bother buying a new cot; there are plenty of people with second-hand ones to give away. And tell him I said he needs to clear out his climbing gear to make space for the pram – not like he should be clinging to the sides of cliffs any more either way. He's got bigger responsibilities now. Phone if you need owt before then."

"Thanks, Mum. See you next week."

She closed the door behind her. *How could that be Beth's mum?*

"Hello again."

"Hello," Kit said cautiously, checking the room for other relatives who might jump out and snap at him. There was a pile of baby clothes neatly folded on the footstool near Beth's chair, and he was sure they had not been there before. "What's gawpin' mean?"

"It means staring. I hope Mum didn't frighten you."

Kit decided he would pretend she had not. A knight of Camelot would not be deterred by a stern expression. But he still was not sure what he had done to make her so annoyed on a first meeting. "Didn't she want me to come and see you?"

"She didn't mind at all. She only seemed abrupt to you because you aren't used to her. Lots of people from my parents' generation are like that." Beth leaned forward to lift the stack of tiny vests and cardigans from the footstool so that Kit could sit down. Her movement was slow and deliberate.

"They're cross all the time, d'you mean?"

"Oh, that's not her being cross. She doesn't show friendliness the way you'd expect, is all. If you don't know her she might seem a bit grumpy, but she's not really. Lots of people her age are like that, I think. But on the other hand, if you ever end up sat next to my dad on a bus, he'll happily tell you his whole life story like you've known each other for ever. Half the country has probably heard about the time he almost met the prime minister. People round here might be a bit different from what you're used to in London as well."

This went against so much of what Kit's mother had drummed into him about good manners and what she called "courteous behaviour", which was one of her favourite subjects to teach her children. His father talked about something called "cultural differences", but that was only when he had to travel with work and needed to brush up on how to greet someone who spoke another language. Then again, plenty of the words Beth's mum had used sounded foreign to him, as if she had taken the English lexicon and spun her own variation of it. His mother had warned him that people had their own dialect round here.

"Are we really different?"

"Probably more than we realize. Everything seems normal until you find out not everyone else speaks or thinks the same way as you. The one that always threw me and Sean when we met up with friends from Reading was dinner."

"How's dinner confusing?"

"Well, what do you think it is?"

Could it be a trick question? The answer was obvious. "It's what you eat in the evening. Like spaghetti or chicken casserole – that kind of thing."

"Not to me. Here, you have your dinner in the middle of the day."

"But that's lunch! What do you call dinner then? I mean, what do you call whatever you eat in the evening?"

"Tea."

"That's a drink. It can't be a meal too. Unless it's afternoon tea, which is when Mum and Juliet go out for expensive cakes on fancy plates, while Dad and I stay home to eat crisps and watch the football."

Beth laughed, but then she fell quiet and closed her eyes for a moment. Kit guessed the interrogation had tired her more than he had expected. He wished he had a plate of posh cakes to offer her now, to replenish her lost energy. After a short pause, she opened her eyes and continued.

"Like I said, it all seems simple until you find out someone else does things differently. I'll have to teach you proper Yorkshire dialect some time. Anyway, what's brought you here today? Have you finished reading about Odysseus already?"

"No – well, yes," Kit stuttered. "I have finished it, actually."

"You're a fast reader. Was it a good school, the one you went to before the move?"

"I'm not sure." Kit had never given much thought to how his school compared to others. He knew that his parents had been concerned that he went to the "right" secondary school in the approaching autumn term, which before had always meant the same one Juliet attended, and now that they had moved meant St Jude's was the only suitable option. And whenever they had spoken about the other schools nearby they would lower their voices and make "hmm" noises, as if they knew terrible secrets about them. But school was school. Mrs MacAllister had called Kit her "model student" and his best friend Toby her "young prodigy".

"What did you think of the story, then? Did you like Odysseus?"

"I liked how he was clever – he was good at fixing problems. And I liked that he got back to his family in the end and they were all together. But I felt bad for the Cyclops. I don't think they needed to go and blind him when he hadn't done anything to hurt them."

He had raced through that part of the book, gripped by it but horrified at the same time. It was only after the excitement faded that he began to wish the story had been different. You weren't supposed to feel sorry for the monster, but somehow he did.

"Oh yes, that bit is pretty gory, isn't it?"

"But I'm reading the King Arthur book now and that's really good. I like all the stories where the knights go off on journeys to find something like the Grail. Are there any castles near here?"

Beth tilted her head upwards as she thought about this. "Not a lot. I think the nearest one is at Scarborough. Our history is more Vikings and monasteries than knights and castles."

"We did the Vikings in Year Four. They were really violent, weren't they?"

"Well, yes. They did raid and destroy a lot of villages round here. But some of them were also good farmers and poets. Lots of our place names were first used by Vikings. So in a way we're still speaking their language."

"Like Askfeld? Is that a Viking name?"

"Probably. It sounds pretty Viking-ish, doesn't it? But I couldn't tell you what it means; you'll have to ask Sean. He's good on local history."

Kit did not like to tell Beth that he was growing reluctant to speak to her husband about anything.

"Your mum said Sean does rock climbing." That sounded like the kind of cliff-side activity that could feature on the map.

"Yes. Well, he used to, back when there was more free time. I don't think he's been out climbing in over a year now, but all the gear's still in the cupboard in case one day he magically gets a free afternoon." With a sigh, she looked down and twisted the gingham blanket around her fingers.

Kit tried to bring the conversation back round to the reason he had come here again. "How is your map going? Have you drawn any more of it?"

Beth glanced over to the table and Kit followed her gaze. The sketches lay untouched and the easel had been moved to a corner.

"Not lately."

"Why not? Shall I bring them over to you?" Perhaps she could not reach them, being ill and confined to her chair.

"Thank you, but no. I'm beginning to think it's a bit of a hopeless case, to be honest. I hadn't reckoned on how big a task it would be. It's not like an ordinary map, where you just plot the roads and houses. It'd be easy enough to buy that sort of thing in a shop. When I had the idea for this, I wanted it to show experiences and memories, so how you use it will depend on a lot of things. It's about the changing moods of the land, the places where storms are at their angriest over the sea, where the kittiwakes come and nest each spring, or where you're far enough from the glow of town lights to stargaze. It's about the sky and all its different complexions, layered over the sea and the land. When I think about trying to chart all of that, it's overwhelming." Beth seemed to catch herself, and her demeanour changed. "Sorry, Kit. I didn't mean to get all gloomy and poetic on you. It was nice of you to ask about the map."

"You're not giving up on it, are you?" Kit bypassed the sketches and ran over to the map on the easel. He spotted the small town of Utterscar, just up the coast from Askfeld. One of the houses there would soon be his new home. Close by, there was a portion of the land's edge labelled *Scar Bay*. He liked the sound of that: it had a dramatic, piratical feel to it.

"I haven't decided."

"Well, if it helps, I've got something for the map. I found your lookout point."

Beth pulled a quizzical face. "You did?"

"Yes!" Kit pointed. "It's here, just off the cliff path. It's four hundred and twenty-three steps from the front door. I counted on the way back."

She grinned. "Four hundred and twenty-three exactly? Well, I can't let that level of research go to waste." Sitting forward, she reached for the pencil on the small table beside her. "Could you bring me those sketches?"

He gathered up the papers and planted them in front of Beth. "Here," he pointed again. She chewed the top of the pencil.

"Let's mark it in then. And how many steps did you say it was? We'll draw the path, maybe a line of tiny footprints showing the way."

She circled the spot that Kit had indicated and began to draw the steps between Askfeld and the lookout point.

"What did it look like? How would you find it again?"

"It's just a gap in the spiky yellow bushes on the left. It looks a bit like a tunnel. Too small for an adult."

"The gorse must have become overgrown since I was last there. You used to be able to walk through most of the way, and only crouch for the last part." Beth jotted some notes next to the trail of footprints. "It's a wonderful spot, isn't it? I'm glad someone else knows about it now. If you were a bird on that lookout point, and you flew out in a straight line over the sea, like this," she drew an arrow eastward from the shore, "you could keep going and not see any land until you reached… Denmark, I think. Somewhere snowy, anyway. Thank you, Kit. Why don't you add it to the main map, since you found it?"

She handed him a broad-nibbed ink pen. Kit hesitated as he looked from it to her. His first thought was, *What if my hand slips and I ruin the map?* But the excitement of being allowed to take part in its creation was too much for him, so he stepped up to the easel.

"Just here?" he asked, and Beth nodded. He drew a small cross at the lookout point, an X to mark the spot. One day he would tell Beth's child how he helped to make this map.

"Perfect. A talented map-maker already."

"They're called cartographers, the people who draw maps." He had read about this for some geography homework last year, and had liked the sound of the word. It had an earnest, studied feel to it.

"Are they? Looks like we'll both end up teaching each other new words at this rate."

Kit looked over the sketches and scribbles, trying to decide which part of the map he would find for Beth next. In places her handwriting was not the easiest to decipher.

"I thought the North was full of hills," he said, looking at the blank terrain that surrounded Askfeld. "Why's it so flat here?"

"You're thinking of the Yorkshire Dales or the Lake District. Over here, we're on the edge of the moors, so it doesn't look the same. It's not all wool mills, sheep farms, and flat caps either."

He asked her what she meant.

"Well, if I came to the street where you used to live in London, would I find it full of cockney-speaking chimney sweeps and beefeaters marching on royal parades?"

He laughed. "No, of course not!"

"There you are then. Things don't always match their reputation."

Maps never told you that kind of thing, but maybe they should. Instead of county borders, they could show you where a word changed meaning, or an accent became hard to decipher. Landmarks would be replaced by local foods, and helpful labels could advise on common misunderstandings for visitors.

"Your map's going to be so much more useful than normal ones."

It would be full of the things that actually mattered.

CHAPTER SIX

THE BIRDWATCHER AND THE PILGRIM

GLOSSARY OF NEW WORDS (PART ONE)

Askfeld – a Viking name, from Ask (ash trees) and feld (field). So it means "field of ash trees".

"Ugh!" Juliet eyed the torrent of rain that cascaded out of the gutter. She and Kit had spent the whole morning indoors, watching as the weather turned worse and worse.

"I guess Mum'll work all day, since we can't go outside," Kit said, wiping the mist of condensation from the window. He traced a smiling face on the glass with his index finger and then erased it.

Catherine was upstairs, absorbed in a set of minutes for a meeting she had not attended. When Kit had complained to her that the rain would mean they'd be stuck indoors all day, she had only muttered under her breath, "Don't blame me. Moving up North was your father's bright idea." It felt like a clue to the mysteries in his red exercise book, so Kit promptly went next door to write it down. He had made no headway in deciphering the comment, though. His mind was half on the map and all the places he needed to explore and discover if he was going to help Beth complete it before her child was born. There was no chance of any of that today, so he and Juliet resigned themselves to staying indoors. They had brought books and games down to the guests' lounge. The basket of firewood beside the hearth had been refilled since yesterday, yet neither could bring themselves to ask Sean to light the fire on what was technically a summer's day. Instead, Kit had pulled one of the blue gingham blankets around his shoulders like a cloak and buried himself in a book. Juliet, however, was less content to entertain herself.

"I'm so bored. There's been no signal or wifi all morning, and I think I'm going mad just sitting here watching you read. Tell me about one of your books."

"Which one?"

"I don't know. Whichever one's most interesting."

'The challenge would be picking something she didn't dismiss as childish nonsense. Kit ruled out the superheroes as too far-fetched for Juliet's tastes, and thought instead about the stories he had borrowed from Beth.

"Well, there's this one here about a witch called Morgan le Fay. I kind of thought Morgan was a boy's name, but she's a woman anyway. She hates King Arthur and plots to kill him quite a bit in the stories. But one day she sends a messenger to Camelot saying she wants to be friends instead, and she sends a gift of a really fancy cloak, all covered in jewels."

Juliet arched a single eyebrow. "It's a trick, right?"

"Exactly! Merlin sees through it straight away, 'cause he's super clever, and tells Arthur not to try on the cloak just yet, in case there's some dangerous magic involved. He tells the messenger to put it on first, so they can see that it's not enchanted. The messenger's one of Morgan le Fay's maids – I forgot to say that – and she does as Merlin says, but as soon as the material touches her shoulders, it catches fire and she's burned to a crisp right in front of them!"

"That's so unfair to the maid. She wasn't the one who cast the spell on the cloak. Why did she have to die?"

"No, but she was in on the plot to kill Arthur," Kit explained. Juliet had misunderstood and was siding with the enemy. This was part of the problem with telling her stories; she tended to confuse or overcomplicate the division between good and evil.

"Why did Morgan whatshername even want to kill the king in the first place?"

"Um..." Kit paused and thought. It had all made sense when he was reading the story, but now he was less sure. "I think so she can be queen once he's dead. She's Arthur's stepsister, so maybe she thinks it's not fair she can't inherit the crown."

"Well," Juliet continued, folding her arms to underline her verdict, "I'm not sure it's a great story, but it's better than all the drama going on with everyone from school at least. Amy and Seb split up and keep writing awful things about each other online. Serves them right, really. No, I don't mean that. It's just that – well – maybe an evil sorceress is easier to face than them." She frowned. Her eyes were full of uncertainty, in a way that was quite un-Juliet-ish. She looked as if she was about to say something more, but at that moment Bert entered the room in a flurry of noise.

"Hullo there, Kit! Being kept indoors by this miserable weather, are we? Same here. No sense going out and getting drenched, is there? This must be your sister, I expect."

Juliet snapped back to her usual self and confidently introduced herself to Bert. There was no trace of the strange fragile shadow that had passed over her face a moment ago. They exchanged names and shook hands in a way that made Kit feel as if he were the only child present in a meeting of adults. He scowled and hid his face behind the book of Arthurian adventures. His hair fell into his eyes when he hunched over, which made reading harder. Recently, his mother had been complaining about it as though he made his hair grow too long on purpose.

"So what do you young folk do for entertainment on a dull day like this? I thought it was all tablets and smart phones and ignoring each other."

Kit lowered the book. "Juliet's phone won't work today. So I'm telling her a story."

"Storytelling, eh? Very good. One of the oldest pastimes in the world, that. And you've got a fireplace to sit round here, quite proper. Is it a good one – your story? Lots of excitement?" Bert sat down in the blue armchair he had previously recommended to Kit.

"It was all right, in spite of some plotholes. But he's got to the end of it now."

"Ah, that's a pity. I've come in at the wrong time, clearly. Unless it's your turn to tell us a tale next?"

Juliet looked startled at the suggestion. "No, I don't think I know any good stories. Just the books I was studying for GCSE English, and I don't want to have to read them again any time soon."

She might have been cleverer than him, Kit thought, but she certainly didn't have anywhere near his imagination. Juliet's mind was a set of filing cabinets, ordered and labelled clearly. But here was a more pressing issue. Juliet had mentioned her GCSEs, and Kit knew that if he did not change the subject immediately, she would start to sink into worrying about the exam results that she would not receive until mid-August, and it would be almost impossible to cheer her up then.

"What about you, Bert?" he asked, moving the conversation swiftly on.

"Well..." Bert stretched out his legs, and as he spoke, the syllables came out sounding stretched too. "Stories – words – that's never really been my thing. I'm a scientist at heart, even if I do have to do an inordinate amount of writing as part of my job."

"What is it that you do?" Juliet asked, with a show of polite interest. Everything about her demeanour, from the way she leaned forward with the question, to her hands folded neatly in her lap, was a perfect imitation of their mother. It wasn't the way she did everything just right that annoyed Kit; it was that he could tell she was thinking more about the "just rightness" of it than anything else. But Bert was not to know this, and took her question in good faith.

"I work at a university. A lot of the time I teach biology undergraduates. The good bits of biology, you understand – animals and plants – not any of this human anatomy stuff. Though it's not too long now until I can retire." The thought seemed to fill him with relief and dread all at once. "Still, you get good summer holidays, which is why I'm able to come and stay here for a few weeks. You can find marvellous seabird nesting colonies at Flamborough, not too far down the coast from us, and of course we're right on the edge of the moors too – splendid for all kinds of plovers and larks and grouse."

"You're a birdwatcher?"

Bert was distracted from answering by the sound of someone else entering the room. Kit's heart sank when he turned to see who it was. Maddie Morley had appeared in the doorway.

"Maddie, come and join us!" Bert called her over with a cheery wave in her direction. Kit wondered if Bert suffered from memory loss and had forgotten how this woman had shouted at them both in the corridor just a few days ago. Today he seemed under the impression that they were all good friends.

Maddie hesitated before replying, as if she also felt that Bert's greeting was much too cordial, and when she agreed, it was with little enthusiasm. She sat down with the group, avoiding any chair that was directly next to someone else. As she sank into the seat, her walking clothes made a rustling sound. She was quite stocky in build, not elegant and willowy like Juliet or Kit's mother, and her hair was scraped back in a haphazard manner, as if she had wanted it away from her face by any means necessary.

"Maddie, this is Kit and Juliet. We were just talking about… what was it that I was saying?"

"That you're a birdwatcher," Kit reminded him. Bert took a moment to remember.

"Mmm. Yes, just about. I used to be quite well regarded for my knowledge on the subject, actually." He scratched his head, moving the unkempt tufts of grey hair into an even more irregular arrangement.

"Used to be?" Kit repeated.

"Well, I suppose there's no harm in you knowing the truth. It's not as if you're going to tell any of the chaps at the university where to find me. You see, the last couple of papers I wrote weren't well received by the rest of the ornithological world. In fact, that's an understatement: one of them was widely ridiculed. And now the British Ornithologists' Union are rethinking their invitation for me to speak at their next conference. If I'm being honest, I'm here to hide away from my colleagues for as long as possible over the summer before the new academic year." He gave a rueful smile at this admission.

"That wasn't kind of people, to laugh at your work," Juliet protested, her brow furrowing at the injustice, just as it had at the thought of Morgan le Fay's maid meeting a gruesome and fiery end.

"Well, in fairness, I did make some wild assertions that I couldn't back up. Just got carried away with the idea of writing something remarkable for once. Didn't verify all my data thoroughly before publishing. I should have known better; it's precisely the kind of thing I teach my students not to do. Let that be a lesson to you all" – he eyed them with mock-sternness – "when you have homework to do: always check your facts!"

"How wonderful, to work with young minds." Maddie spoke at last, and it sounded rather wistful. Kit was surprised to hear her approve of Bert's work, since he had got the impression earlier that she disliked everyone at Askfeld Farm Guest House. Her eyes, however, were not on the others present, but gazing up into nothing, as if she were already lost in her own thoughts.

"They can be a frustrating lot sometimes. Sometimes you wonder what they actually learn at school before they start the course. But there are always some bright sparks in each year group."

"So what birds will you look for here?" asked Kit, thinking that there might be something exotic to add to Beth's map. His dad had taken him to the park once and pointed out a flock of bright green parakeets, which looked like the sort of bird you ought to find in a zoo or the jungle, but he had no idea if they could be found this far north.

"Oh, guillemots and razorbills down on Flamborough Head. Puffins too, if you go to the right points. And I've already been out on the moors and into the National Park a good few times and seen curlews and lapwings. With any luck, I may spot a Northern Goshawk before I leave. That'd be a fine thing to have a photograph of."

"Are they rare?" Kit had never heard of most of these, and wasn't sure how to spell their names if they did end up warranting inclusion on the map.

"Northern Goshawks? Well, they aren't endangered, if that's what you mean. There's a few hundred pairs breeding in the country. But you don't see them as often as pigeons, let's put it that way. I suppose it would be nice to see something truly rare. It might make up for my mistakes this year if I had something interesting to talk about on my return. But I don't imagine that restoring my reputation as an ornithologist will be as simple as that."

As Bert fell silent, the drumming of the rain on the windows grew louder. Kit was a little disappointed: he had hoped there would be a rare and spectacular bird on Bert's list that could feature as another annotated adventure on the map.

"I think it's your turn, Maddie," said Bert, turning in his chair to give his full attention to her.

"For what?" Maddie lurched back to the conversation she had drifted away from.

"These children – sorry, young people – need some entertaining on a grey and dreary day. And what could be more entertaining than conversation with new friends? You must have some interesting stories to tell us about yourself."

Maddie raised her eyebrows at this assertion. For a moment, Kit thought she was going to snap at Bert, but instead she looked from one face to the next and relented.

"Well, I'm not sure there's much to say about me. My name's Maddie, which is short for Madeline but nobody calls me that any more. I've spent the last few weeks walking up the east coast of England, starting from my old home in Norfolk, and this is perhaps the most – no, the *only* – adventurous thing I've ever done in my life. Never was one for spontaneity or excitement, really. If you see me wearing the same clothes a few days in a row, it's because I'm travelling light."

"You mean you're carrying all your stuff and just walking from one town to the next?" asked Kit.

"That's right."

"Wow! That's so cool." He couldn't help his enthusiasm: it was blurted out before he could remember that they weren't supposed to like one another. At Kit's words Maddie seemed to brighten up and she gave him a broad smile. He began to feel that he had misjudged her the day they first met. But then she had misjudged him too, or she would not have accused him of spying.

"I've climbed hills and crossed rivers, walked in thunderstorms with lightning striking the trees about me, and nearly been swept away by the tide on the coast."

It was hard to picture this middle-aged woman being so daring: she looked more like one of the scruffier teachers from Kit's old school than the sort of person to trek the length of the country.

"Where are you going?"

"To the abbey up at Whitby."

Kit was unsure where this was. The trouble with being somewhere new was that all the places people talked about were unfamiliar. Whitby, Flamborough, Scarborough – they might as well have been names from the other side of the world. And yet there was a deliciousness about that foreign quality too. It opened up new possibilities: strange sites usually had room for mystery, for abandoned ruins and buried treasure. You couldn't find that in Richmond Park; Kit had spent enough of his life up to now exploring it to know this for certain.

"But why couldn't you just take the train?" asked Juliet.

Kit groaned. He should have guessed she would be practical

rather than poetic about this. She could not see the value in Maddie's expedition, or how much more exciting it would be to travel on foot than to take the fastest route. Sometimes he wondered if his sister had any imagination at all.

"I'm on a kind of pilgrimage," Maddie explained. "Is that a word you know? Yes, I thought so; you have a clever look about you. So you understand that the journey is important. When pilgrims travelled to significant sites hundreds of years ago, they would have gone on foot, so now I am too. In our busy world, it's good to take your time and get a clear head once in a while."

"Not far to go either," Bert chimed in. "Whitby's only ten, maybe fifteen, miles away. You could do that in a day."

Maddie gave Bert an icy look and made a non-committal noise. Bert seemed not to notice.

"Why are you on a pilgrimage?" Kit asked. He had never heard of a modern-day pilgrim before, and wondered if it was a religious exercise. She had mentioned an abbey, so maybe she was off to visit some monks.

"Well…" Maddie paused, becoming interested in staring at the cold cinders in the fireplace for a moment. "Pilgrimages are often about learning something along the way. And when you're not in school any more, sometimes you have to deliberately set aside time to learn new things."

"What have you learned so far?" asked Juliet, who liked quantifiable data as much as Kit liked unravelling mysteries with "why" questions.

"I'm not sure yet." Maddie smiled, raising her hands in a kind of shrug. "Maybe it will become clear by the time I get to the abbey."

"When will you go?"

"Soon enough; when the weather brightens and I have everything ready that I need for the journey."

She folded her arms across herself and smiled again, but as the conversation moved on to Bert describing the wildlife that could be found near Whitby Abbey, Kit noticed Maddie's smile fade and her eyes drift downward, as if she were no longer really listening but immersed in some other thought.

"And what brought you two here this summer then?" Bert asked them. "Kit tells me you're moving to Yorkshire permanently. Guess you couldn't wait to get to your new home?"

"Yes, we're very excited to be moving into our new house," Juliet replied, with the level of animation she might muster for choosing between white bread or brown at breakfast. She looked down at her hands, scrutinizing them for chips in her grey-pink nail varnish.

"I don't mind being here for now though," added Kit. "We don't have to help out with housework and stuff like we would at home. Mum says it's important for us to do lots. She says we're both really mature for our ages because she treats us like adults and expects us to behave that way." He stopped, embarrassed to register that it sounded as though he were boasting, and quickly changed the subject. "I hope my new room has a window towards the sea. Jules has the best view here. Or at least, it's better than the one I've got. It's not really fair, because she doesn't even like the outdoors much. She'd rather be shopping or revising or texting her old friends from school."

So far, he had only seen photographs of their new house. His parents had been up to view it, but Kit and Juliet had yet to set foot in the place where they would soon live. Juliet had studied the pictures and drawn up a meticulous plan for the layout of her new room on graph paper, making sure everything would fit perfectly. Kit enjoyed the suspense of not knowing for sure what the house was like. He hoped the garden was an overgrown wilderness, perfect for building a den, and that the attic would be a cosy space where he could hide away from the others with a torch and a stack of books. A secret passage was probably too much to hope for, but you never knew unless you looked.

"Ah, of course," said Bert. "You'll both be starting new schools up here in the autumn. You must miss the friends you've left behind. Still, always nice to meet new people."

"Mum said it was for the best," Juliet said thinly.

"Well, parents are always trying to do what's best for their children. I've got two sons, you know, both grown up now. One of them's married and lives in Bristol. No children of their own yet, though they have just bought a golden retriever. The other's a pilot and flies passenger planes between here and the Far East. Always phones me in the middle of the night and says he forgot about the time difference again! But that's me getting distracted." The birdwatcher stopped himself before he pulled the conversation any further away from its original course.

"I still don't really get it," Kit said, seizing an opportunity to voice his questions without their mother present to silence him. "This move, I mean. It's not like we've come for Dad's work, because they're keeping him in the office in London. And Mum likes to pretend she's still at her old job – she phones in to the office any chance and tells them all what to do. So why do we have to be here at all?"

"Leave it alone," Juliet warned, gripping the arm of the chair so that her knuckles turned white. Bert opened his mouth to say something, then seemed to think better of it and instead shifted uncomfortably in the armchair while looking around the room. But Kit could not stop now that he had begun. Maybe if he pointed out the illogicality of it, Juliet would tell him something she knew that he did not. He felt certain she must be in on the secret and know why they were there. He had never heard her ask any questions about it. That strongly suggested she was complicit.

"I've been thinking about it, and I've got a theory. I think we're on the run from the police. Maybe Dad's involved with the Mafia. Or something. But this would be a great place to hide out. No one would think to look for us all the way up here."

"Stop being stupid. You always have to make things so dramatic." Juliet's lip curled in scorn at his hypothesis. It was unlike her to be rude to him when there were strangers present. He must be getting closer to the truth.

"But why else would they make us leave school before the proper end of term and come here before we even have a house? It's all right for you. You got to see your friends one last time at that end-of-exams party, but I'm missing all the fun end-of-term stuff."

"I said drop it!" Her voice had become louder and shriller. The noise startled him into silence. Juliet looked surprised at herself. She stood up and hurried out of the room without another word.

"Well, that girl's carrying something heavy, for certain." Maddie exhaled as though she had been holding her breath during the exchange. She watched the empty doorway through which Juliet had left, with an expression of concern.

"I don't know about that," said Bert. "It's not for us to get involved in Kit's family affairs. But maybe it's better not to be asking your sister too many questions for the time being, lad. No need to upset her more, eh?"

Kit frowned. More and more, the world was a conspiracy of adults who understood something he did not, and were working to keep it from him. But there was one adult who he thought might just help him. He left his books on the arm of the chair and went to find Beth.

CHAPTER SEVEN

SCAR BAY

DAY SIX

Five possible reasons why we moved up here:

1. Dad is working undercover to bring down a gang of criminals, and we've had to flee far away for our safety, so that the gangsters don't kidnap us in revenge.

2. Either Mum or Dad has secretly changed jobs to become a scientist who studies dolphins/fish/crabs, so we need to be near the sea for their work.

3. We're in hiding like Bert and avoiding people who would laugh at us. (In which case, what happened to make them laugh? Did Mum embarrass herself in public?)

4. Our new school St Jude's has a scholarship specially for Londoners.

5. I'm having a surprise party for my eleventh birthday, on a real pirate ship. Dad has stayed behind to buy cake and presents, but we're here so it's not too far to the harbour. Although then I think it'll be a long way for all my friends to come to it.

Beth was not in her room. The only sound from her doorway was faint snippets of the conversation Kit had left behind in the guests' lounge. It seemed colder and greyer without her as Kit stared at the vacant chair and the folded gingham blanket on the footstool nearby. The emptiness of the space made him nervous. Where could she be? She had promised Kit she was not ill enough to die, but what if she had suddenly got worse? Perhaps she had gone to hospital. His heart began to race at the thought of what might have happened. He ran out of the room, slamming the door behind him in haste. He would look for Sean. If Sean was still here, it would mean Beth was OK.

He raced down the corridor towards the reception desk where they had met Sean on their first day. No one was there either. Panic rose and Kit went to the only other place he dared to look. He burst through the kitchen door, causing the two people in there to turn sharply and stop their conversation. Sean looked bewildered; Askfeld's chef scowled as he paused midway through slicing a small mound of carrots.

"You're not supposed to be in here," he said, pointing the knife at the intruder.

Kit ignored him and spoke to Sean instead. "What's happened?" He was breathless from running across the building, but managed to articulate the question nonetheless. The owner and the chef stared at him.

"You tell me. Is something wrong?" Sean asked. From his expression, Kit guessed he did not yet know that his wife was missing. He would have to break the news to them so that they could join in the search.

Then another voice spoke. Someone was coming into the kitchen through the open door behind him.

"There you are, love. I need to speak to you about some of these figures when you've got a moment. Oh, hello, Kit!"

Kit spun round and stared, speechless. Beth was standing there without any kind of support and carrying a lined notepad under one arm.

"You know, you shouldn't really be in here. This is where Nick makes all the food for you and the other guests. If we distract him he might accidentally chop off one of his fingers and put it in the soup! Let's leave him to it. Sean, come and find me when you've got time to talk about the numbers. I'll be in the office."

Still unable to find words to express his amazement at this miraculous recovery that seemed to surprise nobody else, Kit obediently followed Beth out of the kitchen. As the door swung closed behind him, he heard one of the two men mutter to the other, "What on earth was that about?"

There was a small room next to the kitchen, with a plaque on the door that said "Private". It was at this door that Beth stopped, and Kit realized she did not expect him to follow her. But he still needed to know what was going on, so he had to ask his questions before she closed the door on him.

"Are you better now? Did the doctor give you some new medicine?"

"I'm feeling better today than I was yesterday. But I don't know what will happen tomorrow." Even Beth seemed unamazed that suddenly her legs worked normally. He was beginning to wonder if he had imagined her entire illness.

"But you're walking! I thought you couldn't walk. Doesn't this mean you're getting better?"

"I see." Beth smiled at his confusion – a kind smile that told him she had not lied. "Maybe the explanation I gave you before was too simple. I didn't want to confuse you, but clearly you're quite bright, so perhaps the child-friendly version isn't going to cut it after all."

Kit liked the idea of not being treated like a child: a privilege usually reserved for his sister. For once, he was the one being recognized as clever and mature enough. He met Beth's expression with a defiant stare that said, *Yes, you underestimated me*, while she narrowed her eyes and searched for the right words.

"You remember I told you my illness is more complicated than the ones you are used to? Well, some days I can walk around – maybe just a little bit, maybe more – but then the next day I might not be able to get out of bed. It's hard to predict, and we just tend to see what each morning's like." She hesitated. Kit wondered if the thought of tomorrow frightened her, being so unknown. But Beth took another breath and went on, "So, on good days like today, I make the most of it – I get up and stretch my legs. And right now I'm catching up on our finances. Sean never liked dealing with numbers, but I'm quite good with them, if I can just think clearly enough."

"But your map – I thought you said you couldn't do any of those things you did as a child."

"And I can't. I can't make a plan to go on a long hike next weekend, or spontaneously run down to the beach and jump in the waves. Even on good days those things would take a lot out of me, and on bad days I wouldn't be able to get dressed without help, let alone leave the house. It doesn't mean I'll never get to see any of those places again. But my world is changed now. And although I'm recording all the memories I want to pass on, my future adventures will be quite different."

"OK. Sorry I didn't understand."

"It's not your fault." Beth sighed and hugged the notebook to herself so that her chin rested on the top edge of it. Now that she had finished explaining, she looked weary. "It's a confusing thing. Even the doctors have a hard time making sense of it sometimes. Anyway, tell me, where are you off to?"

"Well, I was looking for you."

"I'm not used to being so popular! Do you need another book

to borrow? I found one about Robin Hood that I think you'd probably like."

"No, it's not that."

Beth studied his face. "Something more serious, by the look of it. Come in and sit down then. I can't stand for too long, even on good days, now that there's so much more of me to carry about." She adjusted the stretched fabric of her dress to sit evenly and propped open the door of the study. She moved more slowly now than when she had come into the kitchen. They both went in and sat down on the two black swivel chairs that faced one another across a desk. Beth immediately started spinning round on hers. "I can never resist doing that," she confided with a mischievous smile. "So, what's the problem?"

Finally given the opportunity to tell someone about the mysteries, Kit blurted it all out. "Everyone here says I should stop asking questions. Mum, Juliet, even Bert told me to stop asking. But my dad always says it's good to ask questions all the time. That's how we learn."

Beth's chair slowed to a halt. "I suppose he's right – at least when it comes to learning about long words and far away countries and old kings. But when it comes to learning about other people, the rules are a bit different. We should learn at the pace that person chooses. When we met, I didn't ask you to tell me all your secrets, did I? And you didn't ask me mine."

"Do you have secrets?" Beth was confusing at times, but Kit had never seen her as someone who was hiding information on purpose – not in the way his family was.

"I should think everyone does."

"I'm not sure I do," said Kit, but then he thought about the unfinished map and his quest to help Beth. It wasn't exactly a secret, since he had told Juliet about most of it. But he hadn't told her about his plan to use the map to bring his father here and reunite his family in their new home. He imagined the four of them together in the same room, working their way through all the board games they owned, and the satisfaction he would feel in knowing that he had made this picture possible.

"They're all being weird," he said, changing the subject away from himself and his own schemes. "First of all, Mum and Dad said we were moving up North. That was back in January, right after Juliet finished her mock exams. I remember because she locked herself in the bathroom for hours after the last one and wouldn't come out even for dinner. But they said it would be during the summer holidays. We went and stayed at Grandma Fisher's house for the weekend while they went to look at houses. It took a really long time for them to choose the right one. But they found one: it's in Utterscar, near here, and the people there said we could have it at the start of August. It looks cool in the photos, the bedrooms are really big.

"But then one day Mum announced that we couldn't stay in London any more and it felt like she was on the phone to my school for *days*, getting them to agree to me leaving before the end of term. Dad said she nagged them into it in the end. I missed sports day and the play and Toby's birthday party. And we had to pack suitcases, but leave lots of our stuff behind because the house wasn't ready. Dad said some of our stuff would go into storage, and some of it he'd bring when he came up to join us. He said something about his job needing him to stay a bit longer. I had to leave loads of my books behind, and Juliet was no help; she just sat in her room moping all the time and phoning her friend Amy, who's horrible. I don't know why Jules likes her at all – she laughs at everyone and makes up nasty stories about them. So we had to come and stay here at Askfeld instead of going to our house. I mean, I like it, because I met you, and Bert, and even Maddie seems nicer than people say. But none of it makes any sense. Why did we come here early? And why isn't Dad with us?"

Beth made a "hmm" noise and did not say anything for a while. It was a relief, just being allowed to unload all his questions without being told to stop talking. "I'm afraid I'm no more able to answer any of those things than you are, Kit."

"I think I wouldn't mind not knowing, if we were all together. If Dad was here. He'd know what to do: he always does."

He had expected Beth to reply that she was sure he would be here soon, and it was likely just work keeping him busy, which was what his mother always said, if she said anything at all. Instead, Beth looked sympathetic. "You must miss him."

She was right. Kit did miss him. Kit's dad was the kind of father who took you to the park to play football on weekends, or would let you help with gluing together all the tiny parts of a model plane and not tell you off if you accidentally stuck your jumper to the worktop. He worked long days, often coming home after Kit had gone to bed in the evenings, though Kit liked to stay awake to hear the click of the front door and the low voices in the hallway, but on Saturdays there was always time for them to have fun together. Kit's mum was the one who told them when to tidy up before dinner and reminded Kit he ought to be grown up and helpful, not always running around like a child.

That night the clouds slipped away, having no more rain to hurl down on the coast, and by morning the horizon was a clear blue line under a bright sky. The breeze blew in over the waves, brisk with the promise of fresh new things. Kit leaned out of his bedroom window to fill his lungs with the cool air. It was the perfect day for pursuing a quest. The only difficulty was that both his secret missions, completing Beth's map and solving the Fisher family mystery, required the unwitting co-operation of others. He would have to be clever if he was to succeed.

"Mum, can we go out today please?"

Catherine did not look up immediately, but finished signing off her email and hit the send button first. As she re-read it, she automatically raised her hand to her left ear, forgetting that she had not put in her signature gold earrings the last couple of days.

"What's that, Kit?"

"Can we go somewhere? It's stopped raining."

His mother checked her inbox again, as if expecting a reply already. The message counter remained at a resolute zero.

"I thought you were happy reading."

"I was. But I finished the book about the knights of Camelot. And Juliet's bored and keeps getting me to tell her stories, and then she tells me that the stories are rubbish."

She closed the laptop and stood up. "You know what? You're right. We have been cooped up in here for a while, haven't we? It would be a shame to miss out on this lovely warm weather. We probably won't see so much of it here in the North, you know! Where would you like to go?"

Kit bit back the urge to tell her, as Beth had explained to him, that the differences between the North and South of England were stereotypes rather than rules. Instead, he grabbed at the opportunity to move forward with his quest.

"To the sea."

She laughed. "Kit, we're right next to the sea. Look, you can see it from the window."

"But we can't get to it. Not without going down the steep path you said Jules and I weren't allowed on without you. Can we go to where we can actually walk up to it?" He leaned on the back of the chair, rocking it forward, while she considered the idea.

"A trip to the beach. Why not? But only if you promise not to run off by yourself this time." She waved across the room at Juliet to get her attention, because she had her headphones in. As they talked through the plans, Kit ran to fetch his coat and shoes from his own room. On the landing, inspiration struck him.

"Can it be Scar Bay that we go to?" he shouted back over his shoulder.

"Scar Bay? Where's that?"

"Really close to our new house," he said, impressed with his own cunning. "I saw it on a map."

"Oh yes, that map Sean lent to us was useful, wasn't it? I should buy a guidebook from the shops in Utterscar so we don't have to keep borrowing it from him."

The car park was still some way from the sea, and from there a narrow path stretched down towards the coast. Clumps of grass either side of the track waved about in the wind, breaking up the sandy slope at irregular intervals.

"Let's go!" Kit cried, inhaling the salty air and racing towards the shore.

"Kit, wait. What did I say about running off?"

Begrudging their slow pace, Kit dawdled alongside his mother and sister on the winding steps down to the beach. He blamed their leisurely descent for his unwelcome realization that the path was in fact quite steep, and some of the steps uneven enough to send you toppling forward if you didn't pay attention. He reached for the wooden handrail, annoyed at his new nervousness of heights. He could not forget that sickening feeling at the lookout point, when his feet had dangled over the edge of the cliff.

They were only three miles north of Askfeld, but here the cliffs had stepped back to create a spread of clay-coloured sands, stretching out along the foot of the rock face. He was itching to run across them. At last they reached the bottom of the stairs and stood level with the sea.

"It's so huge!"

The tide was out, exposing broad bare sands stretching so far that Kit was filled with an impulse to run at breakneck speed from one end of the beach to the other. How else could you properly drink in so much wide open space? The shore was riddled with reflective pools where water had collected. He took off his shoes and socks and dug his feet into the soft sands. They sank into the waterlogged ground, leaving clear imprints of his heels and toes.

"Mum, can you take a photo of us and send it to Dad?"

"Oh, yes, that's a nice thought. I'm sure he'd like to see where we've been. Stand still then, Kit, or you'll be a blur in the picture. Smile, Juliet."

At the instruction to smile, Juliet's whole body stiffened and she scowled. It might have been because she didn't like being told what to do, Kit guessed, as it couldn't be that she didn't want to be here. How could anyone not love the feeling of curling their toes into the sand and looking out all the way to the watery horizon? But then, at the last moment before the photo was taken, Juliet changed her whole posture. She relaxed, flicked back her hair, and smiled sweetly.

"Lovely," their mum said, when she had taken the picture.

"Will you send it to Dad now?" Kit asked eagerly. The photograph would be a breadcrumb on the trail he was creating to convince his father that life here was good.

"Later. The signal's not great here. I'll send it when we get back."

She pocketed her phone and smiled at the sight of the sea. With measured steps, she wandered along the sands away from her children, calling back over her shoulder to remind them not to stray too far. Kit was looking in the opposite direction; he had spotted something in the rock. It looked almost like a doorway leading into the cliffs. He attempted to run towards it, and found it was harder to move quickly on the beach, the sand weighing in around his feet the same way deep snow did.

The doorway turned out to be the dark entrance to a cave in the cliff. Around the black arch the ground was littered with stones of different sizes. He crouched down to pick one up. It looked like an ordinary pebble, worn smooth and glistening by the waves' erosion. He wanted to find a fossil to take back for Beth. According to her map, collecting them was something she used to do, back when she was able to go exploring. But he was unsure how to tell what was a fossil and what was a rock.

"Jules!" he called to his sister, who was writing something in the sand with a long stick she had found.

"What?"

"D'you know anything about fossils?"

Juliet walked over so she wouldn't need to shout. "Only what we did in geography last year."

"I want to find one. What do they look like?"

She smirked. "Fossils can look like all sorts of things, Kit."

"Oh." Kit could not hide the disappointment in his voice.

She must have felt sorry for him, because she added, "Ammonites are really common. They're spiral-shaped, like snail shells. I guess you might find some; the conditions look good for fossils. Lots of sedimentary rocks – see all the striped layers in the cliff there?"

Kit picked up a handful of stones and began sorting through them for anything that looked shell-like. When he had finished checking them all, he threw them back and gathered another batch to examine. Juliet watched him for a moment, and then joined in, methodically picking up stones from her right and putting them down to her left to avoid confusion.

"Can't see anything like an ammo-whatsit," said Kit, "except this – is this one?"

"That's a real shell, not a fossil. It's pretty, though. Maybe a periwinkle?" It was white with brown rings around it, and gathered up to a central point. It felt thin and fragile, as if it would shatter if you held it too tightly. Kit set it down carefully on the ground, then moved nearer to the cave and looked inside. It was hard to see anything in the darkness there, but he could hear water dripping from the walls. He stepped forward, accidentally kicking loose some of the stones on the floor. One of them looked as if it had a strange mark on it, so he took it out into the daylight.

"Hey, Jules, what about this? It's not a shell, but I think it's something."

The mark he had seen was an indentation in the rock. It was shaped like an animal's footprint, something with claws. It reminded him of when their neighbour Mr Kendrick in London had resurfaced the driveway, and a cat had walked through the cement before it was dry, leaving an imprint of its paws for posterity.

"Yeah, that looks like a trace fossil. Where did you find it?" Kit pointed towards the cave. "Better not let Mum know you went in there."

Now that she had pointed it out, Kit thought the cave did have an ominous black look about it. He decided not to go back in. It was funny how he hadn't noticed it until now.

"I didn't really. Just as far as the entrance."

Juliet fastened her coat. Kit had been too preoccupied to feel the encroaching cold until now. Grey clouds were rolling in and the sea had turned dark. Looking down the length of the beach, Kit could see his mother walking briskly towards them. She seemed to be calling something, but the wind carried her voice away.

"Cool. Those waves are getting higher," said Kit, and he ran down to the shoreline to stand where the cold water splashed around his ankles. His feet sank into the sand, and when he lifted them up, the imprints became puddles. Further out, the sea was growing restless and throwing white foam into the air. "Look how it hits those rocks over there! I bet ships crash on them when it's stormy."

Juliet stood a few paces behind him, anxiously eyeing her sand-caked shoes as the water drew nearer. She pulled her hood up as the wind grew louder, but she stayed and watched the waves crashing. Here where they stood, the water advanced and withdrew less violently, like a cat taking a swipe with playful paws. Kit occupied himself for a minute or two by jumping over the encroaching water; he was a daredevil facing down the risk of wet feet, but he timed each of his jumps perfectly with the tide.

"Beth says this sea stretches all the way to Denmark."

"Yes, that makes sense. And in that direction –" Juliet pointed north up the coast – "I guess you could sail even further without coming to any land, until you were in the Arctic Circle."

The tide drew in towards their ankles, but Kit was thinking about the dark icy waves hundreds of miles to the north, and how vast a thing this sea before them was. It built sandy beaches for them and uncovered fossils here in Yorkshire, but somewhere far away he pictured icebergs jostling one another, nudged aside by surfacing humpback whales. By comparison, he was so small and powerless. He shivered, and felt tiny goosebumps spread over his arms.

"It's kind of mesmerizing, isn't it?" Juliet murmured. It was the first time Kit had heard his sister say anything positive about their new home. Maybe she felt it too: that electrifying sense that the world was wide and full of wonderful things. Her long hair kept escaping from under her hood and whipping wildly around her face, but she stayed completely still, transfixed by the movement of the sea.

"I've been calling you from halfway down the beach!" Their mother had finally caught up with them and sounded hoarse from shouting against the wind. "It's going to rain; we need to get back to the car. Come on!"

Reluctantly, they tore themselves away from the sight of the stormy waters.

"To think this is supposed to be summer!" She marched them back up the slope to the car park so abruptly that Kit had to climb the steps with his laces untied and his socks still in his coat pocket. Despite her sense of urgency at the changing weather, Catherine insisted they all beat the sand from their soles before climbing back into the car.

"It is beautiful, in a dramatic, wild kind of way." Juliet cast a last look back at the darkening horizon before she claimed the front passenger seat.

"We're too close to Brontë country, that's the trouble," their mother muttered as she slammed the door shut a second before the rain began.

CHAPTER EIGHT

EXILES

DAY EIGHT

Before we moved up here, I think we only ever went to the seaside once before. Juliet and I built a massive sandcastle – not like the little ones you get from turning a bucket upside down; this had a moat and a garrison and a keep behind the defences. The tide came in and filled up the moat, but it also knocked over our watchtower.

Dad gave us some money to spend and Mum let us buy ice creams from a van. Mine tasted salty, but I think that was just the spray from the sea getting on it.

Kit burst into the room. In one hand he brandished a sketch he had worked on that morning to plot out yesterday's trip to Scar Bay, and in the other he held a borrowed book and the fossilized paw print from the cave.

"I've got the next part of the map!"

Beth did not react.

"Beth?" He wondered if she was lost in a daydream, although if that were the case it did not look like a good one. Still she did not turn to look at him.

"Sorry, Kit. Not today," she said, keeping her eyes fixed straight ahead. She had turned herself away from the view through the window, which Kit surmised was because it was all but obscured this morning. Askfeld was shrouded in white fog, which lingered over the old farm buildings and kept the guests indoors again. It had prowled in from the sea just before dawn, like a wild creature set loose over the coastal lands, and showed no sign of letting go of its grip.

"I don't understand." She had black wrappings around her lower arms, like gloves with the hands chopped off. "What are those things you're wearing?" he asked, pointing, to be clear that he did not mean the dressing gown she had put on over her clothes.

"Wrist supports," Beth answered, through gritted teeth. "Please, Kit."

He wanted to ask what was wrong. Her skin was pale and her whole body looked strained, as if the act of merely sitting there took a great deal of exertion. Yet there was nothing obviously changed since yesterday when she had been walking around and spinning on office chairs. Perhaps he should phone a doctor for her. Before he could find the words to form the right question, another voice in the room made him jump.

"What are you doing?" Sean had appeared in the doorway behind him.

"I was just –"

"Does your mother know you're here?" he asked, and Kit thought he heard a warning note in Sean's voice. Sean walked past him and placed on the table next to Beth's chair a mug of tea and a small rattling box from which he took out two white pills.

She frowned. "Sorry – not those ones."

"Another thing you're not allowed to take while pregnant?" Sean put the pills back in the box and set it down on the table. "Would you like me to look for some paracetamol instead?"

She nodded, but still looked unhappy.

He wanted to let Beth know about the fossil they had found, which would surely cheer her up, but Sean would probably not approve of his involvement in the map. He didn't seem to approve of anything Kit did. He needed a secret way to pass on the information. Suddenly struck by inspiration, he slipped the sketch inside Beth's copy of *Odysseus' Adventures: An Epic Retelling for Young Readers*, placed the fossil on top of it like a paperweight, and put them both down on the windowsill.

"Here's your book back – thanks for letting me borrow it," he said, hoping she would see the stone and that Sean would not. Standing at the windowsill with its collection of glass jars and paint brushes, he looked out: the fog was so heavy it was impossible to see where the land ended and the sea or sky began. By going to the window he also had an excuse to walk past the map and take a furtive look at it before he left the room. As he did, something caught his eye. Beside the wavering line of the coast was a small picture of a wide-winged bird soaring over the sea, and next to it the faint but legible caption: *Albatross?* Kit's dismay turned to hope again as he realized he knew exactly what his next task would be.

"Sorry for bothering you. I hope whatever's wrong gets better soon," he said, doing his best to imitate Juliet, who was so much better than he was at winning over disgruntled adults. Inspiration struck a second time, though this was a thought that made him feign casually glancing around to conceal a possible shudder: what was in that box of pills Sean had brought? He had been assuming they were a medicine that would fix whatever was hanging over Beth today. But hadn't she said herself that this was not the kind of illness you took a pill for and got better?

Ever since the day Juliet challenged him to identify the villain in his quest, Kit had seen more and more signs that Sean was acting suspiciously. He clearly did not want his wife to receive visitors, given how secretive he had been about this room on their first day at Askfeld, and today's behaviour only supported that theory.

Swapping the pills was exactly the kind of thing Morgan le Fay would do. She sent Arthur gifts that were bewitched, to harm him. She wouldn't hesitate to put poison in place of a healing potion. But it was a flight of fancy, and Kit knew it. People did not poison one another for no reason in the real world, even if they were suspicious and unfriendly. Juliet had most likely been right to scorn the idea that Sean meant Beth any kind of harm. Still, it would not hurt to make sure. He pretended to be interested in her most recent watercolour sketch, a simple seascape with towering clouds, because it was on the same table as the box. The pills pictured on the side were white and round, which gave nothing away, and the label itself read *Nefopam*, which told him no more. It was an unfamiliar, chemical-sounding word, and he was no closer to putting his mind at rest.

"Off you go then." Sean nodded over to the door, as if he thought Kit needed reminding how to find it. He did not like leaving without doing anything more to help Beth, but at least there was another lead for him to follow up now.

He went to the guests' sitting room and found it was fairly busy. A family he had not seen before were playing a noisy card game. The eldest son, a little older than Kit, was evidently winning, and the others were making a great show of competition against him. In the corner, someone was sitting in an armchair, though they were mostly concealed by the broadsheet newspaper they were reading. Only a pair of legs in mud-marked trousers were visible, and the top of a head covered in grey tufts of hair.

"Bert?" Kit asked. The newspaper folded downwards and the birdwatcher's face appeared.

"Hello there, Kit. Not stuck indoors again, are we? I think 'dowly' is the local term for weather like this. A good, expressive word, isn't it? Sounds like the sky is doing it all on purpose, just to spite us! Tough being kept indoors though, isn't it? When I was your age, we spent entire summers outside, catching frogs in jam jars and climbing trees. I do worry for young people today – it isn't good to have so little fresh air in your lungs. Shouldn't be at all surprised if it takes its toll on the whole generation's health one way or another. Not that I'm trying to scare you. I'm sure you'll be just fine."

Kit was growing used to Bert's rambling trains of thought by now. The birdwatcher said whatever was running through his mind, even if it meant circling a topic or swooping off to another idea. It was so unlike the carefully curated fragment of information he was used to gleaning from his family.

"You know you said you wanted to see a really rare bird while you're here?"

"What's that?" Bert frowned over the top of his newspaper. "Oh yes. Always makes for a more interesting time if you spot something you wouldn't normally see. Would be nice to have some good stories to tell when I get back as well. Anecdotes have a way of distracting people from your failings, I find. People can think all kinds of things about you, but tell them a gripping story and they'll forget it soon enough."

"Does it matter what kind of bird it is?"

"Well, no. I'm not especially devoted to birds of prey or passeriformes, the way some are."

A cheer mingled with groans sounded from the other side of the room as somebody won that round of cards and the others lamented their loss. Kit decided not to ask what *passeriformes* were. It would only distract Bert with tangential trivia, when there was the chance of something far more important here.

"What if it was an albatross?"

"An albatross? Well, that would certainly be beyond remarkable," Bert chuckled, "but just about impossible in this country. They're not found in these seas, you know. You have to be near the Pacific or Antarctica to be in with a chance of seeing one. And as I am sure you are aware, being a very bright young spark, neither of those is anywhere near the British Isles."

"But if there was one here?"

"Well, then I'd say it was extremely lost. Which is usually the case with rare birds, I suppose. But what's this fixation you've got with albatrosses suddenly?"

"I – I saw something that made me think..."

Kit suddenly realized he had not figured out how to tell Bert about the albatross without mentioning Beth's map, which felt like something that not everyone should know about. It was her collection of memories, and her gift to give to her child one day, not a chart for the whole world to use. Still, this snippet of information might just be the perfect distraction to cheer Bert up and give him something to hope for while he hid away this summer in disgrace.

"Ah, well, if you think you've seen an albatross, I'm afraid it's most likely another large seabird. It can be hard for a beginner to tell them apart: lots of them have similar shapes with black and white plumage. Perhaps a great black-backed gull. Yes, from a long distance you might be forgiven for mistaking –"

"No, I don't mean that I think I saw one. It was someone else. They saw an albatross here once and made a note of where it was. On the cliffs. Probably years ago, but maybe it's still there. Lots of birds come back to the same nesting place each year, don't they?"

"Kit, I don't mean to discredit your friend, but I really doubt that they have seen an albatross."

"But you said yourself, birds get lost sometimes!"

"Well, yes, you do get reports of what we call 'exiles' turning up in the North Atlantic, but officially they are extinct there now. And even that would be the other side of the country."

Bert turned the page of his newspaper as if that were the end of the matter, but Kit was not ready to give up yet, and persisted.

"So there have been albatrosses near the UK before now?" He strained up on tiptoes to catch Bert's eye over the top of the paper. The birdwatcher sighed and gave an indulgent nod that said he was only humouring this line of argument.

"Yes, I think I remember reading about some sightings off the west coast of Scotland, but that –"

"Then why not here? If a bird gets lost enough to be on the wrong side of the planet, why not a little bit more lost on the British coast?"

"I suppose… it's not completely impossible, I'll grant you that. But it's still not remotely likely."

"But it couldn't hurt to go and look. Maybe you'd find it."

For the shortest of moments, a light flickered in Bert's eyes at this idea. Then he gave a small shake of his head, as if dislodging the spark of hope before it took hold, and settled for a reluctant "hmm" noise.

"I could show you on a map where it was," Kit offered.

"Go on then. Can't do any harm to look, I suppose. And I can see I'm not going to get any more reading done until I hear you out."

This tentative concession was all the encouragement Kit needed. He ran to the reception desk and brought back the map Sean kept there for giving directions to visitors. It looked very different to Beth's: it was all road names and labels of the nearby towns rather than a sepia-tinted landscape bursting with stories. But there was enough familiar about it for Kit to be able to point to the part of the coast where the pencil markings had been.

"Here, I'm sure it was just here. That's not far from Askfeld, is it?"

Bert said nothing for a minute or two. He seemed to look straight through the map Kit was waving in front of him. When he finally spoke, it was in a very different tone, as if the thought had transfixed him.

"You know, it really would be quite something, to find an albatross. I've never seen one, in all my years as a birdwatcher. There are dozens of different types – did you know that? And their wingspan can be as much as twelve feet across. Ah, forgive me, that's a bit less than four metres for a young metric-user like you. Can you picture it?"

Bert stretched out his arms and leaned as far as possible to the left and then the right to try to convey the distance. He was becoming almost animated now. Even the idea of the albatross was enough to spark his imagination. Kit recognized some of the same enthusiasm he had felt at the thought of his own quest. Perhaps Bert too wanted some kind of purpose.

"Shall we go and look for it?" Kit suggested. "Once the mist is gone?"

"I suppose it couldn't hurt, when the weather clears up, though I don't know when that will be. This fog that comes in off the North Sea, it can stick around for a long time. Yes, come and talk to me about it again when visibility is better out there."

With that, Bert resumed reading his paper. Optimistically, Kit went straight to the window on the off-chance that the fog had vanished while they were talking. However, the dewy grass still petered out into white treacherous mist that gave no warning of the steep drop down to the sea it concealed. Instead, he went back upstairs to look for something he could read, now that he was done with Odysseus and King Arthur.

His stack of comic books sat untouched on the bedside table, caped heroes with clenched fists staring out at him from the covers. Beneath them was his red notebook. He took it out to update it with his latest quest. It was another adventure to record, but as he pressed the pen to the page it occurred to him that they were all connected.

Step one: find the albatross. This will make Bert feel better about facing his friends. Step two: tell Beth about the albatross so she can add it to the map. This will mean the map gets finished sooner. Step three: when the map is ready, call Dad and tell him about it so that he will want to come and live with us here instead of in London.

If he looked at it that way, it was really only one quest in several parts. He would be helping a lot of people along the way too. It was pleasingly neat to solve everyone's problems with one single course of action.

He hid the book under his pillow, because he was not entirely certain Juliet would not come in and start reading it. It was the sort of thing siblings did. And if you complained that they were helping themselves to your belongings, you simply earned a parental lecture on the importance of sharing. Next, he took the top comic book from the pile and went back downstairs. At the foot of the stairs he paused before going into the guests' sitting room and decided to try visiting Beth one last time, just in case Sean had gone now and he might have a chance to explain about the trace fossil. He crept around the corner and found the corridor deserted. Filled with hope, he was about to try the door to Beth's room when he heard voices coming from the office next to the kitchen, and when he began to make sense of the words they froze him to the spot.

"She can't just stay here like this for ever! It's not good for her, and it's certainly not good for the rest of us."

That voice was unmistakeably Sean's. But he sounded different: exasperated and unguarded.

"Well, I don't see what we can do about it," Kit heard the chef Nick answer. "At least, there's nowt I can do except maybe put summat disgusting in her food. You might be able to do more, of course, if it got bad enough that you needed to take action."

"I don't *like* to be talking like this."

"I know, course you don't. But the situation is getting beyond bearable for any of us. And you're having to shoulder the worst of it."

"But she does have a point. We can't really afford to be shot of her, not right now."

"Give it time then. Do what you have to for Askfeld. But get her out of here somehow before this situation drags you even lower."

Kit gasped and ran away down the corridor before he was found eavesdropping on this plot. Beth was in trouble. Despite his fears over the medicine earlier that day, he had not really believed Sean would consider getting rid of his wife. *He did look overworked and grim*, Kit reflected. *Perhaps it had all become too much for him: caring for someone unwell and running a business at the same time. Would he send her away to a care home where she would become someone else's responsibility? Or perhaps it was something more drastic that he had in mind.* Kit thought back to the white pills on the table and wondered if Sean's schemes were already underway.

His first thought was to warn Beth. But he felt certain she would not believe him. Juliet had considered it ridiculous when he first proposed that Sean was not trustworthy, and she barely knew him. How much less likely was it that Beth would believe the worst of her own husband? And even if she did heed his warning, it would not help much, if she could not easily walk most days. She could hardly flee Askfeld at a moment's notice. Kit needed to find out Sean's plan and work out a way to stop it. It was another quest and another mystery to add to his growing list.

What would a knight of Camelot or a Greek hero do? They found ways to save their friends and defeat their enemies by being either brave or clever. It seemed easier to be clever than brave, so Kit decided to start there. He would gather information to uncover Sean Garsdale's plot and only reveal it when the time was right.

CHAPTER NINE

THE SEARCH FOR THE ALBATROSS

DAY TWELVE

GLOSSARY OF NEW WORDS (PART TWO)

Summat *– something*
Owt *– anything (sounds like "out", but Beth says they're spelled differently)*
Dowly *– miserable – a good word to use about the weather, according to Bert*
Gawpin' *– staring at you like you've done something wrong when you haven't*
Flayed *– scared. Not a word I'll need to use much, because heroes are never flayed*

Gathering evidence was tricky. Kit could do nothing to draw attention to his suspicions if he was to catch Sean unawares. He took to loitering downstairs in the communal spaces, pretending to read, while always listening for footsteps in the corridor or conversations over the reception desk. He even went out to the other buildings, half wondering if Sean might have a secret workshop full of incriminating evidence. But there was only an old tractor shed now used for storage, and a block of stables that looked as though they had been partially converted into more guest rooms before the project was abandoned. Sean and Nick seemed to talk about work far more than they plotted nefarious schemes, and the snatches of dialogue Kit managed to overhear were mundane. He learned a great deal about food suppliers and cleaning schedules, that Sean always drank his coffee without milk, and that Nick went to the trouble of gelling his bright red hair into spikes every day even though it was always covered by his chef's hat, but nothing more useful than this. In the end, he decided to risk talking to Juliet.

"Do you know what Nefopam is?" he asked, when their mother was out of the room. He did not think she would understand or approve of the question, and as she was still glued to her emails he could not borrow her laptop and look up the word for himself, so asking his sister was his best hope.

"Never heard of it," she said, not looking up from her book. This lack of response was to signify that she had no interest in the matter, but years of winding one another up meant Kit was sure it would irk his sister not to be able to answer the question. She took pride in her cleverness.

"Not even from Chemistry GCSE? That's where you study drugs and stuff, right?"

Juliet turned the page and fixed a pink post-it note to it as a bookmark. "Believe it or not, it's actually the study of chemical elements and compounds. Why are you interested in random drugs all of a sudden?"

"No reason." Kit shrugged and went to the window. The fog was thinning at last, releasing its hold on Askfeld, though it still pooled over the dark waves far below the cliffs. "S'pose you wanted to make someone ill, or even poison them so they died, what would you use?"

She raised an eyebrow and closed the textbook. "I hope you aren't plotting anything."

Only a back-up plan in case I need to save someone's life one day, Kit thought.

"Course not. But you *do* know how to, right?" He had played the right card. Juliet did know, and she wanted to tell him what she knew.

"Depends how dramatic you want it to be. For a quick, explosive end, you could use something unstable like caesium – just put it anywhere near water and it blows up. But I'd go for something more subtle. One of the traditional slow-acting poisons, where the victim has a headache for a week or two before dropping down dead. Arsenic's a classic; they used that a hundred years ago in the old mystery novels. You could put a small amount in someone's tea each day – it's tasteless, so they'd never notice. And there are some others that wouldn't even show up when they do the post-mortem on the body. You could make it look like natural causes, and no one would ever know the truth of what had happened."

Kit did not know whether to be disturbed at how much thought his sister had already put into this. Then again, there were few topics Juliet had not considered at great length. She didn't often volunteer an opinion, but you could be pretty certain she had decided on one already. He resolved to keep an eye out for arsenic around the guest house. It occurred to him that one possible reason behind Beth's illness mystifying doctors and defying conventional treatment might be that she was not strictly ill at all. What if someone was sneaking dangerous substances into her food to make her believe she was unwell? If it was the sort of plot Juliet could supply on the spur of the moment, why not suppose an adult with unlimited time might have the same idea?

One morning, when he returned earlier than the others from breakfast and found that on this rare occasion his mother's laptop was actually unattended, he took the opportunity to look up the symptoms of arsenic poisoning. The list was long and unsavoury, but he had to admit that so far he had not seen Beth vomiting or convulsing. There must be plenty of other poisons Juliet had not mentioned though, so he could not completely rule out the possibility that her condition was the result of something she had consumed. It would explain why the doctors could not cure her. Remembering his earlier question, he also looked up Nefopam, which turned out to be generally used for pain relief, but on further reading he did find that it might technically be possible to kill someone by feeding them too much of it, particularly if they had an existing cardiac condition. He could not think of a subtle way to ask Beth if her heart was healthy.

That night, Kit's mind was too much of a whirl to fall asleep quickly, and when he finally did, he dreamed that a cackling Morgan le Fay stalked the corridors of Askfeld, trailing a hooded black cloak over the swept floor and bearing a chalice laced with arsenic. He woke, shaking, in the early hours of the morning, surprised to find the guest house so silent when his nightmares had been deafening with hideous laughter. Though only the faintest of thin lights was visible through the curtains, he found that he did not want to go back to sleep immediately, so he turned on his bedside lamp and opened a comic book. He read until it was time to get up, and though Catherine asked him more than once over breakfast why he was yawning so much, he did not speak a word of his nightmare to anyone. A hero was meant to be brave and ready to face anything. What use was he to anyone if he was fixated with fear even while he slept?

The fog cleared in the end, fading away so that the horizon became visible once again. Birds returned in greater numbers to the coastline and fished in the deep waters or scavenged along the shore for debris left by ramblers and tourists. Determined though he was to unmask Sean's true purpose, Kit was relieved to have an opportunity to step away from all these schemes and think about something that made him less anxious. He reminded Bert that they had agreed to look for the albatross, and suggested they had better go today, in case the fog should return soon.

"It's a fair old walk. We'd best get started." Bert hummed to himself as he tied up the laces of his walking boots and pulled on a waterproof coat. "Do you need to tell anyone where you're going before we set out?"

Kit had left his mother trawling through a report that had been written in her absence and which apparently needed major revisions, while Juliet pored over the physics syllabus she would be studying next year.

"I don't think they'll notice I'm gone until I get back."

They set out together from Askfeld towards the coastal path, where the verges grew deep with hogweed and yarrow. As they walked, Bert mused aloud about his summer.

"It's not been such a bad trip, you know. Refreshing to be somewhere I'm not known, and to forget about all the problems at work for a while. I imagine it's similar for you, not having to think about school for a few weeks. I've managed to photograph some kittiwakes. And I saw dozens of puffins at their nesting site. Do you know what the Latin name for a puffin is?"

Kit stared at Bert blankly. "Why would I know the Latin name for anything?"

"Fair question. In my day we used to have to learn it at school, but that was a very long time ago. Can't remember much grammar or anything, beyond *amo, amas, amat* and all that, but I'm not bad on the scientific names of birds. And a puffin is *fratercula*, which means 'little brother'. I've always liked that. Sounds friendly, don't you think?"

Kit wondered what would make a bird comparable to a younger brother, and whether he should feel any affinity towards puffins because of it. Juliet would have said something rude at this point, about how it must mean puffins were irritating and noisy.

"What about albatrosses? Do they have a scientific name?"

"They do, but there are lots of varieties of albatross, and each species has a different one."

"What kind will our albatross be?"

"Well, that's hard to say. But there have been sightings of a black-browed albatross in north Scotland. He's an old bird now, and they say he comes back every summer. One of the mollymawk group of albatrosses – isn't that a wonderful word, mollymawk? His scientific name is *thalassarche melanophris*, which is a bit more of a mouthful, but birdwatchers just call him Albert."

"Albert?"

"Bit easier to say, isn't it? I suppose it's meant to be a joke, too: Albert – albatross." The birdwatcher was quiet for a few moments. "They really are the most remarkable creatures. So graceful, with a wingspan of more than twice my height – it's hard to even imagine! And many of them will fly all the way around the world in their lifetime."

"So they're explorers?"

"Exactly. And they've seen more of the planet than most other animals – or people, I imagine – ever will." Bert paused. "Remind me, who was it who told you about this possible sighting? Someone local, I suppose?"

Kit's face flushed as he floundered for an answer that would not involve giving away the secret of the map. It still felt like something sacred that was not his to discuss with others. He did not like the idea of everyone in Askfeld pouring into Beth's room to inspect the map and offer their own contributions. In part, he feared his own efforts would be less appreciated then. There was a limit to how many heroes a story should have.

"Um, yeah, something like that. A local who knows the area." He needed to change the subject quickly. "Do you think he's lonely? If all the other albatrosses are hundreds of miles away, I mean."

At this deflection, there was the flickering of an awkward pause. Before it could take hold, however, Bert had already begun to answer the question, to Kit's relief.

"Well, they do tend to be solitary birds, you know. Something rather noble about it in a way, the lone wanderer flying over the ocean, don't you think?"

"I really hope we see one." Kit looked out at the sea, half hoping to spot an albatross soaring by at that very moment, even though he knew they were still some way from the site Beth had marked on her map.

"Well, as I said before, it is highly unlikely," said Bert, but Kit thought he sounded more optimistic than earlier. "All the same, it is fun to imagine what they'd say at the British Ornithologists' Union if I told them I'd seen one. I can just picture the looks on their faces."

They had crossed the field between Askfeld and the cliff edge now, and came next to a copse of dark gnarled trees on a steep downward slope towards the sea. The coastal path veered inland around them.

"What's that noise?" Kit asked. Strange bangs and scraping sounds were coming from somewhere between the trees. Bert seemed not to have noticed and uttered a bewildered "Eh?" as Kit slipped from the path to investigate.

It was a wooden sound, percussive and repetitive. He thought of asking Bert whether a woodpecker could drum against a tree trunk loudly enough for this, but the birdwatcher was lagging too far behind, so Kit went on to find out for himself. It reminded him of when his dad had spent a whole weekend building a coffee table, and he had listened to its construction through the kitchen door.

There was someone there. He had spied a glimpse of blue fabric before it disappeared behind the twisted tree trunks. Kit stopped. Why would anyone be hiding out here? Juliet had reacted so strongly to his theory that the Fisher family was on the run from someone. What if that someone was hiding out here to watch them?

Fuelled by the thought that his mother and sister were at the guest house, ignorant of any threat and unprepared for the danger they were in, he moved closer to get a better look. It was an adult, he could tell, though not an especially tall one, who was brandishing some heavy metallic implement. He took a tentative step forward for a closer look, and recognized the figure.

"Maddie?"

The noise stopped. Maddie Morley spun round in the clearing.

"What are you doing here?" she demanded so angrily that for a moment Kit believed he had broken some rule in being out here. But no, he was not trespassing on anyone's land, except possibly Sean and Beth's, and that was allowed.

"What are you doing with that?"

She held a hammer in her right hand, and a long crooked nail in her left. Behind her was the object that had absorbed her attention. It was an old wooden rowing boat, propped up on its side. The chipped grey paintwork was stained with rust-orange patches around the nails that held it together. It looked as if it had not been seaworthy for a long time. So this was why she had asked about buying tools.

Bert caught up with Kit. "Hello there, Maddie. So this is what you've been up to, is it? A bit of salvage work."

He said it brightly, but Maddie must have imagined a note of accusation in his tone, because she responded, "I'm not doing any harm or stealing anyone's property. I found it like this."

"Never doubted that for a second."

"I've asked around and nobody has laid claim to it. So no one can complain if I fix it up, can they?"

Bert and Kit agreed that it was hard to see how anyone would object to it. Maddie threw down the crooked nail and turned her attention to one of the others, still rusting in the stern of the boat. She set about levering it out of the woodwork.

"What are you going to do with it, when you've fixed it?" asked Kit.

"Do? What does it matter what I do with it? Why do you imagine things are only valuable if they are useful for something? Can't a boat just be what it is, and that's enough?" Maddie did not look round at them, but attacked the nail with furious energy. The hammer slipped and caught her hand; she jumped back and cried out a syllable that she quickly rearticulated to be suitable for Kit's ears.

Kit wondered what level of disrepair marked the line between a disused boat and mere driftwood, but knew somehow that this question would make Maddie even angrier.

"If you must know," she paused, red-faced and slightly breathless from the work, "I may even finish my pilgrimage by boat. Whitby Abbey is right on the sea, after all."

"Right. Well. I suppose we'd best leave you to it. Come on, Kit, let's not disturb Maddie any longer."

Bert strode away, back up the slope, and Kit, unable to think of a question that was safe to ask, jogged after him. Up they went, through the trees and dark gorse needles.

"Do you think she'd actually do it, Bert? Mend a boat and go to sea in it?" He wasn't sure it was the sort of thing people actually did outside of books. If it was, then he wished he'd found the boat first.

Bert said "Hmm" in a way that sounded knowing and yet non-committal all at once. "I can't say I've figured out Maddie Morley well enough to know what she might do. But I don't see that bit of flotsam becoming seaworthy any time soon. Do you?"

"It can't be flotsam."

"What's that?"

"It isn't flotsam," Kit explained. "It has to be floating in the sea to be flotsam. Or thrown overboard to be jetsam. And you just said you didn't think the boat would float anyway. I read about it once."

"That doesn't surprise me in the least. I have students who aren't as widely read as you, and they've had a decade's head start. Have you ever thought of becoming an academic researcher?"

Kit answered that he had not. He still was not quite sure what an academic researcher did. Bert did talk occasionally about teaching students, but he seemed to spend a lot of time reading the newspaper and looking for interesting wildlife. They picked up the pace, striding briskly along the cliffs. Their footfall shook the clumps of pink thrift flowers, huddled in gaps between rocks.

"Let's have a look at that map again," said Bert.

Kit handed over the map he had borrowed from the reception desk. Or did it count as stealing if you didn't technically ask permission first? Either way, he planned to return it as soon as they got back, before Sean noticed it was missing. He had even been sure to write on it in pencil, so they could erase the arrows pointing out the spot Beth had circled next to a question mark.

"Not far now, by the look of it. Is that definitely the place your friend saw it? We should be able to get down to the foot of the cliffs this way. That will be easier than craning over the edge from the top to see if anything is nesting there. I don't fancy falling off into the sea. Do you?"

Bert had no difficulty reading the map, even though it was riddled with lines of various weights and colours that signified roads or altitude or boundaries. He found a narrow path that led down from the cliff top and, to Kit's relief, walked ahead on it, making it easy to follow and find the best footholds. When they reached the rocky shoreline, he gave the map back to Kit and took a pair of binoculars out of his rucksack.

The water was a quiet, brooding grey, a glassy mirror to the heavy clouds that had gathered over it. He could almost imagine it was an entirely different sea to the one he had seen from the lookout point or Scar Bay. Beth was right: it had different moods depending on the day. Today's was subdued but with disgruntled depths that grumbled to themselves further out from the shore.

"There's so much more air round here."

"Eh? What's that?"

"The air," Kit repeated, but he felt that he had not explained himself properly. "It's so… wide. You know, how there's no buildings stretching up into the sky and breaking the view. It feels" – he spread his arms out on either side – "open."

He had not done justice to the feeling. He wanted to run and jump, simply to make the most of all this uninhabited space between grass and sky. And yet its vastness made him aware of how small he was, and that in turn made him want to stay very still and breathe in how huge the world was becoming.

"I forget how different life is for children growing up in cities." Bert acted as if he had understood, but this prosaic response jarred against whatever it was Kit had been trying to describe. "Now then, let's see what we've got here."

Kit watched as Bert scanned the cliff face. A cluster of white shapes perched about halfway up the earthy brown wall of rock, but based on the birdwatcher's measured response, he guessed they were not albatrosses.

Sure enough, a few moments later he heard Bert mutter to himself, "Pair of gannets there. And the usual herring gulls." The birdwatcher continued to check and identify aloud the different birds sitting on the rocky ledges.

Kit meanwhile turned his back to the cliffs and studied the skyline instead. A few angular silhouettes of gulls were flying in from the sea, but even without knowing what they were, he could tell they were too small. Then suddenly he spotted a white shape in the distance, broad-winged and soaring over the waves.

"Bert! What's that, over there?" He jumped and pointed excitedly. Bert swung round and stared at it.

"Hmm," he said, and raised the binoculars to his eyes. Kit could hardly keep still with the suspense of watching him and waiting for an answer. "A large bird, certainly… still quite far away… hard to tell… but the wingspan is wide and the body shape is the right kind. Colouring seems consistent. Bigger than a kittiwake, at least."

"Is it an albatross? It is, isn't it?"

"I wouldn't like to say for sure, but from here I'd go so far as to say that there's a slim possibility it could be."

Kit screeched with triumph. He had found it! Bert did not seem to share his enthusiasm yet, but he was smiling at least.

"Here we go, it's flying closer to the land. I should be able to get a better view now. Let me see… ah." And with that last "ah", he lowered the binoculars. His growing smile had vanished.

"What's wrong?" Kit stopped dancing.

"A great black-backed gull. A large adult, to be sure, but nothing more. Not an albatross, I'm afraid."

They both stood, crestfallen, staring at the gull that was circling nearer to the shore. Kit felt decidedly annoyed with the bird for deceiving them. He knew it wasn't the gull's fault it wasn't an albatross. Still, it had given them false hope. Anxious that the birdwatcher would be equally disappointed, he tried to keep their search moving before there was time to reflect too much on this first failure.

"Maybe if we walk a bit further down," Kit suggested. It was, after all, only a vague indication on the map.

"Of course," said Bert. "Birdwatching takes a lot of time and patience, you know. Sometimes I've sat all day in the same spot, just waiting to see what comes along. It's the only way to be sure you haven't missed anything. Really, it would have been a miracle if we'd seen a rare bird so quickly. Let's walk a little bit further. But keep an eye on the tide. We don't want to get cut off from the path."

They wandered along the stony shoreline, Kit kicking at the thin threads of seaweed that were strewn over the rocks. Bert kept looking from the cliffs to the sea and then back again.

"Ah, now there's something we can be glad we've seen." He pointed out over the water. "Do you see that dark shape among the waves, just a bit further out than the headland over there? Here, borrow my binoculars for a closer look. Do you see it?"

"I can see something bobbing about in the sea, but it's not a bird: it's too big."

"That's right; it's a grey seal."

And now that he knew what he was looking at, Kit could make out the facial features: the round black eyes and pointed snout of the seal. It seemed to be floating on its back, perfectly happy to be borne along by the waves.

They took it in turns to use the binoculars to watch the seal. If he strained his eyes to really focus through the lenses, Kit could even make out the individual whiskers around its nose. Eventually, Bert looked up at the darkening sky and said, "Best we head back now."

Kit wanted to stay out longer and keep searching for the albatross, but Bert sounded resigned and had already started walking. As they followed the path back up the cliffs and north towards Askfeld Farm, it began to rain. Kit pulled up his hood and thrust his hands into his pockets to keep as dry as possible, and the two of them walked home with their shoulders hunched and their heads down to protect themselves from the downpour.

"I'm sorry we didn't find your albatross, Bert. Maybe I read the map wrong."

"Never mind, eh. It was always going to be a long shot."

Bert spoke lightly, but as they trudged up the path past the dark trees where Maddie had been working, and across the exposed grass to the door of Askfeld Farm, he gave a great sigh. Kit wondered whether he had been too hasty in encouraging Bert to hope he might make an important discovery here. It had been so rewarding to see the old man shake off some of his cloud of despondency for a while. Now, however, Bert seemed more dejected than before. Kit hoped this was at least in part an effect of the rain, and that life might look better when the skies cleared again.

The birdwatcher had evidently had the same thought. "I think this calls for a hot cup of tea, and somewhere to dry out these shoes."

Bert pushed the door of the guest house open and started stamping on the bristled welcome mat to scrape off as much of the mud as he could. It was only when he stepped aside to take off his boots that Kit saw there was someone in the hallway waiting for them.

It was his mother, and she was white with anger.

CHAPTER TEN

UTTERSCAR

INTERESTING FACTS ABOUT ALBATROSSES:

1. Great albatrosses have the longest wings of any bird in the world.

2. Sailors used to think it was bad luck to kill an albatross.

3. They aren't easy to find.

"Christopher Shackleton Fisher, get inside right now!"

Kit's heart seemed to plummet all the way down into his stomach. His mother never shouted at him in front of others, preferring to wait for the privacy of family. This was bad. He closed the door and kicked off his shoes, which left muddy marks on the tiles next to the mat.

"What were you thinking?" his mother cried.

"I was just trying to find an albatross with Bert," he answered truthfully, the water dripping off his sleeves onto the stone floor of the hallway.

"Kit, you went out without telling me or anyone else where you were going. And with a stranger!"

"Bert's not a stranger. He's a birdwatcher."

"Excuse me, madam," Bert ventured to join in now. "I'm terribly sorry if there's been any cause for alarm. But I can assure you Kit has simply been showing me a good spot by the cliffs to watch some nesting seabirds at low tide. There was never any danger."

"I'm sorry, Mr..."

"Albert Sindlesham. But please call me Bert."

"I'm sorry, Mr Sindlesham, but I don't know you. And the fact that you would take my child off the premises without my permission, without speaking to me first, without even introducing yourself, is completely unacceptable. Now Kit, come with me."

Kit allowed himself to be marched upstairs. A glance back over his shoulder showed Bert looking as dejected as Kit felt. The birdwatcher trudged into the guests' sitting room while the Fishers went up to the first floor. Once the door to Kit's room was closed, Catherine continued.

"Kit, can you even understand how worried I've been, not knowing where you were? What if you'd got lost or fallen from the cliffs? What if you'd been hurt somewhere? You can't just go wandering off like that, not on your own, and certainly not with strangers. It's not just today. It's all the other times you've run off while we've been out. It's like ever since we moved up here you're trying to get yourself into trouble. What happened to promising me you would be well behaved and helpful?"

If only she understood that it had all been in an attempt to do exactly as she had asked. How was he supposed to help anyone if he stayed quietly in his room all the time and never did anything?

"I just wanted to help Beth finish her map," Kit mumbled, too dispirited to maintain pretence or secrecy any longer. Catherine frowned; this was clearly not the answer she had expected.

"Who's Beth?"

"She lives here. She's married to Sean."

"I don't think I've seen Sean Garsdale's mysterious wife the entire time we've been here. Unless you mean that woman he was talking to after breakfast the other day. I thought she was someone they brought in to help with the bookkeeping. What's she got to do with this?"

How was he to explain so that his mother would understand? He had not planned to tell her about the unfinished map, but he could see no other way now.

"She's making a map of all the good places round here. But she can't go outside to see those places any more, so I was doing that for her. She has to stay indoors, you see."

"And I suppose she's been encouraging you to go off exploring dangerous places by yourself? Well, I shall be having words with that woman –"

"No, Mum, you can't!" Kit grabbed Catherine's arm in desperation. "It's not her fault. I wanted to go. She didn't ask me to."

"Well, I imagine she's used to having people do things for her all the time, sitting around and being waited on by Sean every day."

"But she's ill, Mum!"

"Is she? She didn't look ill to me when I saw her. She didn't so much as cough. Some people like to pretend that they're not well, Kit, when they're fine. They do it for attention."

"That's not fair!" he shouted.

"Don't answer back! And don't take that tone with me, either. I don't want you talking to strangers any more. From now on, you stay indoors and you only go out if Juliet or I am with you, do you understand? Now get changed into something dry and put those clothes straight into the washbag: you look a state. I'll be amazed if you don't catch a cold after today." She went to leave the room but turned back at the doorway to add, "You know, I expected better from you."

She marched out, closing the door firmly behind her so that Kit understood he was not supposed to leave. He understood too that he had disappointed her. She had asked him to be responsible and mature. Though he had been doing his very best to follow these instructions by helping everyone, he had made her worried and cross instead. He hadn't meant to do that. But he didn't think her reaction was fair either.

His feet ached from the day's walking, so he sat curled up on the end of the bed and listened as, to his horror, Catherine could be heard downstairs saying, "Excuse me, are you Beth? I'd like a word about the ideas you've been giving my son."

Unable to bear listening in on this, Kit put his head under the duvet to try to block out the sound of his mother's raised voice talking too quickly to let Beth answer or defend herself. If he had not known better, he could have believed it was Maddie shouting.

Kit kicked listlessly at a chair leg. Juliet was practising French vocabulary, which meant there was no hope of a conversation with her that he would understand. Still, it was either this or sitting alone in his room, and Kit knew which he preferred. He still had one of Beth's books left, but he did not like to read it too quickly. He did not know when he might be able to go and borrow another from her, with both his mother and Sean so set on keeping him from seeing her at all now. So he was putting off finishing the last few chapters, because somehow not reading but having a book set aside in case of urgent need seemed better than finishing reading and having no options left.

They had seen no one else all day, except for at breakfast time, and even then Catherine had made them wait until nine o'clock in the hope the other guests would have already eaten. Sean had been particularly abrupt with them, placing their food on the table without a word. Kit was certain it was because of how his mother had shouted at Beth, but Catherine appeared to show neither awareness nor remorse that she was the cause of their unpopularity at Askfeld.

Juliet had her head down as she attempted to recite the list of words she had been memorizing. "*Le foyer, le gosse, le gamin.* Do you have to keep kicking the chair like that? It's really distracting."

He planted his feet on the floor. "Why are you revising anyway? How can you have homework from a school you haven't even started at yet?"

She did not look up from the colourful cards she had painstakingly covered with her notes. "*Parce que* I've already checked the syllabus for my subjects so I can prepare. And I don't know how good the others in my class will be at St Jude's, but I couldn't face Mum or Dad if it turned out I'm the stupidest one there, so I need to go over everything before September."

"Jules, you *always* get perfect marks in everything. There's no way you're going to be the stupidest person in your class." Would their parents be angry if Juliet did badly on a test? He didn't think so. Then again, how could he be sure, when Juliet had never failed at anything? *Fishers work hard and rise to the challenge.*

"What do you know about it? You're not even in secondary school yet. *La famille decomposée, la famille recomposée, concilier carrière et famille.*"

It had not even been a compliment, in Kit's opinion; it was just a fact. Juliet was good at every subject, except perhaps drama. Being on a stage made her uncomfortable. When she was cast as Ophelia in the school production of *Hamlet*, she had been sick the night before the first performance. Kit only knew this because his room in their old house had been next to the bathroom, and the walls were not soundproof. When he asked her about it, she had insisted he imagined the whole thing, but he was certain of what he'd heard. Their parents were always praising her exam marks, and he could not see why she was so worried. If he had been in her position, he would have taken the summer off, and only studied things that interested him.

"You say that now, because we haven't had results day. But when the GCSE results come out… I just *know* I've messed them up! It's OK though, I have a back-up plan of what subjects I'll take if I don't get the grades in my favourites. I just wish I knew more about the other local schools, in case St Jude's refuses to take me after all."

Kit sighed. There was no arguing with Juliet, no convincing her that she really was very clever and had no reason to worry. He had run out of new ideas to persuade her.

"Juliet! Kit!" From somewhere on the stairs, their mother's voice came calling.

"We're here!" Kit shouted back. A moment later she marched into the room, her phone in her hand and a beaming expression on her face.

"Guess what! I've got some exciting news."

"You saw an albatross?"

"What?"

"Never mind."

"I didn't want to tell you until it was all sorted out, but I've been on the phone to the solicitor and the removal company a lot since we came up here, and now the new house is ready for us to move in! We exchanged contracts and completed last week actually, but all our furniture was still in storage and there wasn't much point trying to live there without it. I've just had confirmation that the van will bring our belongings up later today."

Kit jumped up, knocking some of Juliet's revision cards to the floor and ignoring her shout of protest at his clumsiness. "Does that mean Dad can come up now?" If the family could be reunited, everything would go back to normal. It would not matter quite so much that he had failed to finish Beth's map.

"Can we go over and unpack right now?" Juliet asked, picking the cards up and putting them in order. "I'm dying for some different clothes."

"Well, you'll have all your boxes and cases, and your new room to arrange. And in answer to your question, Kit, Dad's staying with Grandma Fisher for the time being, since the old house is sold now. He'll be coming up to join us just as soon as he can, of course."

"Finally!" Juliet looked genuinely relieved, though it was unclear whether it was at the family situation or the prospect of broadening her wardrobe options.

"But will we be able to come back to Askfeld?" Kit faltered.

"Why ever would you want to do that? We'll be in our own home at last. No more living in a draughty guest house and having to share our space with strangers." Catherine looked pointedly encouraging at this prospect. Kit knew he was supposed to be happy about it too.

"But then we won't see our friends any more." He had not finished investigating Sean, or helping Beth with her map, or locating an albatross for Bert. There were too many unfinished stories to leave yet.

She glared at her son, who had refused to take her hint. "Well, before long it'll be time to start at your new school. And then you can make lots of new friends at St Jude's. Friends your own age. You'd prefer that, wouldn't you?"

It was another of those questions that wasn't really a question, and Kit knew it. This time he said nothing.

The next few hours were a whirlwind of repacking their suitcases. Catherine insisted that Kit and Juliet stay in the same room together while she was out buying supplies for a thorough clean of their new house, which Kit suspected was a way of making sure he did not run off to say goodbye to Beth or Bert. He brought armfuls of his belongings into the other room and dumped them all on his mother's bed before trying to squash everything back into the case that had once contained it all so easily.

"Kit, you're supposed to fold your clothes, not stuff them into the gaps like that," Juliet informed him.

"They fit better this way," he argued. His sister shrugged and set to untangling the jewellery on her bedside table. She swept most of it into a drawstring bag, but selected a silver chain which she fastened around her neck instead. On it, there hung a small shining bird in flight. From where Kit was standing, it looked like a seagull.

"I've just got to go and get a book from downstairs," he said.

Juliet raised an eyebrow. "Mum said you were meant to stay here." She moved as if she meant to block his exit, but he was closer to the door than she was, and they both knew she could not stop him.

"I won't be long, I promise. She won't be back before me."

His sister looked troubled by this. Juliet never broke rules. Toby from Kit's Year Six class had told him it was because she was the oldest child, and that was how they behaved. Toby had been a great authority on families and why they were so strange. He used to read his stepmother's psychology books and then come into school armed with technical phrases like "attachment issues" and "oppositional defiant disorder", which he would wheel out into conversation casually, as if forgetting that his peers would not recognize the terminology. Others tended to ignore this, pretending not to have noticed the strange new words, but Kit would always ask for a definition, and Toby was always happy to provide one. On one occasion Kit had asked whether there were any long words in these books that might apply to someone like him. Toby had given a very knowing smile and muttered something under his breath that sounded like "messier complex", but Kit doubted that could be true. He was generally very neat; his mother made sure of it.

He had no book to collect from downstairs, but it seemed a plausible pretence. He needed an excuse to go and say goodbye before anyone stopped him.

Bert was easy to find in his usual spot near the fireplace.

"Bert, we're leaving!" Kit cried. "We're going to our new house."

"What's that? Oh, congratulations," Bert said, though he seemed barely to have registered what Kit was saying.

"Mum says we won't be coming back here."

"I dare say she knows what's best for you," the birdwatcher continued to answer vaguely, which Kit would not accept.

"Are you sad because we didn't find the albatross? Or is it

because Mum was cross with you? Don't worry about that; she gets cross with everyone, but she forgets about it eventually."

Bert sighed. "It's not that," he said. "I've been deluded and irresponsible. I can't believe I let myself think I'd find anything out of the ordinary here. You weren't to know, of course; you haven't spent decades studying British wildlife. There was never any albatross here. Whoever thought they saw one made a mistake, and any real scientist would have known that immediately. My colleagues were right to laugh at me after all. I got carried away again. I should just focus on my teaching, and accept that it's almost time to retire."

Kit could not think of anything he could possibly say to cheer Bert up. He stood there for a moment, watching his old friend stare into space.

"Sorry, Bert," he said, but the words felt utterly inadequate. Disheartened, he left the birdwatcher alone and headed for Beth's room. Sean was in the corridor and spotted him at once.

"Not a chance," he said. His eyes were hard and his expression solemn. "I think you can stay away from Beth, after all you've done."

But I need to warn her about you. If Kit had known they were leaving so soon, he would have sneaked into the kitchen at night to check the cupboards for arsenic. Now it was too late.

Sean stayed in the hallway and watched him slink back upstairs, not going into the kitchen until Kit had reached the landing. As the kitchen door swung shut, Kit heard a voice say, "Who'd have thought one family could cause so much disruption?"

Kit returned to the room where Juliet was packing. He sat down heavily on the bed. *I'm not sure I'm especially good at quests. The people I've tried to help seem more unhappy than when I started.* He wanted someone to cheer him up, but there was little hope of Juliet lifting the gloom, so he would have to find a silver lining himself.

"At least there's one good thing about having to leave Askfeld," he said after a moment's thought.

"What?"

"When we're finally in our own house, Dad will have to come and join us, won't he?"

Juliet turned her back to him and gathered up a selection of colourful nail varnish pots that clinked against one another.

The thought made the day bearable for Kit. He would have to leave this place, but his family would be back together at last, as they should be. He repeated this to himself as they heaved the luggage downstairs, as Catherine thanked Sean for their stay and Sean printed out a receipt for them, handing it over with none of the warmth with which he had greeted them on their first day at Askfeld. He reminded himself of it as he sat in the back of the car and they drove away, without saying goodbye to Beth or Maddie or Nick, and as they arrived in their new house in Utterscar.

It was newer than Askfeld, and when Kit ran his hand over the walls they were not cold and uneven like the guest house. The wooden floors were flat and varnished, and the window frames were white and draught-free. Catherine enthused about "returning to modern civilization" as if they had been staying in a medieval dungeon until now, but Kit felt as though this house lacked something. It had not yet witnessed the centuries of unfolding lives that gave a building its character. In time the Fisher family could stamp personality on this house, of course, but for now it felt a little blank and empty.

Kit ran around, throwing open the door to each room so he could inspect it. To his surprise, his mother approved of his energetic exploration.

"That's right, get some air circulating between the rooms. I'll give the place a good clean before we start unpacking. I've labelled the box with the kettle so it's easy to find."

"Can I see my room?" Juliet asked, and Catherine forgot all about making coffee as she ushered her daughter upstairs to the second biggest bedroom, which overlooked the front garden.

An hour after they arrived, the lorry pulled up outside,

completely blocking the road while two men unloaded the Fisher family's belongings. Their accents were strong and Catherine kept having to ask them to repeat what they said, which seemed to be a great source of embarrassment for her. Juliet located the kettle and brewed mugs of sugar-saturated tea for them as they hauled furniture up the stairs and around awkward corners.

Six o'clock brought a soft golden glow through the windows that did not yet have curtains up. Juliet was still in the kitchen, unwrapping crockery and assigning it to shelves. Kit had offered to help, but after he tried to put saucepans in the cupboard under the sink he was quickly dismissed to another part of the house. His mum was making up the beds in each of the upstairs rooms, and Kit was by now too big to crawl inside the duvet cover and help keep the corners in their right places. He went instead to the study, where his dad's books and files were still in boxes. The desk and shelves were already in place, so he began to unpack the rest. He wanted this room to be ready for when his dad arrived, which would surely be soon now.

He unwound layers of bubblewrap from around a framed photograph of himself and Juliet, much younger than they were now. It had been taken on a holiday about five years ago. They had gone to a farm and been allowed to feed the animals. You could just about see in the picture that the cuff of Kit's green jumper was unravelling where an eager goat had earlier tried to eat more than just the animal feed. Juliet had been nervous of the horses at first, afraid they would bite her if she stood too close. And his mum had been determined to take a photo of them before someone fell over and got muddy, which was, she had said, inevitable. Kit placed the picture on his father's desk, pleased that this memory of the family had been considered important enough to preserve.

There were no photos of their time in Askfeld, aside from that one at Scar Bay. He would have no pictures to help him remember his new friends, unless he committed them to memory now. In his mind's eye, he saw Bert stomping over the heath, a pair of binoculars swinging from around his neck, his grey hair windswept in all directions. Maddie would be finishing off the restoration of her boat, perhaps even launching out to sea for the final stretch of her pilgrimage. And Beth was presumably resting by the window while she contemplated her unfinished map, unable to complete it.

A phone buzzed somewhere in the next room. Kit listened for it to be answered, but nobody else seemed to have noticed the sound. He went into the bedroom and found his mother's mobile balanced on top of a cardboard box labelled "Shoes". Kit checked the screen and then answered it.

"Hi Dad!"

"Kit! How's my favourite son?"

"Dad, I'm your *only* son."

"Doesn't matter. I bet you'd be my favourite even if you weren't the only one. Is your mum there?"

"She's in Juliet's room, making up the bed. This house is really cool, Dad."

"D'you like your new room then?"

"Yeah, it's great." The words came out a little flat. He could not deny their new home had none of the chilly draughts or creaking floorboards of Askfeld, yet still he struggled to summon the enthusiasm he knew he ought to feel.

"What's up? Sounds like something's bothering you."

"Yeah, it's just that I was making this thing – this map for you. Well, Beth's making it actually, but it's got loads of cool places on it that I want to show you. And I wanted to finish it before you got here, but now there won't be enough time before you come, will there? It's OK though, there's still loads of things on there. Beth says there's this lake nearby where we can go and skim stones, only I'm not sure yet how you do that. Do you know how to skim stones?"

There was a long silence at the other end of the phone.

"Dad? Are you still there?"

"Kit, listen… I know we said I'd come up and join you all when you moved into the new house, but I think it's going to be a while longer yet."

"Oh. When?"

"I don't know yet. Work's very busy right now. That's why I need to talk to your mum. Can you pass the phone to her for me?"

"OK." It was all the answer he could muster. He crossed the landing into Juliet's room, where his mum was carefully arranging cushions on top of pillows. In the barely functional shell of their new house, this room was already set up with utter precision. A vase of flowers caught the light on the windowsill, and packs of new pens waited to be opened on the desk. Only Juliet's handmade collages of photos were not yet on the walls, for she would not let anyone else perform that task. It was almost comical to see this room so perfectly arranged, when downstairs the sofa was still in pieces and the coffee table on its side against a wall.

"Who were you talking to just then?" his mother asked.

"Dad. He wants to speak to you." He thrust the phone at her and walked out of the room. He plodded back to the study, closed the door, and sat leaning against it. His dad was not coming. Perhaps he would never join them here. Perhaps he preferred living in the city away from them.

His quest had failed on all counts. He had not been able to help Beth finish her map, or to convince his father to come north and reunite the family. A horrible thought crossed his mind. He had been so certain that Sean was the villain, standing in the way of him doing what he was meant to, but what if he had been wrong? After all, it was his mother keeping him from seeing Beth or going out exploring the map, and it was his father choosing to stay away. Could they be the ones responsible for this terrible mess? But no, that could not be right. After all, both those things were his own fault. He had made his mum worried when he went out looking for the albatross, and he had failed to convince his dad to move.

A worse thought took its place. Could it be that the great secret no one would tell him – the reason for his dad not being here – was that his parents were getting divorced? Now that it had occurred to him, he was surprised he had not thought of it before. About half his class had similar stories from their own homes. Toby's mum had moved to Australia when he was five, and made it very clear that Toby's dad was not welcome to follow her.

It might have been optimism, it might have been stubbornness, but Kit refused to believe it. After all, his mum had always promised to talk to her children like adults, to treat them as though they were clever enough to understand everything, so if she and Kit's dad were splitting up, then she would have told them.

He could hear half of the conversation between his parents, across the landing. His dad must have asked who Beth was, after Kit had mentioned her, because now his mum was saying, "She's one of the owners of the bed and breakfast where we've been staying. Her husband does most of the work, though; she's in bed ill most of the time… I'm not sure. One of these chronic things that's hard to diagnose, I think. Seems to involve tiredness and muscle pain – and I'm pretty sure it must be affecting her mental state too, the way she speaks to Sean sometimes, when he does so much for her. And if you knew the influence she's had on Kit!… What's that?… No, no, I haven't spoken to her about much at all. Why on earth would I discuss our family with her?… Well no, I don't think it would help, actually… Not remotely the same condition. You may think that, but you haven't met her. For that matter, you haven't been here with the rest of us either, to see what it's been like. We don't all have the option to ignore the problems in this family, you know. Maybe if you weren't so *scared* of facing –"

Her voice had grown shriller and louder with the last few words, and there was suddenly the slam of a closing door, perhaps as she realized she might be overheard. The next phrases were more muffled, but still audible. "No, I'm sorry. I didn't mean that you're deliberately… Of course, this is hard for both of us. Look, if you really think it's worth a conversation, I suppose it can't do any harm."

Downstairs, knives and forks were being violently thrown into a drawer, as if Juliet had picked up on the strained tone of their parents' conversation and was echoing it. Kit listened to the sounds of his family fracturing in their separate locations, and wanted to cry. He had thought he could fix everything, but the Fishers were as divided as they had ever been. And here in this new house, he could not speak to Beth or Bert about any of it. Right now, he might even have appreciated a conversation with Maddie. At least he had not tried and failed to help her, the way he had with the map and the hope of seeing an albatross. She would not be disappointed in him like the others.

Feeling utterly defeated, he curled himself up against the study door, put his head on his knees, and stayed there in silence for the next hour.

CHAPTER ELEVEN

LILIES

DAY TWENTY

These are the things I still need to do to set up my room:

1. Put my books on the shelves.

2. Find somewhere to display the model car I built last Christmas.

3. Hang up my new uniform for St Jude's in the wardrobe (Mum already put away the rest of my clothes, but then she said I needed to start looking after my own room more).

4. Find somewhere to hide this notebook so no one can read it.

Obviously I haven't done very much unpacking yet, and we've been here almost a week now. I just can't believe that we're going to be staying here for ever, when Dad still isn't with us.

"Where are you going?" Kit asked his mother, seeing her gather up the keys, lipstick, and umbrella that belonged in her handbag.

"Just popping out for a little bit. Don't worry – you two don't have to come."

From behind a textbook, Juliet announced this was not a problem: she had another three hours' work to complete today. The house did not yet have a working internet connection, and she swung between being irked by this and glad not to have the distraction.

"Where are you going?" Kit asked again. She had donned her smart blue dress and was holding an envelope and a bunch of flowers, which meant this was more than just an everyday trip to town to buy milk or pick up contact lens solution. She looked reluctant to answer him, but after a couple of seconds sighed.

"I'm going back to the guest house to take a thank-you card to Sean and Beth for all they did for us while we were staying there," she said, then added, "It's the proper thing to do in this situation."

"It seems stupid to me," said Juliet. "You were paying them to have us to stay; it's not like it was a favour that you owe them for."

"Juliet!" her mother snapped sharply, then seemed to regret it. Juliet looked deflated, faced with the rudeness of her momentary bold opinion. "Normally, I'd agree with you, love. But we were there a long time –"

"Not as long as Maddie," Kit chipped in. "No one knows when she's going to leave. I bet she wouldn't get them a card though. I don't think she likes them very much. Can I come with you?"

Catherine's shoes tapped on the hard kitchen floor. She warned Kit that it would be very boring for him, and wouldn't he prefer to stay here with Juliet where he could watch television? It was another question where Kit chose to pretend ignorance, and not give the answer his mother was encouraging.

"But I want to come. I want to see them too."

"If you come with me, you'll be leaving your sister all alone in the house. You don't want that, do you? And have you loaded the dishwasher yet like I asked you?"

Kit did not see how staying here with Juliet would benefit either of them. She was guaranteed to ignore him, or else be annoyed by him. They had so little in common these days. The games Juliet had once taught him, she now viewed with contempt and described as childish.

He jumped up, gathered the stray plates, and hurriedly rinsed them in the sink before letting them clatter into the dishwasher racks. His sister winced at the noise.

"Oh, let him go!" she said. "I'll get more work done if he's not running around disturbing me all the time. I need a bit of silence."

There seemed no further argument to be had on this, so Kit was allowed to go with his mum, on the condition that he did as he was told when they were there. There followed an extensive list of all the ways Juliet could contact them if she needed to, which of course she already knew, but it seemed to reassure Catherine to go over the information again. Kit bounded out to the car, simultaneously buoyant and anxious at the thought of seeing everyone at Askfeld again.

For the first part of the journey, Catherine was quiet, and the only noise besides the car engine was the rustle of tissue paper around the bouquet on the back seat. After they had driven about a mile down the single-track lane lined with beech trees and dry stone walls, she said, "You spent a lot of time with Beth Garsdale, didn't you?"

Was it a trick question? His mother had been so angry to learn of him befriending strangers. He mumbled his answer that yes, he had been to see her a few times.

"Tell me about her."

Kit could not guess the motive behind this question. "She's nice. She's going to have a baby. And she has lots of books, and she paints sometimes."

"Is she kind to new people? Does she like talking a lot?"

"She was friendly to me. Sometimes we talked loads, about all sorts of things. But some days she wasn't feeling well: she gets tired and is in all this pain, and they haven't found a medicine she can take to make it better yet. When that happens she doesn't want to see people so much. And some days Sean didn't let me see her either."

"Ah yes, poor Sean," said his mother, and Kit remembered that she had not heard the threat in Sean's voice when he sent Kit out of Beth's room, or overheard the conversation with Nick the chef that day about getting rid of Beth somehow.

"He's not so nice," he began.

"Kit, you shouldn't say things like that. If you don't have anything good to say about someone, don't say anything at all. He works very hard, I'll have you know."

Coming from Catherine, there was no higher praise or greater virtue. Kit knew his mother had no time for the idle. He fell into pointed silence, hoping his refusal to say another word would signal some of his concerns about Sean. But if his mum picked up on the message, she did not show it. Eventually, he gave up.

"What's Dad scared of?"

There was a pause, so long he wondered if she had heard him.

"What do you mean?"

"When you were on the phone, you said something. I think you said Dad would be here, with us, if it wasn't for something he's scared of."

"How many times do I have to tell you? It's rude to eavesdrop on other people's conversations." She was right, but she was also changing the subject.

"Please, Mum." He had worried, ever since he overheard that conversation, about what could be so terrible that it frightened even his father. His dad wasn't scared of anything; that's why he was in charge of getting rid of spiders at home. Catherine sighed.

"All right. Your dad doesn't like seeing a problem he can't fix. He's especially bothered if he thinks he might have had a hand in making something go wrong in the first place. Like… imagine if Grandma Fisher was ill. She's not, of course, but imagine. Dad would be a bit concerned. But if he had knowingly sent her into a room full of ill people where she might catch their germs… well, in that case he might feel so bad he would be afraid to even visit her and ask how she was doing. You see, we weren't talking about anything dangerous. Nothing for you to be anxious about."

It was maddeningly cryptic, as usual. Before he could probe any further, they pulled up at the guest house. Both paused to take a deep breath before getting out of the car. Apparently his mother was as nervous as he was.

"Here goes," she said, with a smile at Kit that was unusually confiding. She put a hand on his shoulder and they walked together up to the building. Sean was at the reception desk, and looked surprised to see them. Behind him on the wall hung a large slate tile, on which chalk letters informed guests that today's low tide would be at two minutes past one, with high tide at seven o'clock this evening, and that the weather would be mild and cloudy.

"I just wanted to say thank you for all your help over the last couple of weeks," Catherine said, placing the card down on the counter top. "And these are for Beth, to apologize for my tone with her."

Sean nodded an acknowledgment of the gesture, but it felt a little formal. "You didn't need to do that."

He looked down and shuffled some papers on the desk. It might have been the effect of the grey shirt he was wearing today, but Kit thought he looked tired. Catherine persisted, forcing him to look up and engage her in conversation.

"Is she… available today? I'd like to give them to her in person. And I know Kit would like to see her again, if it's not too much trouble."

Sean looked from the woman in front of him to the bouquet of orange and pink lilies, and then down to Kit. He did not appear overjoyed at the thought of letting them see Beth. "Let me see how she is first. Wait here, please."

The time they spent waiting in the hall might only have been a couple of minutes, but it felt unbearably long. The anticipation was tearing Kit in two directions: on the one hand, he hoped to have a chance to see Beth again, to ask after the map and explain why he had suddenly abandoned her without saying goodbye. Then again, he was afraid of what Catherine might say. She had made it clear she thought Beth was lazy and selfish to sit in a chair most days rather than rush around in a whirlwind of activity. He wished that he had spent more time on the car journey explaining Beth's illness, so that his mother might be more sympathetic now.

When Sean returned, his grave face gave nothing away until he stopped in front of them and said, "You can go in now, but Beth's tired, so I'd appreciate it if you kept it short."

"Of course, I completely understand," Kit's mum reassured Sean, though Kit was fairly certain that she did not understand at all. "And don't worry, we won't stay long. Juliet's at home by herself so I'll need to get back to her soon."

At the door to Beth's room, Catherine hesitated.

"Why don't you go in first, Kit?" she suggested, and he gladly took her up on this.

Beth was waiting for them in her usual spot by the window. He studied her face and her movements for any evidence supporting his theory that she was being poisoned. But if anything, she looked healthier than when he last saw her. Her skin was full of colour and warmth, her eyes alert. It seemed as though her bump had grown since they first met.

"Mrs Garsdale," Catherine began, but Beth interrupted her.

"I think we're rather past those niceties. Don't you? You'd better call me Beth."

Kit's mum faltered. Politeness was one of her fail-safe ways of winning people over, but Beth was having none of it. Kit could see why. You couldn't very well use your first conversation to shout at someone and accuse them of all sorts of things, only to jump back to formalities on the next occasion as if you were just meeting for the first time. Catherine held out the flowers instead.

"A peace offering. I'm so sorry for how I spoke to you before we left."

"They are very pretty colours," Beth said, but she made no move to take them. They were too garish, Kit realized suddenly, and completely the wrong sort of flower. Not that he knew much about flowers at all, or about Beth's particular tastes, but he felt that his mother should have brought Beth something that grew wild and windswept near the sea, rather than the obviously expensive lilies she had chosen. They just didn't look like the right sort of gift.

"It has been pointed out to me that I made some unfair assumptions about your health and your influence on Kit. And the way I articulated that was equally unacceptable. I want you to know that I understand not all illnesses look the same; I should know better than anyone that some of them are all but invisible."

He had not heard his mother try to apologize to someone before. He didn't think she was doing a very good job of it, but at least she wasn't shouting this time, or accusing Beth of sitting around and being waited on by others. She was still holding out the bouquet. Kit spotted the wrist supports on Beth's arms and realized that the reason she was not moving had nothing to do with rejecting the gift.

"Are your arms hurting again today, Beth?" he asked. "I can put these in one of the jars for you."

He took the flowers from his mother, who looked relieved not to be brandishing them any longer. There were a number of old glass jars by the watercolour set, already filled with water to clean Beth's paintbrushes. He picked out the sturdiest one to support the weight of the lily stems.

"Thank you. I'm not very mobile today, but the painkillers should kick in soon enough. And you are not the first person to misunderstand my illness, Catherine. Still, I accept your apology. Shall we move on?"

Catherine gave a nervous, grateful laugh. Kit placed the lilies on the windowsill where the light would shine through them. He glanced around the room and was relieved to find that the easel was empty today, the unfinished map stored away somewhere. He was not sure his mother would have appreciated it fully, and he did not want it to be seen by anyone who could not understand its value. Still, he hoped its absence didn't mean Beth had given up now that she would have nobody to help her with it. He could not think of a subtle way to ask her about this.

"So how do you like your new home, Kit? Have you unpacked all your games and books?"

"Not quite. There are boxes everywhere. We have a lot of stuff."

"It only looks like a lot when it's all clutter and cardboard," his mum interjected hurriedly. "We haven't accumulated too much. Our last house was really quite small by comparison. Living in the city is so expensive."

The bit about the house was not true. The Fisher family home in London had been spacious, with four bedrooms and a study, not to mention the workshop in the garage. Kit was not sure why his mother would lie about it.

"It must be a big adjustment for you all, moving up here."

Adjustment implied that it was possible to get used to the change. It presumed that one day Kit would wake up in their quiet house by the sea and not mind that his father was miles away, or that he couldn't get anyone to tell him once and for all why they were there. Kit had not yet considered the possibility that he would adapt to this situation and accept it, rather than fight it, and he did not much like the idea now. Adjusting was the sort of thing Juliet probably excelled at, slipping chameleon-like from one situation to the next and knowing just how to behave, but to Kit it sounded a lot like giving up.

"Kit, I'd like to speak with Beth alone now. Why don't you go and read your book by the fireplace in the guest lounge?"

Kit dragged his feet behind him as he left the room. He clicked the door closed before pacing up and down the hallway, but there was no sign of Sean now at the reception desk or in the guest lounge. Perhaps he was in the kitchen. With the rooms so deserted, Kit felt safe to loiter in the hallway for a while, so he sat himself down in a corner, still technically following his mother's instructions to read his book, just somewhere near enough to overhear snatches of the conversation.

"...I'm not sure what else to do," his mum was saying, as he came back to within earshot.

"Well," he heard Beth reply, "maybe it's not enough to simply take someone out of their environment and expect all the problems to melt away. Maybe it's just as important to connect with the new surroundings, to be distracted from all the old worries."

"What do you think would help, then?"

"Everyone's different. But if it were me, I'd want to get outside and go for a long walk over the moors or down to the sea, every day. I'd want to fill my head with the changing moods of the sky and be so consumed with following the nesting of the gannets and counting the starfish in rock pools that what someone somewhere had said or thought about me once upon a time just couldn't matter any more. If I could, I'd be out there right now, clambering up barrow mounds to imagine what the world was like thousands of years ago."

"Oh yes, I've read some recent studies on how being outdoors lowers cortisol levels. Do you think managing stress hormones is something to focus on?"

Beth replied that this was not something she knew much about, but she knew that being in the open air made a difference to her. Kit had always known that Beth missed being able to walk around whenever she liked, but hearing her speak like this about the countryside made him feel even sadder for her, that she was missing out on something so beautiful. Perhaps it was only the lack of it that helped her see the poetry in the landscape. He could go out whenever he wanted, and he was not sure he had ever appreciated it enough until now.

"Out of interest," Beth continued, "what made you change your mind about me? A few days ago I wouldn't have expected us to be having this conversation."

"It was my husband's idea, to be honest. He thought that, given your… situation, you might be more understanding than most towards someone in a different but equally complicated predicament. And he and I – well, we could use the advice."

"I hope I've been able to help then."

Catherine sighed. "I need to find a way to get this family back on track somehow. The normal channels haven't worked, and at this stage I'll try just about anything."

"Me too," Kit said aloud to himself, sitting alone in the corridor where no one else would overhear. He sighed and stomped down the hall, tired of being inside with his ear pressed against a door. The sky outside had brightened, and even the gravel on the driveway was heating up under the sun's rays. He dragged his feet through the stones, ploughing furrows from the front step out towards the sea.

Up ahead, the gravel crunched under a pair of shoes that sounded heavier than Kit's own footsteps. He watched a stranger approach Askfeld. There was a parked car some way down the track behind him, blocking the way in or out for other guests. He wore an old shirt tucked into his trousers, and a pair of dark sunglasses, which he removed when he saw Kit in front of the house.

"Hello, young man," the stranger said with a broad smile. Do you know where I can find Sean and Beth Garsdale?"

Kit did not like that smile. It stretched right across the lower half of the man's clean-shaven face, but no higher. He would have been better off keeping the sunglasses on and concealing his flat hard stare. A real smile should crinkle up around your eyes and make them sparkle just a bit. The lie of this stranger's expression put Kit on edge, and he found he did not want to be helpful for once.

"No."

"All right. Suppose they tell you to say that to people you don't know, right? Say no to strangers and the like – very good. Don't you worry. I just want a little talk with them, nothing to be anxious about. I'll have a look around and maybe I'll bump into one of them. What do you think?"

Kit decided to give nothing away, and instead blocked the doorway to the house by making a great show of retying his shoelaces right there on the doorstep. When he looked up again, the smile had vanished from the man's face. The stranger shrugged and strolled off towards one of the outbuildings. Kit watched him from the step, guarding the way into Askfeld until his mother came and told him it was time to leave.

"You seem very quiet." Catherine glanced over at her son when they had driven halfway back to Utterscar without a word. "You know, that might not be the last time we visit Askfeld. I had a long talk with Beth and she's not at all how I expected."

Kit vaguely registered this as good news, but his mind was racing away with the mystery of the cold-eyed stranger.

"I can't imagine how worrying it must be for her, living with so much that's unknown. To go to bed and not know if you'll wake up unable to walk the next day! And adding a baby into that mix too. She seemed so calm about it all."

Beth was a peaceful person; Kit had seen that about her when they first met. But she might not be if she knew about the man who had been creeping around Askfeld. What was he doing there and what did he want with Sean and Beth? Perhaps it was a clue to whatever Sean was up to, and this stranger was a part of the plan.

CHAPTER TWELVE

SKIMMING STONES

DAY TWENTY-FOUR

Mum let us get takeaway fish and chips for dinner AGAIN last night. That's the third time in a week. She says it's part of the adventure of moving house that you get to do things like that. I'm not sure she fully understands what an adventure is.

Catherine poured a dollop of Greek yoghurt over her cereal and selected the ripest blueberries from the punnet to scatter on top.

"I have to go into town today to run some boring errands. But you don't have to come with me if you don't want to. And no, Kit, I'm not going to Askfeld this time, if you were hoping for another visit there."

"I've still got lots to get through on my reading list for next term." Juliet did not look up from carefully dissecting a banana into bite-size pieces on the plate in front of her. Their dad would have told her she looked as though she was training to become a brain surgeon.

"You've been working all summer, love, and there's weeks to go until school starts. Why don't you take a break? Go out into Utterscar for a bit. Did you have a look at what's listed in the local newsletter that got posted through our door?"

Juliet rolled her eyes. "Did *you*? It was so boring it was almost funny."

The *Utterscar News* was an A5 black and white publication that looked to have been created and printed from someone's home desktop shortly after they learned how to add borders and unusual fonts to a document. But alongside the Utterscar events diary, it contained personal stories from local residents that Kit had enjoyed. It was fun to imagine the authors behind the anecdotes, and to hope for a chance to meet them one day.

"There must be something that interested you."

"Tragically I may have to miss the judging of the Utterscar Cauliflower Show this year. Maybe next year will be my turn to win a prize."

Kit pictured a stage populated by tap-dancing cauliflowers in top hats and grinned to himself.

"Don't you go laughing at her sarcasm," Catherine chided him. "It's bad enough having one child who answers back all the time. And you mock, but I honestly think some fresh air will do you good. If you won't join in with anything organized, why don't you and Kit go out for a walk today?"

Kit nearly dropped the cereal box he was emptying into his bowl. He had grown so used to his mother keeping him indoors and under her supervision ever since the day he went looking for the albatross that this was the last thing he had expected. Juliet must also have picked up on the surprise, because her next words were: "Seriously? I thought you wanted us cooped up safely in here, where nothing bad can ever happen."

"There's no need to take that tone with me, thank you. I don't mind the two of you going out together, if you're sensible. You're old enough to keep an eye on Kit, and you can phone me if you run into any trouble. Some of my happiest childhood memories are of going out for summer walks with my parents. I'm sure it made us healthier than all the staring at screens you do."

Juliet looked unconvinced at the idea of walking instead of

revising, so Kit interjected with, "It doesn't have to be a boring walk, Jules. I know loads of cool places we can go see."

"Fine. I guess I could do with getting out. I thought Askfeld was quiet, but *this*… I couldn't get to sleep last night without music; it's just eerie lying awake listening to nothing. Don't either of you miss the sound of traffic?"

Kit could not remember when he had stopped being bothered by the change in background noise. Now he rather liked it. Besides, if you opened the front door when the wind was from the east you could hear the comforting murmur of the sea, even from here. Beth had learned to love the stillness of Askfeld, but he suspected that might be beyond the abilities of the busy Fisher family.

Their mother gathered together registration forms for the local doctor's surgery and reviewed her shopping list while Kit gleefully thought about where they might go and what they might find for Beth's map, even though they weren't at Askfeld any more. Juliet, however, would not agree to anything until she had seen the route they would be taking.

"Come on then, where are we going? I'll look up a map. And a weather forecast. That way for once you won't end up running home hours late in the rain."

She knew that he had been in trouble the day he and Bert went searching for the albatross, but she had not used that knowledge to dig at him until now.

"Um, OK. Can you see a lake near here?"

"What's it called?"

"I'm not sure of the name. But I heard there's one not far from Askfeld. Can you find it?"

Juliet sighed and opened a map of the local area, zooming in and out in search of a patch of blue.

"I can't believe I'm using up my data allowance here and you can't even tell me the name! Wait, there's something called Skate Tarn here – is that it?"

Kit looked over his sister's shoulder. It was a blue blob on the map, shaped a little like a teardrop. It wasn't far from the house.

"I think tarn's another word for lake." He held his breath as he watched his sister consider this. If he appeared too enthusiastic, it would only bias her against the idea.

Juliet checked how long it would take to walk there before finally nodding. "OK, we can go there if you like."

"Make sure you take waterproofs with you," their mother said, "and there are some cereal bars in the cupboard if you want snacks for the walk."

Though it was now the height of summer, the day was overcast and cool, and the light had a pale dusky quality to it. The air was still and silent but for the muted distant cries of birds and farm animals. Juliet checked the route again on her phone and strode ahead down a muddy path that ran along the edge of the fields. At first Kit was happy to half skip to keep up with her, but he soon became tired.

"Jules, slow down!"

"Why?" It was a genuine question. Juliet did not seem to have realized the speed at which she had been marching.

"Your books aren't going anywhere. They'll still be there when we get home." Kit had spotted a long branch on the path, the right size for a walking stick or wizard's staff. He picked it up and leaned his weight on it as he studied his sister's haste.

"What? No, it's not that. I'm not really in a hurry." Juliet checked herself and tried to slow her pace.

"Yeah, sure." Kit mimicked the sarcasm his sister had perfected over the last couple of years. He tried raising one eyebrow to complete the effect, but ended up squinting oddly at her instead. Now that she was walking normally, he was able to keep pace with her while still brandishing his staff.

"It's just… I like to walk quickly, I think. And listen to music at the same time. Otherwise, well, you're stuck on your own with your thoughts, aren't you?" She quickly added, "And that's pretty boring."

Kit felt sorry for his sister, whose imagination must be much smaller than his if she could find solitude boring. Maybe it was something that happened as people got older. Juliet looked down and absent-mindedly began chewing her fingernails. She must be very anxious about the risk of boredom.

"Do you have your earphones with you?" he asked, and Juliet nodded. "Well, I guess we can listen to music while we walk, if you like."

She smiled, and plugged her earphones in, passing one to Kit and putting the other into her own ear. Now they had to walk more slowly and watch one another's step to keep pace and not yank the wires.

"Is this song OK?" Juliet asked as the guitar chords started. Kit did not recognize it, but he didn't mind. Juliet cared a lot more about music than he did. She actually learned the lyrics to songs, and sometimes sang along to them in her room when she thought no one could hear.

"Yeah, it sounds good."

They walked like this along the track, awkwardly manoeuvring their way around a big puddle without losing balance or earphones. The path entered an area of woodland, cutting a straight line between the trees and then winding round to follow a beck downhill. At last they found the tarn.

The water was still and flat, reflecting the cool grey of the sky. It was surrounded by dark pine trees and the ground up to the water's edge was stony. There was no one else around.

Kit ran straight to the water to see how clear it was. He could see all the way to the bottom of the lake. He turned round to find Juliet arranging stones and taking close-up photos that he guessed would shortly be posted online with artistic filters.

"Want me to take a picture of you by the lake?" he offered.

"Oh, no thanks. I look awful today."

Kit shrugged. Juliet said things like this. Her friends from school, the girls at least, used to come out with similar phrases. He didn't really understand the tiny details that distinguished looking good and looking terrible to them. As far as he was concerned, she always looked like Juliet, and there wasn't much variation unless she was really tired or upset. Sometimes he was very glad he wasn't a girl.

"You don't take as many photos of yourself as you used to in London."

"Um, I suppose not. I'm half thinking about deleting my accounts anyway."

He stared. Juliet had spent the last three years obsessed, in his opinion, with curating her online image. Now she wanted to erase it. He was torn between concern that this was out of character and hope that his sister might be better company if she were less distracted. Hope won, and he decided this was a good choice.

"OK. Do you know how to skim stones?" he asked. "I asked Dad if he'd teach me, only..."

He thought back to the phone call, and then wondered what his dad was doing right now. *Was he trapped in an office, desperately wishing he could escape and join his family? Or was he happy to still live in the city?*

"I don't." Juliet looked down and kicked at the ground. "There was a boy in my class – Richard – who knew how to. He showed everyone on a school trip to the reservoir once. He made one stone bounce six times before it sank. But he wasn't someone many people listened to, or liked. You know the kids who always say odd things, or the wrong things? He was super-enthusiastic about all these weird hobbies, and people tended to ignore him. They'd do impressions of him when he wasn't around, and everyone would laugh. So I didn't ask him how he did it. But maybe we could figure it out. I can look it up."

"What do you think?" she asked, when the video had finished. "It looks a bit tricky."

"I want to try!" Kit grabbed a handful of pebbles and sifted through them to pick the flattest one. He threw it at the tarn's even surface, and it immediately sank into the water, sending ripples radiating out from the spot. Undeterred, he found another stone and threw it, with exactly the same results.

"You're throwing it wrong," Juliet told him. "It's supposed to be underarm, and flat over the surface of the water. Something like, um, this… OK, not exactly like that, obviously, but that's the general idea."

It occurred to Kit, as he passed another stone to Juliet, that he could not remember the last time he had seen his sister fail at something.

"OK, so flat and underarm, like this?" He tried again. The pebble still sank, but this time it felt more like the motion they had seen the American man demonstrate. He repeated the movement, and this time the stone jumped once off the surface of the tarn before sinking.

"You did it!"

Juliet cheered and Kit shrieked. "Did you see that? It bounced!"

"OK, show me how you did it now," Juliet said, standing back to observe with arms folded. Kit threw another stone, and this one bounced three times in a straight line across the lake. Juliet copied him, but her stone was swallowed up by the water. She sighed.

"I can't do it!"

"It's OK, Jules, keep trying." Kit collected a few more flat stones for them to use. They carried on throwing them, Kit's dogged determination maintaining both his own enthusiasm and his sister's when she wanted to stop. Eventually Juliet managed to skim a stone for two jumps, and her face broke into a broad grin. Kit double high-fived her to celebrate her victory.

"I hope I get a chance to tell Beth about this!"

"What's Beth got to do with it?"

"She's the one who told me about the lake and the stones."

"Wait." Juliet frowned. "Has today been about you finding more stuff for your map again? Is that why you dragged me out here?"

When she put it like that, it *did* sound a lot like Kit had deceived her. But that had not really been the point. He regretted having told her about the map now.

"But it was fun, right? We had to test it out to see if Skate Tarn really is a good place for skimming stones. And now we know!"

Juliet gave a disgruntled nod. "I guess she's saved us a lot of work in looking up places to visit."

Kit looked back at the path that had brought them here. "You're going to say we have to go back now, right?"

Juliet looked at the map on her phone. "You know, we're about halfway to Askfeld here. If you want to, we could walk the rest of the way and you can tell Beth about the lake."

Kit was afraid that if he hesitated, Juliet might change her mind, so he grinned and bounded back to the path with a shout of "Turn left!" following him.

At Askfeld's sturdy front door, Kit hesitated.

"What is it?" Juliet asked.

"Sometimes Sean doesn't like me going to see Beth. What if he stops us today?"

"Well, you said that Beth is ill. And you can be pretty… energetic. Let me talk to Sean."

She led the way into the house with Kit trailing behind her. Sean was at the reception desk, counting out stacks of coins and ten pound notes from the till. The tide and weather had been updated on the slate behind him.

"Good afternoon, Sean," said Juliet. Just like that, she had gone into what Kit called her "grown-up mode".

"Afternoon," he replied. "What are you two doing here? Your mum OK?"

"Yes, thank you, she's fine. We've been out walking. It's lovely weather!" Juliet almost faltered for a second as she glanced outside at the grey looming clouds she had just described as "lovely", but she ploughed on. "How are things here? Have you had any new guests arrive?"

"A couple. But you'll still recognize some of the faces here."

Maddie must have extended her stay again. Kit wondered if she would ever leave Askfeld and finish her journey up to the abbey. Bert would still be going out with his binoculars and notepad, hoping to see something interesting. Kit hoped he was not too disheartened from the day they failed to find an albatross.

"And how is Beth?"

"She's doing well this week."

"Is she well enough for us to quickly say hello before we go back home?"

Sean paused, and Kit smiled at Juliet's cleverness. It would be hard for Sean to claim that his wife was too tired or ill to see anyone when he had just admitted how well she was. He might have imagined the scowl he thought he saw Sean flash at them as he nodded and they walked past the reception to Beth's room.

"Kit! This is a nice surprise. I hadn't expected to see you again so soon." Beth put down her book, sliding in a watercolour sketch to mark the page where she had paused. "And you must be Juliet. I've heard a lot about you from your brother and your mum. Come and sit down, both of you."

She took her feet down off the footstool so that they could squeeze onto it, side by side.

"Is it a good day today?" Kit asked. Beth weighed this up.

"Pretty good, I think. Certainly enough that I'm very happy to have some visitors. So tell me what you've been up to since the move."

"We learned how to skim stones!"

"Did you? I used to do that when I was your age. My dad and I would go over to this lake and we had to make it to seven skips before we were allowed to go home. Did you go to the tarn near here? I think I remember there's one not far away."

"We did; it's called Skate Tarn and it's shaped like a raindrop and there are lots of good stones by it. You told me about it the first day we came to Askfeld, but you said you couldn't remember what it looked like. So we found it for you. Juliet, show Beth on your phone where we went."

Juliet obliged and showed Beth the route they had taken.

"We can put it on your map!"

Beth pulled out her sketchbook and copied down the shape of the lake from Juliet's phone. Juliet, meanwhile, had seen the real map propped up on the easel and now wandered over to take a closer look. Since Kit's last visit, the sea had come to life. It was not a single sea, but a pattern of its many different moods. At the top of the painting it was the colour of storms and shipwrecks, while at the bottom it was the deep serene blue of a clear day. In between was every other face it might reflect back at the changing sky: from overcast grey to starlit indigo, all marbled together.

"It's… it's quite unusual, isn't it?" she remarked. At once Kit wished he had not brought his sister here. Of course she would look through the eyes of a geographer, measuring it against the rules of cartography and seeing all that was technically wrong with it. That was how Juliet saw the world. She would care more about gridlines and scales than the fact that there might just be a lone albatross out there on the sea. He readied himself to defend Beth's work.

Juliet straightened up. "Kit told me the map is for your baby." Kit relaxed as he realized she was keeping her criticisms to herself.

"That's right. A childhood's worth of adventures, plotted out on paper. Though I'm not sure how we'll get on with skimming stones. Sean doesn't know how to, and I may or may not be able to manage the walk."

"I'll teach him when he's old enough!" Kit declared. "I'm quite good now."

"Are you having a boy?" Juliet asked.

"I don't know yet, but Kit has decided that's what he wants it to be."

"It's got to be a boy," Kit said resolutely. "With all these cool adventures planned for him, how can it not be?"

"Girls can have adventures too," said Juliet. "After all, most of these are things Beth has done."

Kit tried to picture a younger Beth running around outside, barefoot on the dunes. He could just about remember a time when Juliet had been interested in playing ball games or hide and seek, before she had become so careful and serious. But even back then, she had never wanted to climb trees or pretend that they were saving the world from an evil sorcerer. Kit had played out those games by himself.

An idea occurred to him. "What does Sean think of the map? Can he help you finish it off, now that we're not staying here any more?"

He was sure of the answer, but he wanted to see if Beth or Juliet shared any of his suspicions. He watched their faces carefully.

"He knows about it and thinks it's a nice idea. He was the one who bought me the materials to make it. But he's got a lot of work on, running Askfeld. We're short staffed, and Sean's main way of dealing with that is to try to do everything himself."

So Beth knew her husband was not willing to help with the map. Her tone of voice said that she did not mind, but Kit was satisfied that he had made a good start towards helping her see that Sean might not be all that he seemed. Perhaps he could gradually introduce the idea so that it would not be too much of a shock. He didn't want to do anything that might make her illness worse, not since the day he saw her in so much pain.

Would Beth's child understand the difference between good and bad days? Would he be able to spot the signs early enough to know what to expect from one day to the next?

"Is it the fog?"

"Is what?"

"Is it the fog that makes you iller? It was all grey and cold last time you felt really bad. I noticed."

Beth considered this with a thoughtful smile. "I suppose it's connected, in a way. The chill in the air and the damp hurts my joints."

"And when it's foggy you can't go places – you can't see far enough ahead. I remember playing tag at school once and we had to stop because it was so misty we couldn't see and were scared of running into each other. So on foggy days you have to sit still, right?"

"Right. And sometimes it feels like the mists have got into my head too, stopping me from being able to think clearly or feel the sunlight." She paused, smoothing out the folds of the blanket over her legs. "They have a name for it, round here, the mist that rolls in off the North Sea. They call it the fret."

"Fret?" Juliet repeated. "I thought that was another word for worry."

"You're right."

"Maybe it's because worry is like mist – you can't get hold of it or chase it away." Kit shuddered at the thought of fog creeping into Beth's room and clinging to her.

"It must be so hard for you," said Juliet. "How do you keep from getting overwhelmed by it all?" It was an unusually earnest and forward question from his sister the etiquette expert.

"The most important thing for me is to keep on reminding myself that I'm no less worthwhile a person on the days when I can't get out of bed. Whether I rattle through a to-do list or stare at the ceiling all day doesn't make the slightest difference to who I am or what the people who matter think of me."

The idea appealed to Kit, but he couldn't see it sitting easily with the Fisher family mantra. Juliet, Catherine, his dad, they all worked hard every day. That was who they were.

"How did you get on with *Robin Hood*, Kit?"

So far it had not been the source of any nightmares, the way the villains of King Arthur haunted his dreams. "I'm only halfway through, but I like the idea of all the outlaws living in the woods. I think that would be difficult, having to find all your own food and stuff."

"You know, there's a place not far from here called Robin Hood's Bay."

"Did he live there?"

"Hard to say. Most likely not. But the story goes that he defended the coast from pirates who came to plunder the poor fishermen's earnings and steal their boats."

"When is your baby due?" asked Juliet. She *would* think to ask that kind of question, of course. Kit had never thought of it.

"Due date's a month tomorrow. Not that you ever really know for certain when they're going to arrive. Now, Juliet. Tell me about you."

Juliet looked down at her hands. "I'm fifteen. Nearly sixteen – my birthday's in two weeks. I've just finished my GCSEs. Next year I want to take French, History, Geography, and Physics at St Jude's."

"And what are you really good at?"

"Um, not much." She shrugged and moved over to the window. The grasses had not been cut back in weeks and were bobbing their heads in the sea breeze.

"That's not true!" Kit contradicted her. "She always gets full marks in everything. Except for drama."

"Right, so you're clever and humble with it," said Beth. She set down the rough version of the map so that Juliet had her full attention. "Well, tell me what you like doing instead."

"I enjoy… well, I used to go out shopping with my friends on the weekend. But now they're all in London and I'm here. We stayed in touch every day at the start of the summer, but lately I've not heard so much from them. I think they're realizing that I'm not coming back." She sighed and leaned against the windowsill.

"Do you miss them?"

"Some of them." Juliet sounded surprisingly measured in her response. Kit had assumed, given how much time she had been spending on her phone, that she must desperately miss all of her class and be trying to stay in contact with them at every moment. "A couple of the girls in my year were really nice. But it's actually quite good, not having to think about the group all the time. Mum and Dad think they were a bad influence and that it's better for me to be away from them."

Kit made a mental note to ask Beth what her secret was that people were immediately comfortable talking to her. This was more information than Kit had got out of his sister all summer.

"The people we spend time with can have a big impact on us," said Beth. "What have you been doing to entertain yourself this summer without them?"

"Listening to music mostly. I haven't been able to practise my piano for ages; it's been in storage while we moved. I'm supposed to be doing my Grade Seven as soon as Mum finds a local teacher. But I can still listen to stuff while I'm revising. I guess it's good that there's so much work to do. I'm not as inventive as Kit; I don't have a 'quest' to keep me occupied."

"What quest is this?"

"You know – helping you with your map. He's rescuing the damsel in distress, one grid reference at a time."

Beth looked over to Kit, who suddenly felt embarrassed. True, he had thought of the map as his mission, and even discussed it with Juliet, but he had never told Beth about his efforts to save her from a life of solitude or from whatever horrible plans he suspected Sean was hatching. Beth's large, searching eyes seemed to take in all this in her calm way. He looked down to avoid her gaze.

"I can see why you liked those Camelot books so much now. I think helping me with my map is a very noble quest."

Kit raised his head in surprise. Beth wasn't angry with him. But she hadn't finished yet.

"But there's one thing I think you've got mixed up. In the legends, the person who gives the hero the commission or quest isn't usually the princess who needs rescuing, is it? It's the wise sorcerer."

He thought about this. Beth was right: it was Merlin who pointed Arthur towards Excalibur. And it was Athene, goddess of wisdom, who gave Odysseus all he needed to claim back his home.

"So you see, Kit, I'm not really a damsel in a tower, despite appearances. You don't need to worry about saving me from anything. But I'm very impressed and grateful for how well you've responded to this quest to fill in the map. If I had a magic staff, I'd probably conjure up a reward for you." She picked up a paintbrush and waved it with an overly dramatic flourish. "Just bear in mind that sometimes the people who need our help the most aren't the ones who look ill or desperate. Sometimes you can be a hero by spotting those closer to home who just need some kindness and encouragement to help them out from under a cloud."

It made sense. Beth was wise, and sometimes didn't say everything very clearly, just like the way wizards always spoke in riddles. Kit could accept that. But then she didn't know what Sean had been saying behind her back. Besides, a hero had to save someone. It didn't have to be a princess necessarily, but it had to be someone. Otherwise how would anyone know he was a hero, and not just any old character?

He frowned over this as they left Askfeld. Though it had turned out well in the end, he wished Juliet had not said anything to Beth. He made this known as soon as they were outside.

"I hadn't told anyone else about it being a quest to help Beth. Only you knew that. What if she doesn't want to be friends with me now she knows?"

He waited for his sister to say he was overreacting, that it was his own fault for not making clear that the quest was a secret. Instead, Juliet's eyes widened and she chewed her lower lip. When she replied, her face was full of worry.

"I didn't think of that. I thought you told Beth everything – you have all these secrets together like the map. I'm sorry. That was really stupid of me."

She was so downcast, Kit jumped to reassure her that it was not the end of the world. After all, Beth had coped with him bothering her on bad pain days, running into out-of-bounds rooms, and bombarding her with questions about her illness. She would probably let this most recent mistake slide too. It had no effect on his sister, who stared at a scuff mark on her shoe and mumbled apologetically.

"I can't believe I was so thoughtless. I didn't mean any harm by it."

She was starting to annoy Kit, so he changed the subject. Did Juliet know anything about puffins? Bert had told him the scientific name for them, but he could not quite remember it. He tried to impress her with albatross facts instead. They began the walk across Askfeld's grounds, towards the path.

There was a bang and a shout. Juliet jumped out of her despondency in surprise.

"What's that? Is someone hurt?"

Kit shook his head. "I know what that was. Come on!"

He ran off in the opposite direction from the house, as his sister shouted in protest after him.

CHAPTER THIRTEEN

DRIFTWOOD

POSSIBLE REASONS WHY MADDIE IS SO ANGRY WITH EVERYONE:

1. She's from another country and we've accidentally offended her without knowing it (like how Beth's mum didn't mean to seem like she hated me).

2. Something bad happened to her. Maybe she was attacked by robbers on her way here, but when she arrived at Askfeld, Sean and the others refused to help or call the police.

3. She's thought of somewhere that would have been a better place to go on a pilgrimage to and is cross that it's too late to change it after all this time.

He led the way over the grass from Askfeld, towards the dark crooked trees that spilled down towards the sea.

"I thought we were meant to be going home," Juliet called as she ran after him. "Mum won't like it if we're back too late. And if you think I'm going to take the blame for this…"

Kit ignored her threats, knowing that if he kept running, Juliet would have to follow. She wouldn't leave her younger brother alone and risk getting into trouble for that irresponsibility.

Further up from the copse was a field where the grasses had been allowed to grow tall and golden this summer. The noise was coming from this direction, higher up than the last time he had been here. It rang out again: the sound of wood and metal colliding. There was something not quite right about it this time though. It was not the steady rhythm of a hammer working nails into place.

Juliet caught up with him and hissed, "I think someone's crying. Whoever it is, they probably want to be left alone."

But it was too late to turn back. They could already see the upturned boat, lying like a beached whale where Maddie had dragged it up the steep cliff path from the shore, the one that had been designated not safe enough for Kit or Juliet to use. He had half expected the little vessel to be transformed by now, with new timber and bright paint, ready for its next voyage. It looked, if anything, worse than before. There was now a gaping hole at the prow end.

Bang! Maddie kicked the boat with a wordless cry of frustration. Then she saw she had an audience.

"Oh!" She quickly wiped her face with the back of her hand. Her eyes were red and swollen.

"I'm so sorry, Maddie," said Juliet. "We didn't mean to disturb you. Come on, Kit, we need to get back home." Apparently Juliet had no questions about the broken boat on its side in the meadow, or what was upsetting Maddie so much. But Kit would not be led away so easily.

"What happened?"

Maddie sniffed and seemed to force her eyes wider and brighter before she answered.

"This boat's much harder to repair than I thought. Turns out the wood's rotten in a few places. I dragged it up here into the sunlight hoping it'd dry out, but it hasn't helped."

"Is that why you're crying?"

"Kit, I don't think that's any of our business."

Maddie bent down to examine the sizeable damage to the prow, and Kit peered over her shoulder to see if it was as bad as she claimed. It would fill with water in no time in its current state. There was no way this boat could make the journey to Whitby. It would be a shipwreck on the seabed before it had cleared the cliffs below Askfeld.

"You can mend the hole though, right? You just need some new wood that isn't rotten. Can we help?" His dad would have known where to find the right materials for the job.

"You remind me of Charlie," Maddie said, straightening up. She smiled, but her eyes were still full of tears. "You're the same age as him, I think."

"Who's Charlie?"

"He's a very kind and clever boy, who I used to look after. He never used to let me give up hope either, until…" She changed her mind about completing this sentence.

"Are you a teacher?"

"Not quite. And certainly not any more."

She ran a hand over her face to pull back the strands of hair that had escaped and were now in her eyes. Then she walked down to the stern end of the boat and began chipping away the remaining flecks of paint. Kit wanted to say that he had watched his dad at work often enough to be fairly sure it was better to replace the rotting planks first before sanding down the existing wood, but Maddie was starting to look more relaxed now, so he let her continue.

His silence was rewarded, because as she worked, Maddie said, "I used to work at a special school, for children who have developmental difficulties. It was a residential school, so some of the boys and girls lived there during the term. And I helped to look after them in their school home."

"But you don't work there any more?" Kit decided to join in with the work, so he began scratching away the grey paint too. Juliet hung back and watched them.

Maddie took a deep breath and then sighed it back out. While she did this, she looked down the slope, over the tops of the trees to where the waves rolled in. The sight seemed to calm her.

"No. I left earlier this year. That's when I started my pilgrimage."

"But why? Didn't you like it there?"

"Like it? I loved it! I loved each and every one of those children. I would have jumped in front of a speeding bus for any of them without a second thought. No, I left because I had to."

Juliet, who had been pretending to look at her phone until this moment, stopped now and sat cross-legged on the ground beside them.

"Did you get fired?" Kit asked.

"Kit!" exclaimed Juliet. "I'm sorry, he asks a lot of questions. You don't have to tell us anything."

Maybe it was the fact that Juliet had joined the conversation, but Maddie started speaking differently. "Actually, I don't mind. You're the first person to dare ask me about it. Most people dance around the subject, dropping hints that they're curious – and I can see why. It is a bit odd, a woman my age quitting her job and spending months hiking and staying in hostels and guest houses. But so far no one has had the guts to ask what happened. I don't know how easy this will be for you to understand, but I've seen enough of the two of you this summer to know you're both bright, so I'm going to do my best to explain."

Juliet looked solemn as she nodded, accepting the mantle of being mature enough to cope with whatever Maddie was about to say.

"This time last year, the school recruited a new member of staff. Let's call her… Elsie. Elsie was supposed to improve the school and its ratings. You know about Ofsted, safeguarding, government targets, and all that from your own schools, I'm assuming? Well, she watched us, to see what we were good at and what we were bad at."

Juliet shuddered. "I would hate that. Like having exams every day."

Kit pulled a face at his sister. He could not help it; he was irritated to hear her making everything about her exams, when whatever Maddie had been through was clearly much worse. Juliet hadn't walked the length of the country in response to her troubles, so why did she pretend to understand? Maddie seemed not to notice, however, as she continued.

"And I don't exactly know why, but Elsie just didn't like me. Everybody is different, and sometimes people just don't click, for one reason or another. She gave us all 'feedback' on how to improve at our jobs, and some of the things she said about me were fair, I suppose. So I tried to take it on board. It's always good to learn, to change, to try to improve. But it was like she could only see what was wrong with me. I don't mean what I was doing wrong. No, that would have been OK. But she saw something she didn't like in me and so that's what I became."

"It sounds like she was bullying you," said Kit. Back in the spring term, they had all been called into a special assembly to talk about bullies. Mrs MacAllister had marched up and down in front of them talking about how unacceptable it was to pick on other children. Kit had only half listened, because he knew her irate speech couldn't be intended for him. He would never call someone names, and he couldn't remember an occasion when anyone had ever bullied him either.

"I don't know," said Maddie, and she really did seem torn in two directions. "I'm not the easiest person to work with. Lord knows I've given the owners here enough trouble during my stay. I doubt I'm the most popular person at Askfeld this summer. But I just can't believe I'm every bit as awful as she made out."

She stopped working at this point and frowned, as if she still had not quite made up her mind on this matter.

"I'm sure you're not," Juliet began, but she faltered, uncertain how to offer reassurance beyond basic politeness. Maddie smiled and waved away Juliet's efforts, as if to say she knew full well it was not the responsibility of a teenager to help improve her confidence.

Then she looked instead at the rowing boat, threw up her hands in surrender, and sat down in its shadow opposite Juliet.

"Thanks for your help, Kit, but I think it's time I accept this boat isn't going to sea again. We can't always fix everything."

So that was the line between what was salvageable and what was just driftwood. It lay in someone's choice.

"What did this Elsie woman say about you?" Juliet had thrown out her respect for people's privacy and was leaning in.

"First, she recommended I be given less important tasks around the school. The sort of things where it wouldn't matter if I got it wrong: stapling bits of paper together or counting out pencils. She moved me away from spending time with the children and took over that herself. I would still see them, of course, in the corridor outside the photocopier room where I started spending most of my time, but I wasn't supposed to have any sort of influence over them any more. That became Elsie's role instead. But it didn't stop there. She and I continued to have meetings where she would tell me her plans for the children, and in the next breath she'd tell me why I should not be a part of those plans.

"In the end, she made it very clear that it would be better for the children if I left. She never fired me, never told me I had to leave, never really did anything I could have made a formal complaint about, but her views were plain enough." Maddie put her hands to her face, stretching the skin back from her cheeks and then locking her fingers behind her neck.

"But that's not fair! You cared about those children. And you don't seem like someone who would ever hurt anyone," Juliet commented.

"I did care about them. I do. I cared about what was best for them more than about keeping my home or a job that I loved."

Juliet frowned. "You mean, you didn't stand up to this woman? You just… left?"

Maddie smiled, and it was a gentler, less strained thing now. "Believe me, I wanted to fight it with all my being. I wanted to stand up and say, 'This isn't right!' and I wanted to tell the children I wasn't leaving them willingly; that I loved them all and would have gladly stayed for ever. I wanted them to know the truth – that there was an adult here who loved them unconditionally. But that wouldn't have done any good. At the end of the day, it was clear to everyone that Elsie and I could not work together, so one of us had to leave to keep the peace. I was the lower-ranking worker there, even if I had been around longer. And I would have done anything to maintain some stability in those children's lives, at any cost. Some of them have had horrible experiences by the time they arrive at the school, and others just find day-to-day life much harder than you or I would. The last thing a lot of them need is to feel caught in the fight between two adults' egos. So I just said I was very sad to be going, but that I would always remember them.

"Every day since then I've thought about them all. I've wondered how Charlie's swimming lessons are going. He was so proud when they let him move up a group and swim with the older children. And I wonder who will tell them how wonderful they are now, or whether Elsie knows how to make sure they feel secure so far away from their parents. And I wonder how much they will have changed already, what obstacles they'll have overcome and new skills they'll have learned. And then I remember I won't be able to find out the answers to any of my questions."

"That's heartbreaking," Juliet breathed. Kit said nothing. He suddenly found Maddie a little frightening. That any adult could have such enormous emotions inside them shocked him, and he was more afraid now of her sadness than of her flaring anger, which was only a shade of sorrow after all. She looked at him with a concerned expression and perhaps she realized how much of the storm they had seen, because she quickly sat a little straighter and brightened up.

"Saying goodbye is always sad, but that's why I started my pilgrimage. By walking a long way and visiting all these different places, I've met a lot of new people. And that helps – it gives me some better memories of this summer."

"How far have you walked now?" Kit asked.

"From my old home in Norwich. At the last count it was nearly two hundred miles."

"And you're going to stop when you get to Whitby Abbey?"

"That's always been the plan. Though lately I've been thinking that maybe it's the wrong destination after all. Lindisfarne would be the perfect place to end a pilgrimage. But even then I'll have missed out on all the Scottish coastline, so perhaps I should extend it further north again."

"What will you do when you've finished walking?" He was beginning to feel as though he were interrogating her.

"I don't know."

"Maybe you can find a new school to work at, with new children. Do you think the ones you left behind miss you as much as you miss them?"

"Most likely they have got used to me being gone by now." She leaned back against the boat and it supported her weight. The sea and sky stretching out before them had the same muted tone today. In the quiet grey light, a hush seemed to hang over it all. "It's a funny thing, this sea." Maddie did not look at either of them, but seemed to address her next thoughts to herself, or to the still waters ahead. "I've walked alongside it for so many miles now, and you get to know it, like it's the constant, silent companion in your travels. On days like today it's so peaceful and I could find something deeply spiritual in this place. And then you see the lifeboats rushing out one night in the middle of a storm to rescue some poor soul who's been swept out too far off course, and you realize it could knock you off your feet in an instant. So gentle and yet so dramatic." She ran her hand over the feathered heads of the grasses surrounding her boat.

Kit decided to take a risk and share something with her. "If you want the best place to see it, there's a gap in the gorse just over there." He pointed across the field to the tangled vegetation on the other side of the path. "It comes out onto the cliff top, and then you have this view of the sea and the sky and nothing else for miles and miles. It's amazing."

Maddie thanked him, and said she would have to investigate it. Kit hoped Beth would not mind him sharing one of the secrets of her map. It felt as though Maddie needed the cheering up.

"Staying at Askfeld, I can see there are others just like me. We've all been washed up on this sea of unfinished stories, and we're – I don't know – waiting, or hiding, or gathering strength for the next mile, but we haven't found our endings yet. We don't even know if we could face them if we did."

Juliet stood up. The abrupt movement broke the spell of Maddie's words with a jolt. Kit grimaced. It had all been too poetic for his sister, and made her uncomfortable. She could not understand as he did.

"I'm so sorry to hear what happened. I wish there was something we could do to help. Still, I think we need to be heading back now, Kit. Mum will probably get home before we do at this rate, and I don't want her to worry."

Kit shot an apologetic look to Maddie as he followed his sister away. He understood at last why she had not finished her pilgrimage, and why she kept on extending her stay at the guest house. She was afraid of ending that part of her story, in case it didn't go the way she had hoped. There was always a risk she might leave Whitby Abbey still feeling as pained as the first day of her journey. He understood that fear: just occasionally he had found himself wondering whether the unfinished map would be enough in the end to bring his father home. If the map was completed and the Fisher family were still fragmented, he had no new ideas for how to fix that problem.

As they walked north past Askfeld and the tarn back towards Utterscar, Kit thought about what Beth had said, about the people he could help being nearby. He could not shake the image of Maddie sitting under her shipwreck, so far from the life she had loved. If only there was something he could do to show her that she was not driftwood.

CHAPTER FOURTEEN

BETWEEN THE SALT SHORE AND THE SEA STRAND

DAY TWENTY-FIVE

If the sea was a person, it would be:

1. A wise old man with a long white beard, who's just watched the world go by for years and is never surprised at anything.

2. A boy my age who's fun to play games with (on days when the water's sparkling because the sun's so bright).

3. A really angry teenager who storms out of rooms and breaks things (on stormy days when it crashes on the rocks).

"What are you doing?"

Juliet had caught him. She stood in the doorway, arms folded, fingers drumming against her forearm. They had driven over to Askfeld for Catherine to catch up on her emails, and Kit had seized an opportunity while she was out of the room to borrow her laptop. Juliet had been revising outdoors, her vocabulary lists spread over a bench bathed in sunshine, but she had come back for her bag when she ran out of highlighter pens. "Please tell me it's not what I think."

He had been searching online for special needs schools in the Norwich area. The handful that he found all had websites, and by searching through the old news and events sections he soon found reference to a Miss Morley helping out with the annual sports day, and a photograph of Maddie surrounded by children in white polo shirts. She looked different in the picture. She was smiling, and her hair was neatly curled rather than straggly and weather-struck. She wasn't looking at the camera; she was focused on listening to one of the girls sitting next to her who had just craned her head round to say something.

"Well, that depends. What do you think it is?" he asked, deciding to be contrary rather than confess everything.

"You've decided you're going to fix things for Maddie somehow. I don't know what you're planning, but I know you, and I'm certain you're interfering in something that's none of your business."

"You said that before she told us her story, and then she told us it anyway. So maybe things are more our business than you think."

"Suddenly an expert on other people's problems, are you? It's laughable how much you don't understand!"

Kit scowled. Juliet could just have easily said "funny", but he knew she was deliberately using the longer word "laughable" to show how grown up she was, to distance herself from him. He resented how she viewed him as a child and herself as an adult, when there was only a gap of five years between them.

"What I don't understand is why you're so spiky these days. You just complain and criticize all the time!" he retorted, making a show of being very interested in what he was reading on the computer, so that he could ignore his sister. He wanted to appear cool and aloof, as she so often did, but could feel his face burning with indignation.

"Only when there's stuff that needs pointing out. Anyway, it's better to be argumentative than too scared of conflict to ever disagree with anyone, like your weird birdwatcher friend."

Kit snapped his head back up at this. "What about Bert?"

"Can't you see it? He's one of those people who'll run a mile before telling you that you've done something wrong."

"No, he's not! You've barely even talked to him anyway." How could she presume to be an authority on Bert, or any of his friends?

"Sure he is. Everyone says so. For someone who eavesdrops so much, you do miss a lot. You know his wife left him because of it, right? Apparently every time she tried to bring up a problem, he'd just avoid talking about it and say he had too much work to do right now, until eventually he was spending all his time at the university so he wouldn't have to get into an argument. In the end she gave up and moved out. That's why he spends all his time traipsing round the countryside alone, looking for rare birds. And it's why he talks so much nonsense all the time, to avoid letting the conversation ever get uncomfortable. Mum heard about it from someone here at Askfeld."

He weighed this up. Could it be true? Bert had never mentioned having a wife, just some grown-up children. He was willing to bet the "someone" gossiping to their mother was Sean, and told Juliet as much.

"Might have been. Why? Oh right, because then you don't have to believe it. Because Sean's the villain in your made-up story, isn't he? Even though Beth made it perfectly clear she doesn't need you to rescue her from anything."

It occurred to Kit that Bert might actually be somewhere in the guest house today, and even within earshot of this conversation. He did not want to be overheard gossiping about his friends, so he said nothing and waited for his sister to get bored and go away.

After a pause long enough to make it clear the conversation was over, Juliet uttered a noise of disgust and walked out. Kit breathed a sigh of relief. Clicking on the contact page of the website, he made a note of the school's address on the back of his hand, since he had not thought to bring any paper with him. Then he closed the browser window and sprang away from the computer as Catherine returned.

"Mum, have you got any envelopes?"

"Yes, I think there are some back at the house. Why?"

"I want to write a letter."

"A letter? Who to?"

He was prepared for this. "Toby, from my class." Toby was one of his friends whom his mum had always liked. Toby was polite and dressed smartly even when it wasn't a school day. He called Catherine "Mrs Fisher" whenever he came round, and took his shoes off in the hall. His stepmother was on the board of governors and wore a lot of perfume.

It worked. "Of course, dear. I keep forgetting that you must be missing your friends. I think they're in the kitchen by the recipe books. Have a look when we get home. And I have a book of first class stamps in my handbag. Do send our regards to Toby's parents when you write."

"Thanks, Mum."

"How would you like to go out somewhere new today? I think we all need a break from unpacking boxes and sitting indoors. Don't you?"

Kit grinned. "Where can we go?"

"I don't know – there are some nice seaside towns within driving distance. Let me have a look at the map."

For a moment, Kit thought she meant the unfinished map, but then he remembered she could not know about it, and was probably talking about the road atlas she insisted on keeping even though the car had satnav. He hoped they could go somewhere nearby enough for him to find something for Beth's map anyway.

He heard his mum go and talk to Juliet, who would not agree or disagree regarding any plan until she had voiced a string of questions about where they were going and for how long. Negotiations and map-checking went on for some time before Kit heard his name being called and went to find them.

"How about we go to Scarborough for the day?" his mum said. Kit's heart sank. That was off the edge of the map. There would be nothing useful there. Then he remembered Beth telling him that there was a castle, and he cheered up a little.

It was breezy but a clear sky stretched over Scarborough when they finally found a parking space and clambered out of the car on a small side street. Kit took a deep breath through his nose to take in the smell of this new place.

"I can smell chips."

"I expect they sell a lot of fish here, being so close to the sea," his mother said, putting the car keys back into her handbag.

"Look!" Kit pointed. "There's the castle."

On a headland at the north end of the bay, what remained of Scarborough Castle stood like a beacon overlooking the town.

Catherine asked if they wanted to walk up to the castle, and Juliet shrugged. This was close enough to agreement for Kit, who marched ahead up the hill. It quickly became a steep walk past rows of neat red-brick houses with flowers lining the window ledges, and then a flight of steps where he had to wait at the top to make sure he hadn't actually lost his mum or Juliet by walking too fast. When he was sure they were still following, he ran on to the slope up towards the gatehouse.

While his mother dealt with the boring matter of purchasing tickets for entry to the castle, Kit looked around the little gift shop. His eye fell on a selection of wooden toy swords. A few years ago, he would have begged his parents for one so that he could pretend to be a knight. Then he would have insisted someone else buy a second, so they could battle up and down the castle walls. His dad would have been the most likely to yield, but there was a time when even Juliet might have been willing to challenge him to a duel. That was before she got a phone, before she had essays to write in the evenings and make-up to apply before weekend shopping trips. Now she was much too grown up to be interested in that sort of game. Kit reminded himself that he ought to be too old for it as well. The children at his new school probably didn't play at sword fighting.

He ran over the barbican bridge until he stood beneath the keep. The side nearest him was completely missing, the tower's insides exposed as if it were one of those cutaway book illustrations that let you see inside buildings. He imagined soldiers marching up the stairs to the arched windows, their armour catching the sunlight as they steadied crossbows on the ledges, took aim, and…

"It says here," Juliet interrupted his reverie, reading aloud to the rest of them from an information board, "that half of the tower was destroyed during a siege in the Civil War. The castle was held by people on the king's side, and Cromwell's men attacked it."

"Who were the good guys in that war, Jules?"

Juliet looked confused. "What do you mean?"

"Was the king's side good, or Cromwell's?"

"I don't know. It's not that simple. History isn't like that."

Some of it was, Kit thought. The Romans were ruthless, clever and cruel, while the Celts were brave and tragically doomed to lose against the invaders. The Vikings were vicious invaders who murdered monks, no matter what Beth might say about them doing some good. Kit had not studied the Civil War, but his hunch was that the king had been unfairly attacked.

"I wonder what the café is like here," said Catherine. "They tend to be quite good at these historical sites. We could have tea and cake after we've seen the whole castle."

As they walked along the perimeter wall of the outer bailey, Kit imagined himself as a soldier on patrol, keeping an eye out for pirates or Viking raiders coming over the North Sea. The vantage point from the top of the wall was good; from here on the headland he could be the first to spot sails on the horizon. Beside him, Juliet was battling the fierce gusts coming off the sea and scraping her hair back into a bun to keep it from becoming any more windswept.

After a proper tour of the castle, which involved climbing as high as they could into the ruins of the great tower and peering out through the arched windows (Kit refused to grip on to the wall in case Juliet spotted and laughed at him for his new-found fear of heights), their mother ushered them into the tearoom. She bought a pot of tea for herself and Juliet to share, orange juice for Kit, and then they were each allowed to choose a slice of cake.

"Can we sit outside?" Kit asked.

"No, let's stay indoors. You'll get cold if you sit still for too long out there."

He offered to get up and run around after every third mouthful of cake to keep warm, but his mother just laughed and picked a table near the door.

"Well, we couldn't have done anything like this in our old home!" she said, smiling brightly at them both as she poured the tea with effortless precision. Kit admired how she could do that without spilling a drop.

"You used to take us to historical sites all the time," Juliet pointed out, "and we've had school trips to the Tower and the Imperial War Museum pretty much every year."

"Still, they weren't right next to the beach, were they? We couldn't have cake in a castle looking out over the North Sea back then. Kit, use the fork you've got; you'll get chocolate icing all over your hands. Here, take this napkin to clean them. I'll fetch some more."

Juliet picked at her scone, pulling sultanas from it and chewing them slowly. Catherine sat back down, sipped her tea, and looked quite content. Two elderly ladies in anoraks were leaving the tearoom, but stopped at the Fishers' table. One woman was tall with sleek grey hair cut short around her face and a delicate silver chain at her throat, while the other had sparkling blue eyes and a complexion that suggested she had spent her life travelling to hot countries.

"Aren't they the spit of each other?" the taller one said to the other.

"You look just like your mother," the bright-eyed one said to Juliet.

Juliet straightened up, self-conscious at being addressed by strangers. "Thank you," she said.

"I think I should be the one taking that as a compliment, at my age!" their mother laughed.

"And do you take more after your father?" the first woman asked Kit. Kit was not sure how to answer. He had the same dark hair as his mum and Juliet, whereas his dad's hair was sandy brown. Perhaps they did look alike in other ways.

"He does," his mum answered for him, and the women smiled.

"Well, we had better go. We've got a few more miles to walk before it gets dark." They left chattering together about mutual friends.

"If I have the energy to be walking miles when I'm that age, I'll be quite happy," said Catherine.

"I guess I'm a bit like Dad," Kit said aloud. "I like books, like you do, but I like making things with him. We both like running too. I wish he was here; it would be more fun with Dad."

"Well, let's hope you haven't inherited his uselessness in a crisis," his mother laughed darkly. Silence fell, full and uncomfortable. Juliet looked down and seemed to be chewing her lower lip instead of the scone on her plate.

"What do you mean?" Kit asked.

His mother's eyes darted around. "Nothing, love. Finish your juice and we can go down to the sea."

"Do you mean the time when he left the potatoes in the oven too long and it set off all the fire alarms and there was loads of smoke everywhere?"

"Never mind that now."

"Because he didn't mean to. Mr Kendrick next door came round to ask to borrow a ladder because he'd locked himself out of the house and needed to climb in through the window, but then he got stuck halfway and Dad spent so long standing outside laughing about it that he forgot all about Sunday lunch and that's why the potatoes got burned."

"Come on, I said drink up. Let's go now." She stood up and put her arms into the sleeves of her coat.

Kit studied her face, and then tried to get a look at Juliet's, but she still had not raised her head. He had the distinct impression that his mother had said more than she meant to, and more even than he had understood.

They left the tearoom, Juliet leading the way this time, marching ahead of them down the slope and through the archway. Their mother half ran in an effort to catch up with her, and Kit wondered if the two of them would lose their footing on the steep road and tumble to the coast. He pictured them rolling down, a comical and undignified whirlwind of shoes and handbags flailing.

When they reached flatter ground, it was on the harbour front. Small, brightly coloured fishing boats were moored in neat rows. Kit moved to the edge of the walkway so that he could read the names painted on their sides: *Stickleback*, *Daybreak*, *Amphitrite*. He wondered what Maddie would have called her boat, if she had not given up on it. A white-haired man with sun-scorched skin that reminded Kit of the texture of a raisin was sitting on the deck of one of these, winding a long coil of rope in his ancient hands. He fixed Kit with a stare but said nothing. *He looks like he knows as much as the sea itself*, Kit thought.

"Look at those," Kit's mum said, pointing to a stack of small cages with wooden bases and sides made of blue netting. "Do you know what they're for?"

"Um… for keeping gulls in?" he guessed. Being by the sea, he would have hazarded fish as an answer, but he could not picture the kind of fish that you could put in a cage.

"Not quite. Fishermen use them to catch lobsters on the seabed."

"I read that some chefs cook lobsters while they're still alive," said Juliet. "I think that's horrible."

Their mother marched them on swiftly. It had been a year since Juliet's last threat to become a vegetarian, and Catherine had combated this predominantly by changing the subject every time it came up in conversation. Beyond the harbour, past the stalls selling chips and sticks of rock and tea in paper cups, was the bay. The tide was out, and from here to the cliffs on the south end was nearly half a mile of exposed sand and pools of saltwater. The seaweed draped over the rocks was lime green and stringy in some places, dark and leafy in others. Glistening water dripped from its fronds down to the grey sands. Behind them was a high wall, and above it a row of beach huts with doors in bold primary colours. A few had deckchairs arranged outside them, whose occupants were reading paperback novels or unpacking picnic hampers.

"'Tell him to find me an acre of land…'"

It took Kit a moment to recognize where the sound was coming from. "What are you singing?" he asked his mother. Back in their old house, he had been used to hearing her sing to herself while she cooked or rearranged her files in the study, but since moving here, she had stopped.

"'…between the salt shore and the sea strand.' Oh, it's an old song called 'Scarborough Fair'. It seemed appropriate. Do you know it?"

Kit shook his head. The wind was blowing in off the North Sea so he unzipped his coat and spread his arms wide. The material flapped about him like wings or sails. *I wonder how big a coat I'd need for the wind to carry me away.*

"I wish we had a kite," he said. A man some hundred metres down the beach shouted an apology as his terrier ran past them in pursuit of a tennis ball and narrowly missed colliding with Juliet. She jumped back in alarm.

"Stay here with your sister," said his mother. "I won't be long."

She walked off back towards the road behind the bay, still singing to herself. Kit obediently stood near his sister, who was staring out to sea.

"I've been thinking," he said, because it was clear he would have to start the conversation. Juliet rolled her eyes, but he persisted. "All the people who've come to Askfeld this summer – they're all there to escape something, aren't they? That's what Maddie was trying to say the other day when she couldn't fix the boat."

Juliet said nothing, so Kit continued.

"Bert was getting away from all his colleagues laughing at him for his mistake. Maddie went on her pilgrimage to stop having to think about her old job all the time. Do you remember on our first day here, how Sean told us what Askfeld used to be called? He said the previous owner called it The Last Resort. Maybe it wasn't such a bad name for the place after all. People go there when they're out of options. And it got me thinking about whether that's why we're here too."

In his head, this had been the moment when Juliet would turn to him and say, "Well done, Kit. You figured it all out. I'll explain everything now, and then Dad can move up here and live with us again." But she did not move or make a sound.

"Are you OK?" he asked, because he was unsure if her eyes were glistening because of the fierceness of the wind on her face or from trying not to cry.

"Of course I am. I was just thinking how I wish I could escape you talking all the time."

He was about to take the bait and retort with an insult, but something made him stop. Instead, he waited. And after a pause, she continued.

"For such a mind-numbingly quiet place, there's so much chatter. I wish I could get away from it all sometimes. Not just other people, like you and those old ladies in the café, but the noise of thinking all the time. Turn off the part of my brain that revises French verbs when I'm trying to sleep."

Was it possible to stop your mind in its tracks? He had no idea. It was not a skill he had ever thought might be useful.

"We could look for grey seals," he offered. That had cheered him up the day he had gone searching for an albatross. "I saw some near the guest house once. And Sean said there are sharks and whales out there, though I'm not sure if I believe him." He had little enough reason to trust anything Sean said after what he had overheard him say about Beth. Thinking about the Garsdales and Askfeld reminded him of the map. He wondered if Beth would have made any additions to it, or if she was stuck without his help. He felt a strange pang of guilt whenever he thought of it: that he had let people down by not seeing it completed before they left for their new home in Utterscar. It was not entirely his fault, since the move had been sprung on him at a few hours' notice, but nonetheless he felt that he should have completed his quest.

"If we wander off, Mum won't know where to find us when she gets back. You're so easily distracted, I'm amazed you haven't got lost or fallen off a cliff yet!"

Kit shrugged and resigned himself to waiting.

When their mother returned, it was with a brown paper bag under her arm.

"What's that?" he asked eagerly.

The paper rustled as she held it out to show them a diamond of blue canvas, thin white wires, and a reel of thread.

"I saw a stall selling kites on the way over here," Catherine explained. This was not the sort of impulsive behaviour Kit expected from his mother. His dad was the fun one – that was how things were. But his mum opened up the packaging and unfolded the kite, smoothed out the crêpe-paper streamers of its tail, and tied the string to the supporting bars, all as if she were completely oblivious to the way she had strayed outside her normal territory.

"Now then, Juliet, would you like to hold the string? There you go. Kit, you take the kite now and run over to those rocks. Hold it high above your head. You'll need to wait for a good gust of wind. When you feel it, let go!"

He took the kite and ran as instructed, while Juliet let out the string. At the rocks, which were still slippery from the retreating tide, he found a place to stand and lifted the kite up on outstretched arms. As the wind blew in, it filled out like a ship's sail and the cord became taut. Kit jumped into the air and let go of the kite as he did. It swooped up, carried high by the breeze and then began to circle back downwards. Kit heard his mum telling Juliet to pull in the string, and as she did, the kite stopped its descent and rose up again.

"It's flying!" Kit cheered, watching the bright blue shape flutter, with lilac streamers dancing behind it.

When the wind dropped and the kite fell to the sand, Kit ran to fetch it and bring it back in.

"Can I hold the string this time?" he asked. Juliet handed it over to him.

"Juliet, do you want to take the kite?" She did not, so their mother carried it away while Kit tried not to let the string tangle as he rolled it back out. Juliet stood behind him as he tugged at the string to try to keep the kite airborne. A seagull flying in to land had to make a swift detour as the kite charged towards it, and the two of them laughed.

"You nearly hit that bird!" said Juliet.

"I didn't mean to."

"See if you can aim for the next one that comes in." She smiled mischievously, and Kit knew she did not mean it. He found it was too hard to control the direction of the kite; it depended too much on what the wind was doing and he could not send it towards a target.

"This is good. I've missed this," he said.

"Missed what? Kite-flying?"

"No, you being fun Juliet again, not boring, serious, too-much-work-to-do, too-many-friends-to-see Juliet."

"Oh." Juliet was silent for a while. "We used to get on all right, didn't we?"

"Yeah, before you moved schools."

"Well, we'll both be at St Jude's together from September. It's really weird that you're old enough to be in secondary school already."

"There you go! You talk like a grown up all the time now. You sound just like Mum, or one of those old ladies from the café."

"Well, I'm not a kid any more. People grow up. And what's expected of you changes."

"Like what? You mean your exams, or having friends who say nasty things behind each other's backs?" These things were obviously bad, but he could not shake the feeling there was something else she had neglected to tell him.

She looked away. "Doesn't matter."

"When I'm your age, I'm going to make sure I still read good books and play football on Saturdays and fly kites at the beach."

Juliet made a "hmm" noise and watched the kite soaring above them. "When you start at our new school, just be careful when choosing your friends, OK? The people you hang out with at school have a way of shaping you and getting under your skin. So pick the right people."

Kit thought this advice was a bit rich coming from Juliet, whose friends had always seemed melodramatic and selfish, as far as he could see.

The kite danced and twirled overhead, its streamers performing pirouettes in the air.

CHAPTER FIFTEEN

THE CONSPIRACY

DAY TWENTY-NINE

The best things about my family are:

1. Dad – he's fun, and knows how to make stuff and always has time for games. And I don't know why he isn't here, but even if he isn't, I bet he misses us.

2. Juliet – she's really clever, which is sometimes annoying because Mum and Dad go on about it all the time, but it's helpful when I don't know the answer to something and I can just ask her. Also, I don't think she's completely lost her fun side, even if she has been really gloomy all year.

3. Mum – she's not as much fun as Dad, but she spends more time with us, and she never forgets to say well done when I do well in a test at school. Also, she reminds me that I need to be helpful to others, which is the sort of thing a hero should never forget.

The next opportunity to visit Askfeld did not arise for a few days. Eventually, Catherine had to spend a morning driving to the next town, leaving the other two at home. Juliet had seemed resigned to the fact that Kit would want to walk to the guest house, almost before he suggested it.

When they arrived, Juliet sat outside on the bench Sean had set in the garden, hammered together from weathered pieces of grey wood brought in by the tide. Here she could gaze out to sea. It surprised Kit that she was content to sit like this, but he didn't challenge her, since it meant he was free to speak to Beth. The waves were playing against the rocks today, a curious deep blue that one moment seemed murky and foreboding and the next looked perfect for a summer swim. It reminded him of how Maddie had described the North Sea: gentle and yet so dramatic all at once.

On clear days like this, Askfeld owned its cliff-top location with a sense of presiding over the coast. Its white walls gleamed in the sunlight and Kit knew the front door would stand wide open in welcome. He had meant to go indoors straight away, but as he crossed the garden and rounded the corner of one of the dilapidated old farm buildings, he stopped and ducked back out of sight. Sean was there, his back to Kit, and he was talking to the stranger with the false smile who had come to Askfeld looking for the Garsdales before. From here, Kit could not make out what they were saying, but Sean kept glancing back to the house and holding up his hands. The stranger was not smiling today. He jabbed an accusatory finger at Sean's chest and then moved as if to walk right past him towards the guest house. Faster than Kit had ever seen him move, Sean jumped to block the stranger's path. Then his shoulders sank and his head fell forward as he reached into his back pocket and took out his wallet. He produced a handful of crumpled notes and counted them out into the stranger's hand. The other man still looked angry, but he seemed a little mollified. The stranger left, and Sean went back into the house.

What could Sean be paying this man for? Kit was quite certain he wasn't one of the usual suppliers to Askfeld, because he had spent so much time watching them come and go when he had stayed here. So it had to be something out of the ordinary, and nothing good if that man's lifeless smile was any indication of his character.

The words Nick had spoken to Sean weeks ago in an empty corridor of Askfeld returned to him. "Get her out of here somehow before the situation drags you even lower."

It would certainly explain Sean's anxiety about being seen with the stranger, if this man was part of the plot to remove Beth. If money was exchanging hands, the conspiracy must be progressing faster now. It was time to warn her, before it was too late. With a growing sense of dread in the pit of his stomach, Kit ran inside to find her.

At once, he knew something was not right. The door to Beth's room was wide open, revealing her empty chair and the map. But he could hear raised voices coming from the office where she kept the finance records.

"It's not complicated. We can't go on like this," Beth was saying. Kit breathed a sigh of relief: she was still here, at least. Sean had not got rid of his wife yet.

"You say that like it's news to me." Sean's voice was loud and clear through the closed door. "What do you think I've been working so hard for, all this time?"

"I'm just saying maybe we need to look at some other options."

"You mean *I* do. We're not having this conversation again."

"Well, what better ideas do you have?" It surprised Kit to hear Beth shout.

"At least keep your voice down. The guests don't want to hear you. It's unprofessional."

"Unprofessional! What about letting this place fall apart because you're too proud to ask for help? Is that your idea of professional?"

"You talk like I've not done everything I can to keep us afloat."

"For goodness' sake, stop trying to be a hero or a martyr and accept you can't do it all by yourself!"

"I never set out to, but that's just how things have turned out. I didn't ask for any of this."

The shouting suddenly stopped. Silence fell in its place. It was such a stark contrast that Kit tiptoed towards the office door to listen more closely, just to be sure they were still there. Through the wall he could hear the soft sound of someone crying.

"I'm sorry, love, I didn't mean that." Sean was speaking at a normal level again.

"But you did. And it's true. It wasn't meant to be like this. The dream was always the two of us, running our own place. You didn't sign up for a back-breaking workload alongside caring for me."

"I didn't. I didn't have the imagination to see it coming. But if you'd told me back then it would be like this, I wouldn't have walked away."

The voices grew quieter now, and though Kit strained, he could not hear what they were saying. After a minute he heard someone moving inside the room, and ran back around the corner into the guest lounge just in time to avoid being spotted by Sean as he closed the door behind him. Nick must have come out of the kitchen shortly after, because Kit heard him speak next.

"Everything all right?"

"I guess you heard all that?" Sean sounded tired.

"Not much. There owt I can do to help?"

"No. Unless you can answer impossible questions." Realizing the voices were coming nearer, Kit looked around frantically for somewhere to hide. He did not want them to know he had been listening. There was a gap between the large armchair and the wall, where he might not be seen. He squeezed himself into the space and sat very still as Sean and Nick came into the room.

"This is about Askfeld's future, right?"

"Yes. And I don't know what to do. Say you'd sworn you'd

never ask a certain person for help, but everyone was telling you it was the only way, would you do it?"

"Sounds like you already know what you have to do – you just don't like the idea of it."

Sean gave a hollow laugh. "That's about right."

"Just make the call. It might be the answer to all our problems."

Kit heard a heavy sigh, followed by a long pause. He did not like the sound of this call that Sean was contemplating. Could it have something to do with the stranger he had given money to just now?

"Families can be hard work," Nick continued, "but you need to do what's best for you, and this place."

"Hold on," Sean said. A cupboard door creaked open, and something clinked like glass.

"The single malt? This really is hitting you hard."

"I just need a drink before I can talk to him."

A heavy bottle connected with the wood of the table. Kit didn't know what single malt was, but it was a general rule that drinks he had not heard of before were alcoholic.

"None for me. I need a clear head in the kitchen."

"Like hell am I drinking alone! If you're going to talk me into this, you're having one too. I've seen you 'testing' the cooking wine before now anyway, so don't think I buy this disapproval either. Just be ready to hide the glasses if any guests come in."

There was the sound of liquid being poured out, once, twice, and then the faint metal scrape of a cap being replaced. The two men sat in contemplative silence for a while. Kit became acutely conscious of his breathing, and tried to keep it shallow and quiet so he would not give away his location behind the armchair.

"Beth loved this place the minute we set foot in it. It was run down and riddled with mould then, but she knew we could turn it into something better. We spent months scrubbing down the walls and painting them, buying in furniture and ripping up the weeds in the garden. We'd only been married six months, and having our own bed and breakfast was a dream come true.

"It crept up so gradually, I didn't realize at first there was anything wrong. The evening of our first anniversary, I remember watching her get ready to go out to dinner, and seeing how much pain she was in just trying to put her arms through the sleeves of her dress. She didn't want to admit how hard she found something so simple."

"Must have been a shock when she got ill."

"The doctors couldn't decide what it was. They'd try one diagnosis and then switch to another. And when something didn't fit, they'd tell Beth it was all in her head. But they hadn't seen what I had – how some days she physically couldn't get out of bed. How she'd get exhausted and not be able to sleep because she was in too much pain. And when they finally gave us a name for what was wrong, they said they didn't know how to treat it."

"But you get prescriptions for her, don't you? I've seen you taking bottles of pills to her."

"Some of them help. Some don't. Everything's an experiment to see what works. And I know it breaks her heart not to be more involved in running this place."

Kit was sure Sean was wrong about this. He would have noticed if Beth had been so sad about her illness. They had talked about it often enough.

"I remember when I first got here, how she used to burn herself out trying to keep working. She doesn't seem to do that any more," said Nick.

"You're right. I think it was the pregnancy that changed how she saw things in the end. She couldn't justify taking care of herself and not working alongside me, until someone else depended on her being healthy. This year I think she's finally learned how to rest. I don't mind the extra work when she's so peaceful about her situation at last."

"Yeah, but it's also a weight for you, mate. Even with me here, you're doing two people's work, and looking after her."

"And I can't afford to hire someone else to work here, but I can't keep on top of everything I need to do either."

"Well, you know what you've got to do when that glass is empty."

"Nick, you don't understand –"

"Doesn't matter. I still know you need to try. For the sake of Askfeld, if nothing else. This place is too important to you to let it fall apart now."

The room fell quiet again, until a heavy tumbler thudded down onto the table.

"All right. Let's get this out of the way."

Two sets of chair legs scraped against the floor.

"I'm going outside," said Sean. "I think I need to be alone for this call."

Nick stayed behind and cleared away the empty glasses and the whisky bottle. Only after he had returned to the kitchen did Kit exhale loudly and crawl out from behind the armchair. Sean was about to do something terrible. He had to warn Beth. He ran to the window, where he could see Sean trudging over the gravel to a secluded spot, phone in hand. He had the duration of the phone call to tell Beth what he had overheard. After that it might be too late.

She was not in the office where the argument had taken place. Kit went next to Beth's room. She was standing in the middle of the room with a furrowed brow.

"Beth!"

She jumped, and then gripped the back of the chair to steady herself. "Kit, you scared me."

"Beth, I need to tell you something."

"Not now. It's not a good time. My mind's got into a muddle. I was fine this morning – I did some work on the accounts. But now I keep getting halfway through doing things and forgetting what they were."

Kit looked at the table behind her. There was a ham sandwich on a plate, next to a glass of water.

"I think maybe you were about to have lunch."

Beth turned round slowly and saw the sandwich. "Oh yes, of

course," she murmured, then sat down to eat. Kit let her take a bite before continuing.

"I do have something important to warn you about though."

She chewed the bread slowly. "Can't it wait?"

"No. It's about Sean."

"What? Is he OK?"

"Yes, he's fine. But I think he's planning something. Something bad. He wants to get rid of you."

Beth put the plate down and stared at him. "Kit, that's a horrible thing to say. What on earth are you thinking?"

"He's planning to get you out of Askfeld so he won't have to look after you any more. He's on the phone right now with someone who can help. I think maybe it's the man he's paid to take you away. I heard him and Nick talking ages ago about how they couldn't carry on letting you stay here, that you were making things difficult. And just now Nick convinced him that if he didn't, Askfeld would have to close down. I had to warn you, so we can stop him!" The words tumbled out with barely space for breath in between.

Beth was stony-faced throughout Kit's explanation. Then she reached for her glass of water, but her hand shook and she overturned it by accident. The water spilled over her lap and down the side of the chair, but she did not jump up to fetch a tea towel, the way Kit's mother would have. She sat there, letting it soak through all the layers of fabric.

"You think," she said slowly and deliberately, as if each word cost her too much to waste a syllable, "Sean hates caring for me so much that he would – what? Send me away? Poison my meds? What exactly do you imagine he would do?"

Kit had to admit he had not figured out all the details of Sean's plan, only that it was being put into action as they spoke. To his horror, the door opened and Sean entered the room. He looked drained and weary.

"It's done," he said.

CHAPTER SIXTEEN

UNDER A WIDE AND SILENT SKY

I know it's normal for heroes to fail at some point. Like when the superhero gets captured by the villain and has to listen to a long speech about his evil plans. But is it the same when ordinary people mess up? What if you can't make things better by coming back to save the day?

"What did he say?" Beth reached out to take Sean's hand in hers.

"He said yes. He wants to meet with me first, but he'll do it." Sean sighed and leaned against the back of Beth's chair.

She rested her head back and closed her eyes. "Thank you. I know you must have hated asking him. Maybe it's time you reconnected though – it's been three years now."

Kit stared from Sean to Beth, and back again. *What was going on?* Sean had spotted the upturned empty glass, and the water still dripping onto the carpet. Without asking how it happened, he picked up the tumbler and went to the kitchen to refill it and fetch a towel. When he had gone, Kit sat down on the stool by Beth's feet. She folded her arms and looked at him expectantly. When it became clear she was not going to speak first, Kit asked the burning question.

"You knew who he was phoning?"

"Yes."

"But I thought…" he began, hearing the sentence trail off as he found he couldn't bring himself to say everything that he had suspected.

"You thought a lot of things, clearly. I guess I'm going to have to explain it to you, before you get any more ideas. Askfeld is struggling to make ends meet. Sean is overworked, and I can only help on days when my brain isn't full of fog. We need another member of staff, and we need better advertising so more guests will stay here. But we don't have the money. If we don't act quickly, we'll be bankrupt, and this place will close down."

Beth had to be mistaken. Kit had seen large amounts of cash change hands less than an hour ago.

"But the man outside – Sean just gave him a load of money, and I thought –"

"You thought he was what? A hitman? Nothing so dramatic, I'm afraid, though still unpleasant. We owe one of our suppliers and they got tired of waiting for the payment, so they sent someone round to demand the money. Sean came straight to me and told me about it – that man was threatening to take our belongings if we didn't pay up, so he panicked and gave him everything he had in his wallet towards the debt. That's why we were arguing."

"But then I heard him talking to Nick about how families make things difficult."

"Yes. Sean and his dad don't get on. That's who they were talking about."

"I thought they meant you and the baby. What's Sean's dad got to do with it?"

"He's a rich man. Or at least, compared to us he is. I asked Sean to talk to him and ask him for a loan. But they haven't spoken in years. Sean's dad doesn't think Sean has done enough with his life. He thinks he should have got a better job, a cleverer wife, an apartment in a big city. On our wedding day, he left early to show his disapproval and that's always upset Sean. But I knew he still cared. I knew if Sean asked for help, he'd give it. But people – even good people – can be proud. We argued about it today because Sean didn't want to ask for help from a man who turned his back on him, and who thinks so little of me."

"But what about the other conversation I overheard?"

"What exactly did you hear?"

"Um, first Sean said, 'She can't stay here like this for ever,' and then Nick said he could put something in the food."

Beth thought about this for a moment and then nodded in understanding. "Maddie. They would have been talking about Maddie. And they didn't mean it – they were… we were all just exhausted over how difficult she's been at times. Sometimes she shouts at Sean for no good reason, and she can be very rude to the other guests. It doesn't make our jobs any easier."

"What's this about Maddie Morley?" Sean had returned with a fresh glass of water and some paper towels. He mopped up the mess on the floor and the chair. Kit shrank back in fear of what would happen when Beth told him what they had been talking about.

"I'm just explaining to Kit that even though sometimes our guests can be difficult, it doesn't mean we hatch elaborate plans to get rid of them."

Kit's eyes widened in momentary relief; Beth had decided not to tell Sean the accusations he had just made. Sean laughed. "Not if they're paying for board! Do you want anything else to eat? You've hardly touched your sandwich. Let me see what else we have in the kitchen. I think Nick was making soup."

Kit frowned. He had been certain that Sean was the enemy: everything had fit that theory so well. Yet Beth had an explanation for everything. It was less neat and clear-cut than Kit's own version of things, but it did make sense.

"You know, Kit," Beth said once Sean had left for the kitchen, "it seems to me that all this misunderstanding wouldn't have happened if you hadn't been eavesdropping on people. It's a risky thing, to listen in and only hear half the story. Suppose I'd believed you?"

Kit thought about this. He had not planned what they would do next. He imagined he might have helped Beth escape Askfeld before Sean could do anything, perhaps bringing her to live at their house in Utterscar, where she could hide from danger. Maybe then he would have sneaked back into the guest house to gather more evidence until it was possible to call the police and arrest Sean. But it would have been a false charge after all. Kit pictured Sean languishing in prison while Beth raised her baby alone. Not alone, though: Kit was sure his family would have helped her. Still, it would not be the same as the child having its father. Kit knew that only too well; he missed his dad every day, but he had nearly inflicted the same thing on another person before they were even born.

"I'm sorry," he said, unable to look straight at Beth, so he stared intently at his shoes instead. They had been brand new and gleaming white at Easter; now they were caked in sand and mud. "I didn't think about that."

"And that's saying a lot from someone who thinks as much as you do."

Was she laughing at him? Kit had to look up to see her expression. It was hard to read: her jaw was set firm but her eyes still seemed gentle. Either way, it was not mocking.

"I only wanted to help," he explained. Those had been his mother's instructions on their first day at Askfeld: to be grown up and helpful. It was trickier than expected.

"I know. I know you would never mean any harm. But if you keep trying to help people without understanding the whole story, you might end up making more trouble, for yourself and others."

Like letting Bert think there was an albatross, only to see him be disappointed. He needed to be more careful to protect what was left of his quest at Askfeld, and there was something gnawing at him about that now.

"You know you said that man wanted to take away all your

belongings if you didn't pay him? He wouldn't take the map, would he?" He would not be able to bear it if, after all that work, the cold-eyed stranger took away Beth's map before she had a chance to show it to her child.

"I think he would go for things that look valuable first: electrical appliances, furniture, that kind of thing."

Kit was only partly reassured. What could be more valuable than all those memories carefully painted into the promise of an adventurous childhood? If the stranger realized that, would he confiscate it to punish Beth and Sean for not paying their debts?

"Now then." Beth sat up straight with a new burst of energy. "Pass me those paints. And the watercolour paper."

Kit did as she asked, but wanted to know what she was planning to do. Askfeld was at risk and she meant to paint in response.

"I have every faith that Sean and his dad will patch things up, and that his father will lend us the money we need. And when that happens, a shop-bought thank-you card won't quite cut it." She sounded so confident that Kit found himself believing it, too. She mixed up a blue wash and brushed it over the page. It was an act of defiance against circumstances, preparing this gift for someone who loathed her. Kit loved it. He watched as the blue background took on life as sea and sky, with a thin horizon painted in to distinguish them. Beth added green and gold grasses in the foreground, tiny black birds and at last the outline of a child gazing out to sea. She might have been imagining her own child, but Kit thought it distinctly resembled him.

He found Juliet exactly where he had left her, a book open on her lap, chewing her nails and staring off into the distance. They walked home in silence. On the way, he wished, not for the first time, he could be a character from one of his books. Their worlds were straightforward, their quests clear. If someone could just point him towards a monster that needed slaying, he would find that so much easier than trying to understand the complicated lives of the people around him.

"Kit, there's a parcel here for you!" his mother called up the following morning. "Did you give our new address to your friends from school?"

Kit clattered down the stairs to snatch the brown parcel from his mother before she had time to spot the Norfolk postmark. Hugging it against his chest, he ran back to his room and closed the door before tearing through the packaging.

The top letter was the only one actually addressed to Mr Christopher Fisher, so he opened that first. It read:

Dear Christopher

Thank you for writing to tell us about Miss Morley's adventures. The children were all delighted to hear what an exciting time she has been having. We have been practising our letter-writing this term, so many of the boys and girls wanted to take the opportunity to send some messages to Miss Morley, as you suggested. Please tell her she is much missed by many of us here and that we wish her all the best in the ups and downs of life.

From Miss Entwhistle, Class 4B

Beneath it was a collection of folded pages, covered in lines of large, untidy handwriting. He glanced over them briefly to be sure that they were all good messages. While Kit knew it was wrong to read other people's letters, he wanted to check there was nothing in there to upset Maddie. She had enough to be sad about already. But every page was from a child who had clearly loved her and wanted the best for her now. Some told her they missed her, while others shared their news from the school. Not one of them mentioned Elsie, which meant it was safe to show the letters to the pilgrim. He put them all back in the brown packaging and hid them under his coat when they drove round to Askfeld later that day. Sean had said Catherine was welcome to come back and use the wifi until the house was connected. Kit had to admit that since the day his mum had taken the flowers for Beth, Sean had seemed much friendlier towards them all.

While Catherine found new reasons to email her former employer, and Juliet caught up on all that she was missing out on via social media, Kit searched the guest house for its veteran residents. He found Bert first, hunched over a pad of paper, scribbling a list of bullet points in illegible scrawl.

"Hullo. Almost didn't hear you come in there," he said as he noticed Kit. "Just writing some notes on an idea I've had – for a new paper I'm going to write and hopefully get published next academic year. Only this time round I'll have learned from past mistakes to be more careful with my data. High time to move onwards and upwards, I think! But what's got into you? You seem to be hopping with excitement today. Not your birthday, is it?"

Kit shook his head and grinned. He was buzzing with the knowledge that he had at last done something that would make a real difference to another person here. He might have failed to find an albatross, or bring his father home, or even finish off the map, but he could not wait to see Maddie's face when she read the letters. Surely then she would be able to finish off her pilgrimage and go home.

"Do you know where Maddie is?"

"Finishing lunch in the next room, I believe."

Kit ran next door, with Bert following him at a slower pace. Maddie was sitting alone at a small table, chewing on the crusts of her cheese and pickle sandwich and turning the teapot almost upside down to be sure she had poured out every drop.

Kit thrust the letters at Maddie, forcing her to put down the pot.

"What's this?" She looked at the pile of papers in her hands.

"From your children. The ones you're missing."

Maddie frowned, and turned over the first of the letters. As she unfolded the paper and caught sight of the uneven handwriting, her frown faded and her whole face changed.

"How did you…" she began to articulate, but then lost interest in explanations as she read the words in front of her.

"'Dear Miss Morley,'" she read aloud, "'I hoop' – she means hope, but Holly's always found spelling a bit tricky – 'I hope you are happy and have lots of friends to play games with like we used to. Love from Holly.' Bless her!" As she moved on to the next letter, a small smile began to grow across her face. With it, the life flooded back into her complexion, softening contours that had seemed harsh before. Kit watched the transformation and for the first time could see what Maddie must have been like in her old job. The woman in front of him looked kind and caring, not solemn and strict. Her eyes were beginning to shine where tears were forming in them.

"Charlie got his swimming badge after all!" she murmured, too delighted with the news to keep silent. Her eyes glistened as she drank in the words on each page.

"Looks like you might have found the cure there," the birdwatcher said with a nod of approval, moving towards the door to leave now that he had seen the outcome. Kit stayed behind to watch his success play out, extremely satisfied with the effect of the letters. He pictured Maddie being able to go on with her life, no longer worrying about her children. He had done it! He had managed to help someone in the end.

Maddie had come now to the longest letter, the one Hannah from Year Six had written in perfectly neat handwriting, with little stars in place of the dot above each letter. Her eyes flicked back and forth along the lines, but something was not right. The frown returned and the muscles in her face tautened. She leaned forward over the page.

"What? No, no, she can't have."

"Is something wrong?" Bert had spotted it too, and paused in the dining room doorway.

"After everything..." Maddie seemed to be reading the letter a second time, perhaps to make sure she had understood it, then she let the paper fall into her lap. "She's left."

"Who's left?"

"The woman who took over from me. The one who wanted me out." Her voice was shaking and she had turned pale. Kit felt a sharp jolt in his stomach as he realized that when he checked the letters for any mention of Elsie, he had forgotten that it was a made-up name. "Just for a moment there, I thought... but no. I went quietly because I didn't want to upset the children. I thought it was best for them to have as much stability as possible, and here was someone so confident that she was the one to provide it. But apparently, after a year in the job, she quit, and they're having to find someone new."

"Ah well." Bert tried to sound bright and reassuring. "That just goes to show you were made of sterner stuff than her. Not just anyone could do your job."

"But it means it was all for nothing." Maddie spoke each syllable through clenched teeth. "She convinced me I was doing the right thing by leaving her in charge. That it was best for the children. But it wasn't. Because now they'll have to get used to someone new all over again."

Chair legs scraped over the floor as she stood up from the table, gripping the letters in one white-knuckled hand, while she placed the other on the gingham tablecloth as if to steady herself.

"I'm sure she didn't plan for it to be like this," Bert said. "She probably wanted what was best back then too. Circumstances change –"

"She took my children from me!" Maddie slammed the flat of her palm on the table so the cutlery rattled. Her interruption startled the others by its shrill volume, and the dining room fell silent. She seemed to take herself by surprise too, because she put a hand over her mouth and hurried out of the room.

"Oh dear," sighed the birdwatcher. "Who could have seen that coming? Where are you going now, Kit? I wouldn't follow her if I were you."

But Kit ignored him. He was to blame for Maddie's distress, and he needed to find out how to fix it. He came into the hallway just in time to see the front door slam. When he opened it and looked out, Maddie was striding away at an impressive pace. Kit followed her, but at a distance, because he had no idea what to say when he caught up with her. He wanted to explain that he had meant well, that he had wanted her to know that the children had not forgotten her. It would be little comfort now.

The content of the last letter, and its impact on Maddie, still confused him a little. But he had understood enough. He of all people could see that Maddie had made it her quest to protect her children. But her attempt to find purpose in that quest had been thwarted, and now her story made no sense to her. *So where was she going?* Perhaps she had finally decided to finish her journey to Whitby. If that was the case, though, she was taking the wrong direction. She still had not noticed Kit following her, and he decided to hang back behind the dark gorse. If she spotted him now, he was not sure what he would dare say to her.

They came at last to a place where the path opened out into a wide field where the dry grass was golden and almost waist high. Kit recognized it by the shape of the broken rowing boat protruding over the top of the grasses. Maddie waded out into the middle of this space until she stood beside the wreck and looked around her. There was no one else in sight, and Kit stayed hidden behind the gorse. The land stretched flat and the sky was clear and distant. She must have been satisfied that no one was around, because suddenly her whole demeanour changed. First her shoulders sank and she put her hands to her head. Then she fell to her knees in the middle of the sea of grass and began to scream: a sound full of rage and pain and futility. Kit understood then that this was something he was not supposed to see or overhear, and he slipped away quietly, leaving Maddie alone under the sky to pour out her grief.

He wanted to return to Askfeld unnoticed. The failure of his latest scheme stung, but more than that he felt he owed Maddie the kind of privacy that would be destroyed if he underwent a grilling about what had just happened.

But when he opened the sturdy front door that was always unlocked during the daytime, he found Beth sitting behind the reception desk, talking to Juliet and Bert. It was too late to sneak away quietly; the three of them spotted him at once.

"Best laid plans, eh?" The birdwatcher shrugged and smiled, but his brow was furrowed.

Juliet was less forgiving. "You never know when to quit interfering, do you?"

For a moment, Kit wondered if she knew he had accused Sean of trying to dispose of his wife, but he did not think Beth had been angry enough to tell others about his mistake. Juliet folded her arms as if to form a barrier between herself and her brother's stupid actions.

"I only wanted to cheer her up," he said.

"Why do you have to be the one to fix everything? Why does it have to be Kit the Hero? If you stopped for a second to ask someone for help, maybe you wouldn't keep making these messes for everyone else."

It reminded him of the quarrel between Beth and Sean. She had told her husband he needed to ask others for support instead of doing everything alone. But the whole point was that Kit was supposed to be the helpful one. "I –
I guess…"

She took a step closer, making full use of the fact that she was a good six inches taller than him to look down as she continued. "You don't get it, do you? You think if you just find something big and impossible to hope for and you call it a quest, then it's bound to work out the way you want; that people will magically get better or find things they've lost or be happy again. But sometimes impossible hopes are just that – impossible – and you need to learn to just leave them alone."

She stalked off to return to her reading. Kit's shoulders slumped downwards, and he looked to the two adults present for any sign that he should not take his sister's words to heart.

"I haven't made that big a mess, have I?"

Bert scratched the back of his neck for a few seconds before answering. "Well, it's hardly for me to say, of course, but I suppose it's possible – that is, I often find it's best to let other people be, rather than to give them false hope. But you know, we're all different. Now I really must go, lots to do today." He hurried away upstairs, muttering to himself, "Yes, yes, that's right. Lots to do. All for the best."

"Why is hope a bad thing?" Kit asked Beth, who had been studying the guest-book entries. She closed the book and rested her hands on top of it with a sigh.

"Hope is a wonderful thing," she answered, "but sometimes it can feel terrible and cruel too. Especially if it's followed by disappointment."

"I don't understand."

"Well, when I first got ill, I thought every time I went to the doctor that this was the day they'd give me a drug that would make it better, or that they'd find me a specialist who understood. But it didn't happen. And having hoped for things to improve made it harder to be content when they stayed the same, or when the pain got even worse."

"What happened then? Did you give up hope?"

"Never. But I decided I could learn to live with things the way they are, while also wanting them to get better."

Kit sighed and leaned forward so his chin rested on the reception desk. How could he accept things as they were, when he was the cause of so much trouble?

"I told Bert there might be an albatross round here. I made him hope and now he's sad about it."

Beth nodded. "I expect he liked the idea of impressing all his friends with the story. There's an old rumour about an albatross being sighted round here years ago, though no one's ever proven it. My dad claimed he saw it once, down over the cliffs. He used to tell the story whenever we had visitors round. In fact, that's where you got the idea from, isn't it? I put it on the rough version of the map. You should have asked me about it. I could have warned you there was no evidence it ever existed."

So it wasn't even a confirmed sighting. He had pinned everything on a maybe. But Kit wasn't sure it would have made much difference, even if he had known that before. A maybe could be enough.

Beth narrowed her eyes the way she always did when trying to remember something. "'At length did cross an Albatross, Through the fog it came.'"

"What's that?"

"A poem I read at school, many years ago, perhaps even before you were born. There's a dreadful thought. By... Coleridge, I think. I used to be able to recite quite a bit of it, but since then my brain has had to make space for more pressing information."

Kit wondered what he might forget when he grew older: whether the stories of Camelot's knights would melt away, or the memories of this summer at Askfeld. He shuddered at the idea of it all becoming obscured. Then again, he might prefer not to be for ever dwelling on his mistakes.

"Juliet's right. I've made everything worse."

Beth shook her head. "Don't you believe that for a second! You wouldn't let me give up on the map. Without you, I might never have been able to share a lifetime of memories with my child. That's a gift beyond value." Her voice was so full of emotion that he found his own eyes stinging. He ran around to the other side of the desk and hugged her tightly. She made a noise of surprise.

It had been a summer of impossible things, whatever Juliet might say. He had learned to map memories like cities, and found allies in strangers. Whatever happened, he was glad to have made a friend in Beth.

CHAPTER SEVENTEEN

THE THING WITH FEATHERS

Things I must never, ever forget, no matter how old I am:

1. How to skim stones, fly kites, and have sword fights (with pretend swords, because Mum worries that I'll take somebody's eye out one day).

2. My friends: Toby, Beth, and Bert. Maybe even Maddie if she forgives me for the letters.

3. How to be helpful and brave for other people – never giving up on a quest or refusing to save someone in need.

"Today's the day, then," Kit's mother said with a nervous smile across the table at breakfast. "What time will you be able to see your results?"

"School will email this morning. They said it'll be from eight o'clock," Juliet replied, not looking up from the avocado she was pushing around her plate.

"Perfect! I have a video conference call at eight-thirty, so I can stay with you when you get your grades. Darling, don't look so anxious. I'm sure you will be fine. Sean has said we can use the internet at the guest house for my call, since they *still* haven't connected us here, so we'll drive over after breakfast. Kit, make sure you bring a book to read or something, otherwise it might be a dull morning for you. Juliet, I'll make you a camomile tea before we go – I find that always calms me down."

The more their mother talked, the paler and quieter Juliet became. It was as if there was only enough brightness and noise for one person in the kitchen that morning, and Catherine was using it all up. Kit went up to his room to pick out some books.

Nobody spoke on the journey over to Askfeld, so Kit gazed out of the car window up to the brooding August sky. Dark clouds were gathering all along the coast, lining themselves up in readiness. He listened to the whir of tarmac passing under the tyres, and then the bumps of the stones and puddles in the rough track, and finally the crunch of gravel as the car stopped.

Beth was sitting at the reception desk; her stick was leaning against the wall behind her. She was talking on the guest house landline and did not see them come in.

"So the payment has come through? Good. And you'll send me an official receipt of that? Even better. Now that's all cleared up, I should warn you that we will be using our newly solvent status to hire security staff, and if you ever send someone round to threaten my husband again, they will be marched off our land and kicked squarely into the sea. Are we clear?"

They had never heard her sound like this before. Catherine, who had approached the desk on arrival, took a step back now and murmured, "Oh dear."

"It's all right, Mum. It's good news."

She had done it. Beth had saved Askfeld. In spite of all the bad days of fog in her head, she had wrestled the finances back into shape. Only she had believed Sean and his father could be reconciled, or that she and Sean might find help from someone so hostile. And she had been right – she must have been, since now the debts were paid.

The phone now replaced on the desk, she sighed, leaned back in her chair, and greeted the guests before her.

"You got rid of that man! Are you really getting guards at Askfeld?"

"No, that wasn't true," Beth admitted with a wink, "but it did feel good to say it. However, I'm going to need a lie down to recover from that. As soon as Sean finishes getting the rooms ready. We've had a couple of last-minute bookings." The strain of the phone call was evident in her face. She looked tired and pale, but the triumph of seeing off the debt collectors seemed to have lifted a weight off her shoulders.

It surprised him that Beth had lied. He imagined her incapable of such misdemeanours. Then again, this summer had seen him keep all manner of truths hidden from his family. The guilt of having lied to his mother about writing a letter to Toby had prompted him to actually write one, and thus redeem the fabrication. It was only a couple of sentences, but it felt good to have reassured his friend he was not forgotten.

"And is the map safe?"

"Safe?"

"No one's taken it away, have they?" If the stranger with the false smile had already confiscated it before the debt was paid, he feared it might be lost for ever.

"Oh, of course. Don't worry. It's in its usual spot, and looking more map-like these days."

"But Beth –" Kit's mother ignored this discussion to protest – "you've had to use a walking stick to get from your sitting room to here. Surely that means you aren't well enough to be up and about!"

"To be honest, it's getting hard to tell what's chronic illness and what's just being very, very pregnant. I'm slow on my feet and my joints ache, but I can't be sure why. Still, I can sit here for a few more minutes until Sean takes over and I can rest. Do go through. This week's Wi-Fi password is on the chalkboard in the guests' sitting room. If you'd like anything to eat or drink, I can call through to the kitchen from here and get Nick to bring you something."

"In that case, could we have a strong coffee, a green tea, and an orange juice? You do seem to have grown since last time I saw you. It can't be long to go now."

"I'm thirty-eight weeks yesterday, though they say first babies are usually late." Beth picked up the phone. "I'll call your drinks order through then."

They went into the guests' sitting room, and found Bert there, frowning over a newspaper crossword. Kit waved cheerily to him but Catherine gave only a silent nod of acknowledgment. Kit sighed and realized he probably was not forgiven yet for wandering off in search of the albatross.

She led them to some chairs on the opposite side of the room from Bert, and ushered Juliet into the most comfortable-looking one.

"There you go, love. Do you want to see if there's any news yet? It's two minutes to eight."

Juliet had already opened her inbox on her phone, and seemed not to hear Catherine at first.

"Nothing," she said. She refreshed the page. Kit looked over to Bert, who was still engrossed in his puzzle, and decided his mother would not like it if he went over to talk to him.

"It's still early, of course. Have you got anything else you can read while you're waiting?"

"She can borrow one of my books." Kit pushed them forward on the table for Juliet to see. When she did not respond, he figured he might as well decide which one he was going to choose this morning. He had been reading more stories of Greek heroes, and had got to Theseus and the Minotaur, but today he did not feel like picking that one back up. Maybe Beth was right and all the books he'd read were making him see villains and princesses in towers everywhere. There was one book in the set he'd brought that wasn't a hero's adventure. It was a paperback about a boy and his friends solving a mystery. Kit decided to try that one instead.

It was now ten minutes past eight.

"Perhaps they send the emails out in alphabetical order," Catherine suggested. "In which case, there's a few letters for them to get through before Fisher."

Juliet's phone buzzed and her eyes snapped back to it. "It's from Amy. She got six eights and four nines."

"Yes, well, that girl never did really apply herself," Catherine muttered.

"Amy's surname is after mine in the alphabet. Why haven't I got my results yet?"

"I don't know, love. I'm sure it will be soon. Wait a bit longer, but if they don't come through, then why don't you just call the school office? They'll have the results there: they can read them to you over the phone."

Juliet tried refreshing the website one more time and then took out her phone. "What's the school's number, Mum?"

Kit tried to ignore them and the growing tone of urgency in their voices and movements. It was starting to make him anxious, but there was nothing he could do to help. He focused on the book he was reading, trying to picture the locations as if they were before his eyes. If he tried really hard, he might be able to block out the sounds around him.

"I'm going to have to go now – it's nearly half past and I've got to be on this call. They do need me. Keep trying to get through and let me know when you find out, OK? Kit, wait here with your sister."

She withdrew to the dining room next door, leaving Juliet poring over her phone as though her life depended on it, and Kit trying very hard to be absorbed in his book. Once his mother had closed the door behind her, though, Kit put his book down and went over to Bert. He sat in the chair opposite him, and the birdwatcher looked over the top of his newspaper.

"Hello there, Kit. What's got your family in such a frenzy today?"

"It's results day for Juliet. She's finding out what grades she got in her GCSEs."

"Ah yes, I do recall what that's like. Although we called them O Levels in my day, and there wasn't nearly the pressure there is on you young people now. You know, some of my students make themselves ill trying to do everything at university. Which of course makes it impossible for them to work as well as they could. Terrible cycle to get into. And I'm quite sure it starts in the schools. Yes, well, your sister has my sympathy. Still, I remember you saying she was clever. I dare say she'll have done fine."

Kit was tired of everyone talking about Juliet and feeling sorry for her, when she was the best at just about everything. He changed the subject.

"Aren't you going out birdwatching today?"

"No, not with those clouds looming. Forecast says there's a storm on the way, and I don't want to be outside when it gets here. I don't suppose you like crosswords?"

Kit said that he did, and Bert offered him the paper. A few were already filled in, so Kit read aloud the first one that had yet to be solved. "'Direction of feathers in hospital room', eight letters. It's got feathers in it, so you should be able to get this one, Bert."

"Just because it has feathers doesn't make it a bird."

Kit scrunched up his face and re-read the clue. It had to be a bird, and one that had something to do with medicine.

"Is there such a thing as a doctor bird?"

"Um, yes, as a matter of fact. It's another name for the swallow tail humming bird. A beautiful, iridescent little thing that you can only find in Jamaica. But that's more than eight letters, so I'm afraid it can't be the answer. Not a bad guess though."

"Oh. I don't know then." Kit put the paper down and stared at the ceiling for inspiration.

Bert chewed the top of his pen. "Downward."

"It's an Across clue."

"No, the answer. See, 'down' is what young birds have for their feathers, and a 'ward' is a room in a hospital. Together they make the word 'downward', which is a direction."

He wrote the answer into its boxes. His handwriting was messy, even when forming capital letters.

On the other side of the room, Juliet stood up suddenly.

"Hello, Miss Carter? It's Juliet Fisher. I'm trying to access my results, but I can't see them. I don't know if there's a problem with my email account. Can you help me?" Holding the phone to her ear, she hurried out of the sitting room and into the hallway to take the rest of the call in private.

"Well, sounds like the suspense will all be over soon enough. Listen out for the sound of cheering or tears."

Juliet was not the sort of person to cheer at her own success. Kit decided that silence was likely to indicate good news. And he wanted to think about something else for a while. He asked Bert if he knew about the albatross poem Beth had mentioned to him the other day.

"You mean the one about the ancient mariner? Yes, my younger son bought me a book about famous birds in literature once. A very long poem, as I recall, and not an entirely happy one."

"Why not?"

"Well, the mariner kills the albatross, and soon regrets it, as the crew of the ship think he has brought them bad luck by doing so. The mariner is made to wear the albatross around his neck as a constant reminder of his mistake and his guilt."

"But you told me albatrosses are huge."

"Quite. Birds have hollow bones, which makes them less heavy than a mammal of the equivalent size, but even so, a dead albatross would be a serious weight to carry around. I wonder if the poet knew that."

"How does the story end?"

"Hmm. Good question. I don't remember. I recall something

about the poem being symbolic though… Wasn't it an image of how a person is weighed down by guilt, reminded of their past mistakes all the time, but that God wants to take it away and give you a fresh start? Something along those lines. I don't know – it's a long time since I've read it – and as I've probably said before, words aren't really my thing."

Kit hoped it was a happy ending. He didn't much like the thought of the dead albatross, or the mournful mariner being taunted by his own actions over and over again. He'd always pictured God as a stern old man who would have wagged a finger and joined in berating the mariner. He hoped Bert and the poet were right instead; it was a kinder and more accepting image that left him less anxious. Out in the hallway, they heard the front door slam.

"Have you seen Maddie?" Kit asked. She was the only person at Askfeld Farm he knew who would close a door with so much force.

"Since the day with the letters, you mean? No, our paths haven't crossed in a while. I think Sean said she had gone into town yesterday, and I was out most of the previous day. I went onto the moors in search of black grouse. Got into a bit of a pickle with a particularly miry spot – should have paid better attention to where I was putting my feet. Still, nothing that a bit of dry cleaning can't mend."

"Did you see any?"

"Any what?"

"Grouse."

"Yes. Four, in fact. Not to mention some buntings and warblers."

Kit sighed. "I only wanted to help her – Maddie, I mean. I think I made things worse though."

If it was Maddie he had heard coming back in, at least she had not come into the guest lounge where Kit would have to face her again. That was something. Bert tried to fold his newspaper up but could not make the pages stay flat, so gave up and let it fall to the floor in a heap. "Well, I don't know about that. I'm sure you meant no harm by it."

He seemed uncomfortable. Kit considered that Beth would have responded quite differently, with kindness and confidence and something wise. Bert just wanted to be polite. He was beginning to see that not all adults were alike, especially in difficult situations.

Bert stood up. He tried to stretch, but stopped abruptly when his shoulders clicked. "Did you hear that? Never take your joints for granted!" He walked over to the wicker basket where Sean had left a selection of other newspapers and magazines for guests to read. As he did so, he passed the window overlooking the garden. "Good heavens, there's somebody out there!"

Kit did not see why it should be so surprising for someone to be outside, at a place where visitors were free to come and go as they chose. However, when he joined Bert by the window, he understood.

The rain Bert had predicted had already begun pelting down. It was not the sort of weather anyone would willingly go out in. Yet there, on the grass, lay a body. It was too far away to recognize, but it was a round figure, with hair that might have been naturally dark or simply rendered that colour by the rain. The person was lying on their side, one arm stretched out past their head. On the grass beside them lay something long and thin. What was it? Kit strained to see. It could be a toy sword, like the ones he had seen at Scarborough Castle. No, that was not it. It was a walking stick.

"Beth!" he shouted, and ran to the front door. The reception area was deserted, the white-painted hall cold and quiet. Kit hurtled out into the rain, which bore down on him as if it wanted to drive him back indoors. But he was not deterred. He sprinted across the grass to where Beth lay. Her clothes were soaked through, but her eyes were open.

He knelt down next to her. "Are you OK?"

She did not reply straight away.

"Please be OK."

"I'm fine," she then managed, slurring her words as though she was struggling to force them out of her mouth. "Just need some help getting back up. But don't worry about me."

Bert caught up with them now, having covered the ground at a slower pace. "What happened?" he asked. "Are you hurt?"

"I tried to go after her," Beth said, turning from her side onto her back. "She was in such a terrible state. But I didn't have the strength to keep up, and then I didn't even have the energy to stand any more."

Kit and Bert exchanged a look. "I guess Maddie's still angry with me then," Kit said. The slamming door he had heard must have been the sound of someone leaving, not entering, the building.

"Never mind that now," said Bert. "Can you sit up, Beth? We need to get you back inside if you can make it. It's not good to be out in this weather – not in your condition."

By now Kit's clothes were drenched too. He dreaded going back inside and facing the despairing comments of his mother or Juliet. Both would demand to know why he couldn't have spared the two seconds it would have taken to pick up his coat on the way out.

"No… that's not right…" Beth was mumbling something as they helped her raise herself up. "I have to…"

"Don't worry about Maddie; she can take care of herself. She may be older than you, but she's healthy and fit. She can make her own way back through this."

Beth was now sitting upright, propped up on her arms with Bert supporting her back.

"I think we might need a bit of extra help to get you back indoors. Kit, can you go and fetch Sean or Nick? Tell them not to worry, but we need someone stronger than an old man or a boy to help us."

Kit would have preferred to stay with Beth but knew he could bring help faster than Bert could, so he ran back inside. In the hallway, he paused. He knew Sean was upstairs getting the rooms ready for the new guests, and that Nick would be in the kitchen. It would be quicker to fetch Nick, as he was nearer. This was logical enough to gloss over the fact that Kit knew Sean would want to be told first, or that Kit was still nervous of Sean, even though Beth had set him straight on his theory about the villainous plot.

He burst into the kitchen. Nick jumped, and dropped the saucepan he was taking down from a high shelf.

"What have you been told, kid, about coming in here?"

"It's an emergency!" Kit cried. "Beth's not well and she's outside and can't walk and you need to come now and help her!"

Nick left the saucepan on the floor and followed him out to where Beth was slumped on the ground. The rain had become lighter now and more mist-like as the clouds sank lower over the cliffs. The water droplets did not attack Kit any longer; they simply hung in the air and latched on to him as he made a path through them.

"Anything broken?" Nick asked.

Beth shook her head.

"The baby OK?"

She nodded.

"Then let's get you inside first."

He put her arm over his shoulders and motioned for Bert to do the same on the other side. They helped Beth rise slowly to her feet.

"Can you walk?"

Beth moved her head, but it was not clear whether she was giving a positive or negative answer to his question. Very slowly, Nick and Bert began to walk towards the house, with Beth taking unsteady steps between them. Kit picked up her discarded walking stick and carried it back with them.

"How long was she out here for?" Nick asked the others.

"I'm not entirely sure, to tell you the truth," said Bert. "She was sitting at reception first thing this morning. And then when I went to the window we saw her. But there was a good hour in between where she might have been inside or out here."

Nick looked serious. "I'll go and get Sean as soon as we're back inside. He'll know what to do."

They brought Beth into the guests' lounge, as it was the first room with proper chairs in it. Nick took one of the throws from the back of the sofa and draped it over her as she sat, dazed and shivering, in the armchair by the fire. He went back to the hallway and shouted Sean's name up the stairs. Kit heard the responding thud of feet on the wooden steps.

"What happened?" he asked the others as he saw Beth and ran across the hall to her.

"She went out after Maddie in the rain. She was lying on the ground when I found her," said Kit.

"Did you fall?"

"No," Beth answered, her voice little more than a whisper. "I just ran out of strength and had to stop."

Sean shook his head. "You were supposed to be resting today," he reprimanded her. "I wouldn't even have agreed to you being on reception if you hadn't insisted."

She pulled a face, and looked as if she wanted to reply, but the effort of the words she had already spoken had left her without any further resources.

"Is she going to be OK?" Kit asked. Nobody answered. Sean sent Nick to fill up a couple of hot-water bottles and bring another blanket.

"Whisky's normally the thing to warm you up inside," Bert chipped in. "My father always used to have a hot toddy if he'd been caught in the rain while fishing."

Sean did not look up at him as he replied, "Not at thirty-eight weeks pregnant, it isn't."

"Ah yes, of course. Quite right."

"I'm going to call the doctor and see if he can come out here. I want to be sure there's nothing more seriously wrong, either with Beth or the baby."

As Sean telephoned the GP's surgery, Bert withdrew to one of the other chairs and said nothing more. Kit was watching Beth intently, and it seemed that she had recovered a little energy now, for she looked directly at him.

"Kit," she said, her words still strained, as if forming each syllable cost her dearly. "Look."

"Look at what?" Kit asked.

"Look. Out."

Was it a warning? Had Beth seen something else from the cliff-top garden? He wanted to ask her more, but at that moment two people entered the room and changed the atmosphere entirely.

The first was Kit's mother, who had finished her conference call.

"Goodness, I thought I could hear something going on," she said. "Whatever has happened?"

"Hopefully just a bad reaction to tiredness and rain," Bert supplied, "but Sean is calling a doctor, just to be safe."

The next person to come into the room was Maddie. She looked a little dishevelled and bleary-eyed.

"Ah, good, you're back safely then," said Bert. "You caused a bit of a stir this time, Maddie. However did you manage to escape getting drenched in all that rain?"

Maddie looked at him oddly. "By not going outside. I overslept this morning and thought I'd come down to see if there was any chance of a late breakfast."

Bert frowned. "But you were seen leaving Askfeld. At least, I'm pretty sure that's what Beth said. Didn't you say you'd seen Maddie going out into the storm?"

Beth winced as she tried to turn her head towards him. Nick returned with two hot-water bottles and a thick woollen blanket.

"Here we are. These are to warm you up if you need them. I'll ask Sean where the painkillers are."

Kit frowned as he tried to remember what exactly Beth had said. He couldn't believe she would be wrong about something like this. Then his mother spoke in a clipped, urgent tone that froze him to the spot.

"Where's Juliet?"

CHAPTER EIGHTEEN

NINE FATHOM DEEP

ASKFELD'S CHALKBOARD FORECAST

High tide: 12:36 p.m.

Low tide: 6:44 p.m.

Weather: early morning mists, followed by heavy rain

The question hung horribly in the air of the now silent room. Kit looked around. Her bag and coat were still on the chair where she had sat earlier trying to access the exam results.

"She went to take a phone call," said Bert.

"When?"

"I'm not sure. Sometime in the last hour."

Just before we heard the door slam, Kit thought. His mother turned to Beth.

"Was it my daughter you saw going out?"

Beth nodded. Catherine rounded on Kit next.

"And you just let her go out? After I told you to stay with her!" Her eyes were wide and her face was completely white. Kit could not remember ever seeing her look so angry, even after he had gone out searching for the albatross.

"You told me to stay here, and I did. She was the one who went out," he protested.

"I thought you'd keep an eye on your sister. Why do you think I haven't left her on her own all summer?"

Nick and Bert both looked uncomfortable, and kept throwing sympathetic glances towards Kit, which made him all the more convinced that his mother was not being fair. He had assumed that, as the youngest, he was the one she was most worried about getting into trouble, and that Juliet was being trusted to be in charge and make her own decisions. How was he supposed to have guessed it was the other way around?

"Now, Mrs Fisher, don't you fret," Bert said soothingly. "I'm sure Juliet's not gone far. There's nothing to worry about." He gave a smile that was almost convincing, but then it wobbled just enough to betray his doubts. Looking around the room, Kit could see that no one was about to be persuaded of an idea the birdwatcher himself barely believed.

"Mr Sindlesham" – Kit's mother drew herself to her full height as she snapped out her words – "my daughter suffers from high-functioning depression and anxiety. Why on earth would I take her out of one of the best schools in the country and bring my family to this bleak little corner of nowhere if there wasn't a great deal to worry about?"

High-functioning depression and anxiety. Such heavy words, Kit thought. Such long, clunky, prosaic words for whatever it was that had changed his sister. He remembered how Beth had once told him that her condition had a long name that was hard to pronounce too. Maybe they should employ poets to name conditions with words that conveyed a greater sense of meaning.

Sean came back into the room. "The doctor's on his way."

He looked around at the different faces in various stages of shock.

"It wasn't Maddie who Beth saw going out; it was Juliet," Kit said, when none of the adults spoke. His words seemed to wake everyone from their trance. His mother grabbed her coat and started pulling the sleeves over her arms.

"We'll help you look for her," Bert said, standing up. Kit's mother gave him an impassive stare that suggested he was not her first choice for a helper, but she would not stop him. Maddie and Nick also offered to help.

"And me too," said Kit.

"Absolutely not," his mother answered. "Wait here."

"I'm sorry I can't come too," said Sean, "but I need to stay with Beth."

Kit's mother assured him that she understood his need to take care of his wife, and she led the party of four out into the grey. Kit stood at the window and watched them split into two pairs. His mother and Nick headed inland to the fields and farm buildings, while Bert and Maddie went north along the cliff path. The rain had started again as the clouds rose higher, driven in from the North Sea.

Sean went to rummage around in a cupboard by the stairs and hauled out a fold-up wheelchair.

"Didn't think we'd need this already," he said, as he unfolded the chair next to where Beth sat. "Kit, come and help me. Can you hold the chair steady?"

Kit ran over and grabbed hold of the handles and pushed down on them, while Sean lifted Beth carefully into the wheelchair.

"I'm going to find her some dry clothes," he explained, as he pushed the chair out of the room and down the corridor to the staff end of the guest house. "Do as your mum said and wait here, OK?"

Kit stayed in the lounge, his nose pressed against the glass as he watched for any sign of the searchers returning. The guest house was suddenly very quiet after the flurry of activity and noise moments ago.

Where would Juliet go? What had Beth been telling him to watch out for, while Sean was phoning the GP? He watched the waves rolling against one another over the darkening sea. Askfeld felt starkly exposed to the elements – the price it paid for its view of the sea.

It clicked into place in his head. Of course! It wasn't "look out" but "the lookout". Beth had not been warning him of anything, but telling him a place from her map. The very first place Kit had found. It must be the direction she had seen Juliet heading in.

He jumped away from the window. His mother had told him to stay here, but then she had gone off the wrong way. There were no adults available. It was up to him. He pulled on his coat and went outside, lowering his head against the strong winds bearing down on the coast.

It was four hundred and twenty-three steps along the cliff path. He knew, because he had counted them. He paced them out again now, since the pelting rain made it hard to recognize any landmarks from last time. The fields were shadowed and muddy, the gorse waving wildly in the wind.

At four hundred and twenty-three he stopped to search for the lookout spot. It occurred to him that Beth could not have been certain Juliet was going here, since she would not have been able to see this far down the path from where they found her in the garden. But she must have seen Juliet take the Cleveland Way southward, so if he did not find her at the lookout point, he would just keep walking south until he caught up with her.

He must have counted incorrectly or measured his stride differently this time though, because he was not at the lookout point. He ran back a short way and then ahead, until eventually he found it. He crouched down and crawled through the gap, though this time it was harder, with the trees' lowest branches whipping about him.

The lookout point was empty. Before it, the sea was turning wild as the storm grew. *Whatever had upset Juliet*, Kit thought, *it was the sort of day where the weather could only make you feel worse*. He wished it had been sunny this morning, and that a bright summer's day might have cheered her up. But then he remembered how mesmerized she had been by the stormy waters that day when they searched for fossils. She had loved the brooding clouds and crashing dark waves.

He sighed, and was about to turn away when he noticed something on the edge of the cliff. There was a patch of ground that had given way recently. The mud around it was churned up, and when he looked more closely he could see the deep furrow of a stretched-out footprint there, as if someone had slipped forward and lost their footing. Gingerly he moved towards the edge of the cliff and peered over.

The cliff face descended all the way to the shore below, but it dropped in sections. These ledges did not join up well enough to form a path along the coast, though perhaps an intrepid mountain goat could have navigated them. On the highest of these ledges, just a few metres below where Kit stood, a small figure sat huddled against the rock face. It was Juliet.

"Jules!" Kit shouted into the wind, so loudly he felt as if the sound was grating all along the back of his throat. It worked, though. She looked up.

"Kit!" she shouted back. "I'm stuck!"

"What happened?"

"I slipped. Don't come too close to the edge; the ground's not secure!"

Kit did not want to fall, but neither did he want to back away so that he couldn't see his sister any longer. He lay down on his front so that his legs and torso were on solid earth but his head craned over the edge of the cliff. Juliet's hair was plastered to the sides of her face; her clothes were dark and waterlogged. She was pressed against the cliff face with her knees drawn up under her chin.

"I'll reach down," Kit shouted. "Grab my hand and I'll pull you up!"

He wriggled so that his shoulder was over the edge of the cliff and extended an arm towards her. Juliet looked up at him and shook her head.

"I can't! If I move, I'll fall. I only just managed to land on this ledge and not go any further down. And I hurt my leg when I slipped – I don't think I can put any weight on it."

Kit hesitated, and then withdrew his hand. He needed to think of a different plan to save his sister. At the same time, confusion gripped him at everything the Fisher family had kept hidden from its youngest member, and this tipped into indignation that they had ended up in this place at all.

"How did you even fall down there anyway?" he demanded. "What were you doing here?"

He sounded like his mother, but he was cross with Juliet for springing this sudden change in behaviour on him. The roar of the wind was dropping enough to be able to ask questions without hurting his voice, but the rain and the waves continued to rage.

"You told me about this place, remember? The first time we went out for a walk. You said it was a place you could forget… everything. That you could feel free for once."

It was true: he was the one who had raved about the lookout point to Juliet. But he hadn't told her how he had thought that falling from the cliffs up here might feel like flying.

"I was trying to see how far I could lean into the wind. I wanted that feeling you get, you know, when you tip forward and it holds you up. But I got too close to the edge, and it gave way. I thought I was going to fall all the way down, right into the sea!"

Kit looked at the ledge. It wasn't especially wide, and he could see why Juliet was still scared of how precarious her perch was. Still, there looked to be space for someone else down there.

"Hold on. I'll come down."

"No, Kit! You could fall and break your neck on those rocks down there."

"But it's weird, talking to you from up here."

He crawled to the edge and lowered himself cautiously down. The rock scraped against his elbows, but he barely felt it. Below him, the sheer rocky cliff face dropped all the way down to the sea.

His stomach jolted as he took in the distance between his feet and the water.

Don't look down, or you'll be stuck here too.

He sat down on the ledge and shuffled along until he was next to her. The ledge itself was not far from the top of the cliff. If Juliet wasn't hurt, or paralysed by fear, it would be easy enough to help her back up to the cliff top.

"See, it's not so bad," he said. But now that he was nearer, he could see that she probably wasn't exaggerating. There was a large purple bruise spreading over her leg. She looked so utterly miserable that he put an arm around her shoulders in the safest equivalent of a hug he could manage right now. Juliet burst into tears.

"I'm so sorry, Kit. It's all my fault."

"Don't be silly; it's not like you fell on purpose," Kit reassured her.

"Not just this. I mean all of it. You having to leave your school and friends behind, moving up here, Dad being gone – it's all because of me."

"That can't be right."

Juliet nodded, so that her bird-shaped necklace jumped up and glinted at him.

Like the albatross round the mariner's neck, he realized.

"It is though."

Kit thought about the shrill tone his mother had used; how she had let slip that she had hoped Kit would keep an eye on Juliet this summer and not leave her alone. He was starting to suspect there was an awful lot more that he had missed.

"What's high-fun… high-factoring…" he began, trying to remember what their mother had said to Bert.

"High-functioning depression and anxiety?" Juliet gave a dark laugh through her tears. "Just some long words a counsellor told Mum she could use after a couple of sessions of talking to me. Mum likes them, because it means there's a labelled box to put me in."

"But what do they mean?"

"I don't know, really. It's a clever way of saying I'm drowning in the pressure to be perfect all the time. That I can remember every single mistake I've ever made and they're all dancing around my head when I try to sleep at night. That you think I've turned boring, but I'm spending every moment trying to hide how terrified I am of each new situation and problem I'm supposed to handle maturely and gracefully."

Could this be the same Juliet who spoke to adults as though she was one of them; who was top of every class and surrounded by friends any time she left the house? It had all looked so effortless.

"But I don't think you're boring. It was fun when we flew the kite, and when we learned how to skim stones that time by the lake."

She smiled and passed a hand across her face to sweep away strands of hair. "I liked those times too. I felt better then, like I could breathe again for a bit. But it's no good. I've messed up so badly."

"What do you mean?"

"I thought I could have it all. Most people in my class either wanted to be popular or clever, not both. I wanted to prove everyone wrong – that I was better than that. But you saw through them, didn't you? You never liked Amy or Seb or any of my friends. I didn't see it until the end of term party, when they made me look like such an idiot. And I thought, 'It's OK. I'll meet new people at St Jude's and at least I didn't skip too many revision evenings to go out with them, so I'm sure to get the grades I need.'"

"And did you?" Kit asked, but he already knew the answer.

Juliet shook her head. "I was below my predicted marks in all the subjects I want to take next year."

A part of Kit wanted to tell her they were just grades, and it did not matter all that much, but he knew it might as well be the end of the world for Juliet. She had lost her friends and her position at the top of every class. Those were the things she was known for. And what happened at the end of term party? Hanging over the edge of a cliff, it didn't feel like the right time to ask. He still could not see how any of it made their new home or their father's absence her fault, but he could see that asking her about these things was only going to upset her further. If she continued in this state, she might well end up falling off the ledge. He needed to find a way to get her safely up onto the cliff top again. He wondered if he might be strong enough to carry her. With her rain-soaked clothes clinging to her limbs, he could see how thin she had become in the last few months.

"What if I lift you up to the top?" he suggested. The idea came so instinctively to him; it was what any of the heroes in his books would do in a single-handed rescue.

"Don't be ridiculous. You're eleven. You can't carry me. We'd both end up falling off the cliff."

With a wrench, Kit realized she was right. He was not strong enough. He could not save Juliet alone, so he would have to find help. It needed someone older than him, and with a good head for heights.

"OK, I'm going back to get help. Wait here and don't move. I won't be long."

"Believe me, I'm not going anywhere."

Kit shuffled his way along the ledge, then tentatively stood up and hoisted himself back to the top, scrabbling his way over the lip of the cliff. He rolled away from the edge, making sure not to look down until he was safely on solid ground. Then he crawled back under the trees and out onto the path.

He ran all the way back to the house. Beth had been right all along. She had told him there might be someone close by who needed his help, and Kit had completely missed that it was Juliet. Between Beth's illness, Bert's search for the albatross, and Maddie's tragic story, it had not occurred to him to look more closely at how strangely Juliet had been acting. But now that he thought about it, it had been right in front of him all along. He could not remember the last time he had seen her eat a full meal without pushing it around her plate as if she could not face the idea of food. He could not think of a time all summer when she had laughed, unless it was tinged with sarcasm. Now she was alone on that ledge, and it left him feeling sick. What if she slipped again, or the rock gave way beneath her?

Out of his fear rose a fierce determination. He gritted his teeth as he ran against the pelting rain. *I might have lost my dad this summer, but I won't lose my sister too.* He ran faster.

As Kit arrived back at the guest house, so too did Bert and Maddie. Both had pulled their hoods up to protect themselves from the downpour.

"Weren't you supposed to be staying inside?" Maddie asked.

"No success looking for your sister, I'm afraid," Bert added.

"I've found her!" shouted Kit, running past them into the hallway.

"Well, where is she then?" Maddie called after him, but Kit did not stop. He needed to find Sean. A week ago, he would have been the last person Kit trusted to save his sister, but today he had no choice. The birdwatcher and the pilgrim followed him into the building and down the corridor to the room where he had seen the owners of Askfeld last headed. He knocked on the door.

Sean opened it. "Kit. You've been outside." He looked past him to the others. "Any sign of her?"

"Yes!" said Kit. "I need your help though. She's trapped on the cliff and can't climb back up."

"Oh, the poor girl!" Maddie clapped a hand to her mouth. "We have to go and rescue her."

"Sean does rock climbing," Kit explained. "Beth told me. He can help."

Sean looked torn.

"He can't very well leave Beth alone though, can he?" Bert seemed to say what he was thinking.

"The doctor's on his way," Sean said, "and Beth's in bed now.

She was complaining of bad muscle pains. I can't leave her. But we can't leave your sister either."

"Let me stay with Beth then," said Maddie, stepping forward. Sean's face said that she was not his first choice to watch over his wife. "I know. We haven't been especially friendly since I got here, but I've spent my whole life caring for people. I can keep an eye on Beth until you get back or the doctor arrives. I'm sure it won't be long."

Sean inhaled and nodded, stepping aside to let Maddie into the room. "How far down is your sister stuck?"

"Not far – I can climb it. But she's hurt her leg, so she can't move."

"Right." Sean marched to a store cupboard and opened it. He pulled up a coil of red and black rope and some metal clips. "Can you show me where she is?"

"Yes, it isn't far. It's Beth's old lookout point."

"Bert, you'd better stay here. If Nick and Mrs Fisher return, tell them what's happened and where we've gone."

"Right you are," Bert said in a cheery tone that sounded wobbly, as if he was trying to reassure himself as much as everyone else in the room. He saw them to the door, and then waited in the porchway, watching out for any sign of Catherine coming back. Kit and Sean hurried to the path, Kit leading the way.

"It's here," said Kit, when they came to the spot where the lookout point lay just beyond the trees. "But I usually crawl through the gap under there. I hadn't thought about how you'd get through."

Sean examined the obstacle and then pulled aside some of the branches. He stepped into the gap, leaning his weight against the gorse to hold it back. It was a struggle to push a way through, but he managed to fight his way to the other side. Kit followed, taking his usual path.

"Jules!" he shouted. "I've brought help!"

He and Sean looked down to see Juliet still huddled on the

ledge, white-faced with fear. Sean set about examining the ground and the drop.

"It's not far," he said to Kit, and then shouted down to Juliet, "Can you stand up? We should be able to reach you and pull you back up if you could."

Juliet shook her head frantically but said nothing.

"She can't move; she's hurt her leg," Kit explained.

"That's not the main thing keeping her there. She's terrified. I've seen it before. Sometimes climbers suddenly panic and become paralysed. I can climb down to her, but I need you to help her calm down. Talk to your sister, Kit."

"What about?"

"Anything. What will distract her?"

Kit struggled to think. In recent years, they had found less and less in common to talk about. Juliet always seemed to be focused on her friends or school, neither of which was a good topic to bring up right now. What would make her feel calmer or happier? He was struck by how little he knew his sister.

"Jules," he shouted, "I think when Dad gets here, we should take him to that lake we found and see if he can skim stones as well as we can."

Juliet buried her head in her drawn-up knees. Kit remembered she blamed herself for their father's absence, though he did not see how that could be true. Sean had fixed a metal clip in the rock and was now testing that it was secure. He thought again. He thought of his books and his quest to finish the map, but these were his things and would comfort him, not Juliet. *What did she love?*

"What music did you listen to in the car this morning?"

She looked up at him, confused.

"Come on. Tell me the names of the songs."

Juliet paused, and then listed off words and phrases that Kit did not recognize. But the effort of remembering the songs seemed to steady her breathing so that it shook less.

"Cool. I need to learn more about music. You should teach me. Which of those is the best?"

This question required more thought. "'Fire at Night' is the best one. We used to sing it at the top of our lungs in the common room. But you'd like 'The Wanderer's Song', because it's an epic hero story."

Sean had readied the ropes now and was lowering himself over the ledge.

"You're doing well," he said to Kit. "Keep going."

"I like the sound of that. Who's it by?"

Juliet shouted back a name, but at that moment the wind picked up again and the sound was carried away along the coast like a gull swept off course.

"Sean's almost there now; just hold on! He's going to help you back up. It's going to be OK."

Kit watched Sean's feet connect with the ledge where Juliet crouched. He could not hear the words being said, but it was clear that Juliet was still afraid to move. Sean showed her the rope and the metal clips above them in the rock face, presumably explaining that it was safe to climb up with the help of these things.

Gradually, slowly, Juliet took hold of the rope and let Sean help her to stand up. Most of her weight seemed to be on one leg. The two of them ascended together, and Kit was waiting to grab Juliet's hand and pull her back over the edge.

They emerged back onto the path, Juliet leaning on Kit and limping. As they turned north towards the house, they saw Bert, Nick, and their mother running towards them.

"Oh my goodness, are you all right? What happened?"

Juliet burst into tears as her mother threw her arms round her.

"She fell," Kit explained. The adrenaline ebbed out of him like a retreating tide, and he suddenly became conscious of his grazed elbows and the pounding of his heart in a new wave of retrospective fear at all that had just taken place. He gripped on to the stone wall by the path, needing to feel supported by something solid and unshakeable.

"Mum, I messed up! My grades are so bad. And you only came here to try to fix the mess I'd made, and I know it's my fault Dad doesn't want to be here, and I'm sorry!"

Their mother gripped Juliet's shoulders. "That is not your fault. Don't ever think it is. Your father may not know how to adjust to this, but he wants to be here. We will work this out." Out here, in the rain, she no longer looked like professional, organized Catherine. She looked like an older version of Juliet. "If anyone's to blame for this, it's me. I'm so sorry we didn't see sooner how unhappy you were. I should have done more to help you."

Both of them were crying now. With wet hair plastered across their faces, and in mud-caked shoes, they walked together back to the house, Juliet limping as she leaned against her mother for support.

"You did the right thing, coming to fetch me," Sean said to Kit as they followed the others home. "You probably saved your sister from hypothermia or a horrible fall."

Did it count? He had not done much for Juliet compared to the weeks he had spent on Beth's map, or in pursuit of albatrosses and letters from the children Maddie had left behind. He looked up at Sean striding along with the climbing ropes over his shoulder. It was funny now to think how certain he had been that this man was the villain in his story, and that his wife was the one who needed saving.

Askfeld came into view. Maddie was in the doorway.

"Is Beth all right?" Sean demanded.

"Yes. The doctor's here and everyone is drinking hot camomile tea. But Sean –"

"What is it? Is something wrong?"

"No. She's not hurt by the fall. But those pains she was complaining of – the doctor says they're contractions. She's going into labour."

It was Sean's turn to freeze.

"Your bags are here for you to take to the hospital." Maddie pointed to the holdalls she had put in the porch next to the front door. "I've sorted everything – you just need to drive her there. And she's been handling it amazingly. I don't know if all those years of chronic pain have helped prepare her for this or not, but she's barely wavered from being calm about it."

Sean nodded. "Nick, you're in charge while we're gone. Make sure the Fishers have whatever they need. Ask the doctor to take a look at Juliet's leg before he leaves."

"Yes, boss," Nick grinned. "Don't worry about any of it. Go take Beth to the hospital. You're about to become a father."

He hugged Sean and pushed him in the direction of the door. Then Nick ushered everyone else into the guests' lounge to leave the Garsdales in peace. He announced that hot chocolate, compliments of Askfeld, was now needed, and went to make it.

Catherine sat at the window with Juliet's head resting on her shoulder. The two of them watched the storm pass by. Kit hung back.

"I'm so sorry," she said. Her voice shook. "I've been so busy, I never got round to saying any of the things that matter."

She extended an arm towards Kit and he joined them by the window. Juliet had stopped crying, but was sniffling as she recovered. Catherine continued, "Just because *I* work hard, it doesn't mean you can't rest, or play, or just be yourselves. I've always asked so much of you both. But I need you to know that I love you no matter what you do. Kit, you are allowed to be a child and run around without worrying about other people. And Juliet, you are such a clever, beautiful young woman. I'm sorry for the times it must have felt like I was pushing you to be better, instead of telling you how proud I am of you."

Tears streamed down Juliet's face again. Kit could not think of anything to say, so he put his arms round his mum and sister in a hug, and they sat together like that for some time. Nick returned with mugs of hot chocolate and set them down in front of the Fisher family. It wasn't the picture of family Kit had been holding on to all summer, but they felt more united right now than they had done in months.

CHAPTER NINETEEN

THE END OF THE PILGRIMAGE

MY TO-DO LIST BEFORE THE SCHOOL TERM STARTS:

1. Practise football in the garden so I'm good enough to join the school team.

2. Listen to music with Juliet. I'll let her pick the songs.

3. Make sure Beth's OK after having her baby.

4. Ask Mum if what happened on the cliffs is something to do with Dad not being here.

5. Find a new quest.

Kit and his mother drove round to Askfeld the next day to return the clothes Juliet had borrowed. A quietness hung in the corridors after all the noise and confusion of yesterday. It was like returning to an empty theatre when all the performers had gone home. Maddie was the only occupant of the guests' lounge, sitting with her feet up on a stool, examining an Ordnance Survey map.

"Nick's busy with the new guests who arrived this morning," she said. "How's your daughter today?"

"Better for some sleep and something to eat. We'll find a way through the rest."

Maddie nodded as if she understood what "finding a way" would entail for the Fisher family.

"Are Beth and Sean back yet?" Kit asked, listening out for the telltale wailing of a newborn baby.

"No. I did hear Nick say that Sean phoned and they were coming home tomorrow. But I may not be around when they do."

Kit looked again at the map she was studying. Even in this format, with a pattern of grid squares and tiny printed road names, the shape of the coastline was familiar to him. "Are you finishing your pilgrimage?"

"Reckon it's about time. I've put it off most of the summer, but I think tomorrow I'll make the walk to the abbey."

"To Whitby Abbey? You decided to stick with the original end point then?" She had seemed so fearful of the end of the journey that Kit had assumed she would find excuses to keep waiting or walking indefinitely.

Maddie gave a wry smile. "Can't keep walking for ever, can I? I've always known the pilgrimage would come to an end sooner or later and real life would resume. I've avoided it long enough, and Whitby's as good a place as any to put it all to rest."

"Can we come with you?"

"Kit, you can't just invite yourself along to other people's plans." His mother put a restraining hand on his shoulder. "I'm sorry, Maddie; he doesn't mean to be presumptuous."

"Of course he doesn't. I know that. And I'd be happy for you to come with me. There's no rule that a pilgrimage has to be undertaken alone. To tell the truth, Mrs Fisher, your children are in part what has inspired me to finish this walk."

Catherine looked surprised at this revelation. She gave Kit a questioning look. He just smiled back.

"I think Juliet would like it," he said. "We can walk slowly so that she can keep up, even on her hurt foot." This was enough to sway her, and she told Maddie they'd be delighted to join the walk. While they made arrangements together for a time to set out, Kit took the opportunity to sneak away.

Beth's sitting room felt strangely lifeless without her in it. Kit stepped carefully between the overcrowded bookshelves and the table where her watercolours were still balanced. He wanted to see the map. He had neglected to bring Beth anything for it in a while, but he still thought of it as his original quest, and he needed to see what stage it had reached.

Beth had transferred the sketches and notes to the main map, and it was fuller as a result. She was right: it wasn't an ordinary map with roads and buildings. He traced the thin line of the Cleveland Way along the coast and the set of footprints leading from Askfeld to the lookout point with the number *423* written to tell the walker how many paces to take. The teardrop-shaped lake was drawn in, but Kit had not seen before the two small figures sketched beside it. One had an arm raised as if in mid-throw, while the other watched a tiny dot bounce along the water's surface. *For skimming stones on still days,* the caption read. All over the map were little notes about which season was best for a visit, or places to shelter if a summer's walk turned stormy, or spots you could only reach during low tide. The sea was teeming with seals and dolphins. And in a broad border all around the edge, Beth had painted the shifting character of the sky: the cloud shapes that heralded a storm from the east, bright sweeps of watercolour for the late golden glow in the west, or in silver ink the glimmering constellation of Orion the hunter with his dog Sirius overhead. It was a map that changed according to the time of year or the weather or your mood.

Maybe his dad wouldn't come and see the map, but Kit was proud of the result anyway.

The following day, they arrived at Askfeld early. Maddie was at the doorway, her rucksack on her shoulders already, a walking pole in her hand. It was funny, Kit thought, that after all the delaying of her journey, she should be so eager and in a hurry to set out this morning.

They climbed out of the car as their mother enumerated the same inventory of supplies she had packed into the boot only twenty minutes earlier: "Sunscreen, waterproofs, sun hats, snack bars, water bottles, insect repellent…"

Kit left her to finish her list. Bert stepped out of the guest house wearing his outdoor clothes – a pair of binoculars and a heavy camera hanging round his neck and knocking against one another.

"Hello, Bert! Are you coming with us too?"

"Thought I might join you, if that's all right with everyone. I've made quite a good start on the article I'm writing, so I thought I'd earned a break and a bit of a walk in the sun."

Kit glanced back at his mother. She had only had two conversations with Bert all summer, and both had involved her shouting at him. Would they be able to get along today? She had not heard Bert's announcement, being busy talking to Juliet.

"Will you be all right today, love?"

"I hope so. What if I can't keep up with everyone else though? I don't want to be the slowest one." She tested her weight on her left foot. The doctor had reassured her that nothing was broken.

Maddie had overheard this. "We won't be hurrying. The point isn't to complete the walk quickly. The weather is good and there will be more than enough hours of light for us to take our time. Is everyone ready?"

They were, so they set out. Maddie led the way. The sea was to their right and the land to their left on the path that led northwards. Once the track was clear, Kit ran ahead of the group. He still loved this feeling of being the first on the road: an intrepid explorer discovering new lands. But then he paused and looked back. Maddie was still walking resolutely on, beating the ground with her walking pole. Behind her, Juliet and their mother walked arm in arm, matching each other's step. At the back of the group, Bert had stopped to take a photo. Kit ran back past the others to find out what he'd taken.

"Have you seen something exciting?" he asked. Bert lowered the camera and showed Kit the image on the screen.

"A couple of gannets, captured in high resolution. Can you hear them squawking at each other?"

He could. The sound was something between laughter and arguing. But Kit couldn't think what anyone could have to argue about on a day like this. The sun was out, Maddie was finally finishing her walk, Beth and Sean would be coming home with their baby. Juliet was surely going to be well again if the remainder of the summer was like this. He watched her walking ahead and wondered how he had failed to notice for all those weeks and months how thin and pale she had become. Her T-shirt hung loosely over her torso and her elbows jutted out, all angular bones. Yet today's sunlight gave her skin a healthier look, and he found it easy to believe she was getting better already. He had only to remember to be kind to her. Beth had seen it, of course, and tried to steer him in the right direction: *Sometimes you can be a hero by spotting those closer to home who just need some kindness and encouragement to help them out from under a cloud.*

They walked north along the cliffs and the coast. Kit thought he had waited a reasonable length of time before asking his mother if he could have one of the chocolate bars they had brought, but her reaction suggested he had not been patient enough. He broke off squares for Maddie and Bert, since they did not appear to have brought their own supplies of sweets.

"Are you feeling happier now, Maddie? If you're finishing your pilgrimage, I mean."

He had meant it as a simple enough question, but she took as long to answer as if he had asked her the meaning of life. While she considered it, she turned her face upward to soak it in sunlight, perhaps looking to the sky for an answer. Kit knew not to rush her; he counted his remaining squares of chocolate in silence.

"I am feeling better, thank you, Kit. I've had lots of time to think about it – about what happened. I've decided that however much it hurt, however much it felt like the wrong thing for the children too, Elsie probably never meant to do anything other than what she believed was best.

"You know, when I started the pilgrimage, I think a part of me still hoped someone would turn up to fix everything. Maybe not Elsie, but I liked the thought that the people who employed her might say they were sorry for putting me through so much pain. Does that sound silly?" Kit shook his head as Maddie took a deep breath. She was calm. "I've accepted it's not going to happen. And agonizing about it has been exhausting. So I think it's time I forgave her – for my own sake more than anything – moved on, and thought about something else."

Kit offered Maddie the last of his chocolate, which she broke in half for them to share, so that for a while as they walked side by side the only sound was of chewing. Then the travellers rearranged themselves, so that Kit and Juliet walked with Bert, while Catherine spoke to Maddie. Bert did what Kit had come to realize was the only thing he could do in this situation, and acted as though the last couple of days had not happened as he cheerily pointed out cornflowers, harebells and a patch of musk mallow to Juliet, who stopped to admire the fragrant purple flowers at her feet.

Up ahead, Catherine and Maddie were talking in low voices and Kit soon realized why.

"There was a build-up, yes, of little things over the year. I should have spotted the signs sooner, but it wasn't until she went out with her friends after the exams finished."

They were talking about Juliet. After months of secrecy, Kit was glad to hear his mum finally discussing what had happened, even if he would have preferred her to be telling him instead. He checked that Juliet was distracted enough not to notice she was the topic of conversation, but she was preoccupied quizzing Bert about the entry requirements for an undergraduate degree in biology.

"One of the group must have had a fake ID. I'll bet it was that Sebastian – he walks around with such a smirk on his face, like he's too clever to follow rules. Anyway, they all had a lot to drink, but Juliet wasn't used to it. We don't let the children have alcohol, apart from the occasional sip of champagne at special occasions."

"Do you think it was peer pressure that made her join in?" Maddie asked.

"Probably, but it was still her own choice. That much I could hold Juliet responsible for, but it's what happened afterwards, when she was being sick and unsure where she was. Her so-called friends found it *funny*, would you believe? And they took photos of her in that state."

"Ah. And I take it these photos made their way quickly online?"

Catherine nodded, and her face was grim. "We didn't know straight away. It was another student's mother who told us. Some of the comments… I didn't know teenagers could be so cruel! And we've done everything we can to get them all taken down, so future employers or universities won't see them. But truthfully I think they've done enough damage already. She's been humiliated by friends she trusted. And the stress of it has had a knock-on effect on her schoolwork."

Maddie sighed. "I don't envy today's youth. They have to deal with things that were never a problem for us. But Juliet seems a sensible girl. A few mistakes won't spell an end to good opportunities for her."

"I just hope she stops blaming herself."

Kit watched his sister, who had stopped weighing up degree options with Bert and was pointing out to sea.

"Kit, look! Dolphins!"

Their round backs were silver with reflected sunlight: three bottlenose dolphins swimming northwards. *It wasn't your fault*, Kit thought as he turned back to Juliet. *Well, maybe you could have chosen better friends, but it wasn't your fault that they were horrible to you.* If he thought it hard enough, maybe she would hear it, and know it to be true.

Maddie stopped abruptly, and the whole group stopped with her.

"What is it?"

She pointed up ahead to a shape on the skyline, distant yet rising taller than any of the other buildings visible.

"That's it. That's Whitby Abbey." She stood still and stared at it for a long time as if in disbelief.

"You're nearly there," Kit encouraged her. Maddie nodded, and took a step forward. Juliet seemed also to have picked up on the enormity of this stage in the pilgrimage, because she asked Maddie to tell her about the abbey's history. Maddie's face lit up as she dived into a description of the first monks and nuns who came to this spot by the grey North Sea. All those years of working with children must have brought out the storyteller in Maddie, because it was easy to picture robed figures emerging from the mists over a place they gave the magical-sounding name Streoneshalh. As she talked, the pace picked up again, and Juliet listened with eager interest.

"You know, it was a woman who actually founded the monastery here."

"Really? I didn't think women in history got to do anything interesting."

"Don't you ever believe that! Her name was Hild; she was from a noble family, and she was so well regarded that the kings of the time went to her for advice. She was made a saint in the end, because of what she did."

As they drew closer, the abbey became clearer. Kit could see the dark shapes carved out by the Gothic arches. "It's a shame it's a ruin now. Was it Vikings that did it?"

Maddie laughed. "Vikings probably did raid it at one point, and others too, over the centuries. But it's been rebuilt since then.

There will have been storms and years of neglect and all sorts to bring it to this point. But it is still very striking, as a ruin. Things can be, you know."

"Can be what?"

"Beautiful, even if they aren't as they used to be."

Juliet gave the kind of sigh and smile that would once have followed reading one of her favourite books. Kit thought of Beth's map, incomplete and yet still full of memories and future adventures. Then he thought of his own family. He had spent almost a whole summer trying to rebuild them into what they had been before, with his father here, his sister happy and relaxed, his mother the unshakeable source of stability for them all. But perhaps they too had changed into something different now – not a ruin, or anything as desolate, but another shape that he could accept and love rather than work to change.

"I think I hear a marsh warbler!" Bert declared, wandering off the road to investigate and then returning with a shrug a couple of minutes later.

The road became a narrow path, and the dry stone walls gave way to an open space and a body of water, like a moat except that it did not encircle the buildings. They came to the end of the path, and there was only a stretch of grass between them and the abbey.

"You did it!" Kit cried. The abbey loomed high above them, the summer sky visible through its empty arches.

"I did." Maddie turned round to face the others. "Thank you for coming with me. This has been an important and difficult journey. Do you mind if I… if you don't –"

"If we let you go in by yourself?" Kit's mother supplied. "Of course. We understand."

"Thank you."

Kit did not understand, but everyone else seemed to agree this was the right decision, and it felt too important a moment to demand an explanation. Maddie walked on to the ruins alone, while the others explored the rest of the grounds and buildings. There was a grand house beside the abbey, and in the courtyard before it stood a statue of a man reaching forward, with a sword in his right hand.

"What will Maddie do, now her pilgrimage is over?" Kit asked Bert, while trying to imitate the statue's pose. He managed to hold the stance for a few seconds before wobbling and falling over.

"I don't know if she knows the answer to that yet. I suppose the main thing is that she has finally finished it, so she can at least go and do something else now."

"What about you? Are you going back to your university when the summer's over?"

"I'll have to go and face everyone if I want to keep my job. Besides, I've got some new research ideas to explore. It's been nice to get away for a while though. I'll miss this place."

"You should come back next summer. I'll find some good birds in the meantime, and then you can write about them."

"Maybe. Let's see how things turn out."

"I hope you can come back." It was as close as Kit could come to finding the words to express that he would miss his birdwatcher friend. Bert smiled, so perhaps he understood what Kit was trying to say.

Kit's mum had brought a picnic rug with her and spread it out on the grass outside the abbey. She now produced a flask of tea (you never knew how long it was going to be before you found a café, she explained) and poured it into plastic cups for herself, Juliet, and Bert. Kit did not like hot drinks as a rule, so she handed him a bottle of lemonade instead. Bert was appreciative of the tea, but explained that he was too old to be sitting down on the ground for fear of never being able to get back up again. He took his cup to drink while wandering towards the coast.

"I think I did see a café over there," said Juliet. "Can I go and check?"

"Of course, love. Take some money, and if they have any good cakes to take outside, bring something nice back for us, won't you?"

Juliet ran off to investigate. Kit and his mum sat together on the picnic rug.

"Kit," his mum said, the way she began important conversations, "last night, Juliet and I had a good long talk, about how we can make things easier for her. I know the last few days have probably been quite scary for you, but I want you to know that it is going to be OK."

"I know. Juliet's going to get better, isn't she?"

Catherine paused to sweep her hair out of her eyes. "That's right. But we are going to have to start doing some things differently. This whole move – it was meant to be a fresh start, for Juliet and for all of us. A clean break from the people and places that led to this point. I hadn't really thought through everything though. Somehow I found it easier to uproot us all to a new place than to make any of the small day-to-day changes that needed to go with it. I'm going to stop acting like we're still in our old lives in London. But if it's going to work, there will be changes for us to make – and you can help too."

"What can I do?"

"You can help us spend more time being a family. We need to do things together, get away from our phones and our work and our thoughts, and actually talk to one another. We won't know how to help one another unless we spend time together and listen to each other. I know you've put more work than the rest of us into learning what there is to do round here. So I'd like you to help with some ideas of things we can do. That's what your map has been about, hasn't it? Juliet told me a bit more about it.

"And I want you to know you can come and talk to me about… anything, really. I know this move has affected you – I hadn't realized before just how much you worry about things, but you do, don't you? We didn't tell you about Juliet before, because I thought it was better you didn't have to think about it. Since you know everything now, you're allowed to ask me any questions you like."

It had not occurred to Kit that he might be the sort of person to worry any more than was normal. He was, after all, a hero modelled after Camelot's finest knights. Still, the memories of how he had jumped to a few worst-case-scenario conclusions over the summer made him squirm.

"You don't need to fret about things in silence," Catherine continued. There was that word again, *fret*, that meant fog and fear all at once. "I know that I've not always been good at praising you two for things other than your school achievements. But I want you to know, Kit, that I am extremely proud of *who* you are too. I'm going to try to remember to say that more often. It's never been about what grades you get or how many useful things you do for the rest of us – that's not how families work. They love each other no matter what happens.

"And there's one more thing, which will be another change for us. I spoke to Dad last night, after our long talk. Juliet spoke to him too. And we've agreed it's time for him to come up and join us."

"Dad's coming here? You mean you're not getting a divorce?"

"Is that what you thought? No, of course we aren't. If I'd known that was what you thought… He'll be here very soon. His boss has agreed to let him work from home, so we'll get the study set up properly as an office for him."

Kit did not know what to say. He felt as though he had only just accepted his father's absence and suddenly they were to be reunited! But then he reminded himself of what had run through his mind earlier – that even with his father back, the family had grown and altered; that his quest was not to fix a ruin back into a functioning abbey, but to figure out what this new shape of things would be. And there was another mystery that still needed explaining.

"Juliet said something – when she was on that ledge. She said it was her fault Dad wasn't here. Why would she think that? Dad loves Juliet, doesn't he?"

Tears brimmed in Catherine's eyes. "Of course he does. But he has found all this business very difficult. You know Dad. He's an optimist, and he never believed things would get too bad with Juliet. He thought she was being a normal teenager and just rebelling a little bit, and that if we gave her enough space she'd be fine without any help. And then something happened –"

"The photos?"

Catherine looked surprised that Kit knew about this. But since she had said he was allowed to ask anything and receive an answer, she continued. "That's right. You were in school that day, so you didn't see how upset she was. We were a bit shocked. Both that her friends could be so unkind, and that she was so distraught. We thought she might do something… something serious, so we spoke to a professional counsellor and it emerged she'd been depressed for months, but masking it by focusing on school work and keeping distracted with her so-called friends. Dad didn't know what to do to help. He blamed himself. Well, I may have encouraged the view that it wouldn't have happened if he had taken things more seriously earlier in the year, back when the stress of revision was already taking its toll on her. Remember you asked me once what he was scared of? He's scared that he – and I – pushed Juliet to this point and that he doesn't know how to fix it. That's why he didn't come to Askfeld with us. He thought that he couldn't come here until he could be sure he wouldn't make matters worse."

"I don't understand," said Kit. How could his dad possibly make things worse, even by accident? Just having him present would have surely helped.

"It's complicated, I know. But Dad's way is to make jokes and hope for the best, isn't it? We all like his optimism. But there are times when people need to be taken seriously. Dad thought he might have upset Juliet by making light of her problems. I wish I'd known she felt that way – that she thought she had driven him away. I could have told her sooner that none of it was her fault. Dad knows now everything that has happened this summer. And he knows that we are going to work together to be OK again."

And just like that, the mysteries of the summer all made sense: the sudden move north to give Juliet a change of scene from the world of her cruel friends, even if she had still brought along her reading list and her belief that she was only as good as her achievements. And their dad had never forgotten them or wanted to abandon them. He and Kit were alike in that way: they both wanted to do the right thing and had made enormous mistakes in their efforts.

"When will he get here?"

"Soon. Hopefully a week next Friday."

Kit counted up the time in his head: eleven days. It was strange to think of his father being scared of anything. Adults were more complicated than they liked you to know.

Juliet returned with some shortbread wrapped in white paper napkins and shared out the pieces with them. The three Fishers ate in silence. It made a pleasant change, Kit thought, not to have his mum muttering to herself as she composed emails, or Juliet worrying over vocab lists. For once, he too was content to lie on the grass and watch the clouds drifting past.

After a while, Maddie returned. Her face glowed and her arms swung breezily as she strolled across the grass to them.

"You look like you've just woken up from a good long sleep," Bert remarked. Then they all went into the abbey together and stood in the cool of the main nave, between the centuries-old stones.

"I had no idea anywhere could be so peaceful," said Catherine, and she stood completely still for several minutes under one of the arches. It wasn't somewhere you had to do anything, Kit thought; it was enough just to *be* here. Beth would have liked it.

It was a short bus ride back, which Maddie said would not be cheating now that she had completed her walk.

"Will you get a bus back to where you used to live?" Kit asked, turning round in his seat to talk to her.

"I think it might be time to start over somewhere new," she said.

"There are lots of memories in my old home. Some are happy and some are sad. I'm going to look for a fresh start – a new house and a new job."

Kit had hoped that the end of the pilgrimage might have marked the end of Maddie's sadness at the past. All her anger had evaporated, but it was a shame, he thought, that the memory of what had happened was not yet fully washed away. He was certain that in all the stories of quests and journeys he had ever read, the endings had been more satisfying than this. But Maddie just gave a contented sigh, remarked that her legs ached from the walk, and looked out of the bus window at the hedgerows and dry stone walls racing past them.

By the time they returned to Askfeld, the sun was starting to sink behind the fields in the west, casting a golden glow over the cliff tops.

"What's that?" Kit asked, as they crossed a field to take a short cut into the guest house garden. A table had been set up on the grass. As they drew nearer, they could see Nick setting out plates on it.

"Hello!" he called. "Here's the victorious travellers returned! Come and have something to eat."

Sean came striding out of the house. "Keep your voice down!" he chided Nick.

"Sorry, totally forgot. I'm going to have to get used to this."

There were chairs set up around the garden. One of them was Beth's chair from her room, and she was sitting in it with a blanket over her knees and a small bundle in her arms.

"They're back," said Juliet. She ran over to Beth, and Kit followed.

"Hello, you two," said Beth. "There's someone here I'd like you to meet. This is Amelia Hope."

"That's a beautiful name," said Juliet, craning forward to see a small sleeping face and a pair of fidgeting arms escaping the yellow blanket wrapped around them.

"It's a girl!" Kit said in surprise and undisguised disappointment. "I thought it was going to be a boy."

Beth laughed. "I know you did. I hope you don't feel too let down."

"Can we still show her all the places on the map to have adventures?"

"As soon as she's old enough."

Kit thought about this. Maybe it was not a complete disaster. "Didn't you say that Sean doesn't know how to skim stones?" he asked.

"That's right, I don't think he does."

"Then I'll have to teach her," Kit concluded. And with that, it was settled. Amelia would need an older brother to share some of her adventures and games.

"That would be a lovely thing, Kit. Thank you."

"And can I show the map to my dad when he gets here?"

"Of course. Do you know when he is coming?"

"In eleven days. I've" – Kit checked that Juliet had moved out of earshot – "I've got a feeling he isn't exactly looking forward to it. I didn't used to think he worried about anything. But maybe if we go collecting fossils together that will help."

Maddie was talking to Kit's mother, and it did not surprise him at all that Catherine was asking the pilgrim lots of questions about her professional qualifications and career plan.

"I was thinking I might look at support work with people who have learning disabilities." Maddie said this tentatively, as if trying the words out loud for the first time.

Sean brought a plate of food over to Beth, and took Amelia so that his wife could have her hands free to eat something.

"You were right," Kit said to Beth, "about the quest. Though I can't quite figure out if it's over yet."

Beth just smiled at him. She had been right about so many things. He spotted Bert standing away from the others, looking out to sea through his binoculars.

"What have you seen?" he asked, following the line of sight.

"I'm not quite sure yet," Bert said, with an urgency in his voice. "There's something out there and I don't think it's a gull."

A dark silhouette with wide wings was soaring in on the sea breeze. It skimmed low over the waves and then wheeled up higher, coming in towards the cliffs some way south of them.

"It can't be!" Bert breathed and Kit felt his stomach jump in excitement.

"Is it?" he asked. Bert stared in silence and Kit did not dare speak for fear of breaking the possibility that hung in that pause. The birdwatcher handed the binoculars to him. Kit moved them about, trying to find the right spot to focus on. It was white with black wings. Kit thought he could see markings around its face, like a haughty eyebrow that knew exactly how majestic it was. He lowered the binoculars and looked to Bert for confirmation.

"A black-browed albatross," the birdwatcher croaked, and there were tears running down his face. Kit turned back to the others.

"It's an albatross!" he shouted, waving and pointing. Some of them came to look, but did not understand what was making the old man weep and the young boy jump up and down in excitement.

The albatross swooped in its flight, wheeling close enough for them to see where the wind ruffled the tips of its feathers. It turned sharply so that the sunlight caught on the underside of its wings as it flew home to its roost.

"Aren't you going to take a picture, to show the people you work with?" Kit asked.

Bert looked surprised. "Oh, yes, I suppose that's a good idea. I was so absorbed there, just watching it. Almost forgot!"

He pointed the camera and pressed a button. The tiny click it made told Kit that his work here was done, for Bert at least. He left the birdwatcher gazing at the orange-flecked sky.

"I've got something new to add to your map," he said as he re-joined Beth and the others. "Or I suppose it's Amelia's map now, isn't it?"

The quest, he realized, was never complete, because it was not just one quest. It was a whole pattern of adventures playing out at the same time, and there was always more to discover.

A MAP OF THE SKY

Reading Group Questions

1. Do you think Kit's love of hero stories and adventures has a positive or negative influence on his life?

2. Was Catherine right to move the family to Askfeld that summer?

3. Did you trust Kit's perspective on the story as it unfolded? Were there moments when you disagreed with his take on events?

4. Hope and disappointment are experienced by most characters over the course of the novel. Which character do you think has the hardest time with these themes?

5. At one point, Maddie talks about the North Sea as if it were a person. What kind of personality do you think the book's setting has?

6. What do you think will happen to Bert, Maddie, and the Garsdales next?